# MINE UNTIL MOONRISE

## JENNIFER BERNARD

# CHAPTER ONE

It couldn't be good that Megan's passengers were singing the theme song from *Gilligan's Island*—"a tale of a fateful trip." Or that two of them were snoring loudly. Halfway back to Lost Harbor and they still hadn't sighted anything for the tourists to write home about. She'd better come up with something fast, or her online reviews were going to be brutal.

They were just passing Bird Rock, where thousands of birds congregated in the summer. Surely there had to be at least one species that her passengers could get excited about. Guillemots, auks and sea ducks only went so far. Megan fished under her bright yellow rain jacket for her binoculars. She didn't mind the way the ocean spray misted her face and sent her hair into a soggy, bedraggled frizz—but her precious Zeiss Victory SFs had to be protected at all costs.

"Stop the boat!" she shouted a second later. "I got something!"

The *Forget Me Not* lurched to half its previous speed. Her passengers slid across the bench seats, clutching each other and laughing.

Still captivated by the shape that had just caught her eye, Megan gestured an apology at her passengers. "Sorry, everyone, I get carried away when I spot something extra special."

Luckily, her boat was an old tub built to ride out the worst Alaska storms. Her passengers were unlikely to go overboard, although the chances of springing a leak were essentially a hundred percent. Her boat pilot—she thought of him as Captain Kid, since he'd just barely reached the age at which he could legally captain a boat—had warned her of a new one just this morning.

After a quick check to make sure everyone was still onboard, she aimed her binoculars off the starboard bow. "This is a very lucky day, you guys. Do you see that blob of white just on the tip of that cliff face?"

Everyone looked in the direction she was pointing, to the jagged fortress of rocks. Waves crashed at its base, while seagulls tilted and wheeled above it. Their crying made a lonely sound, even though they were probably just chatting about the nearest bed of oysters.

"That's called Bird Rock, for a good reason. Hundreds of species stop here over the course of the summer. Some of them nest, some are just passing through. But today..." She focused closer on the elegant white plumage with the black cap and deep orange bill.

"Looks like the entire cliff is white," said one of her tourist passengers.

"Yes, there's a lot of bird poop everywhere," Megan answered absently. "You can smell it if we get close. Should we get closer? Ben, can we get closer?"

"Sure thing." Ben—Captain Kid—answered from inside the wheelhouse as he turned the *Forget Me Not* toward Bird Rock.

"Mama, can I drive just this little bit?" Ruby piped up from her usual spot next to Ben. Her little eight-year-old city girl had a new goal in life—getting permission to pilot the *Forget Me Not*.

Not happening. Definitely not happening.

"In ten years, absolutely," Megan called to her daughter from her spot on the stern deck. The tourists laughed sympathetically.

"Sweet saints alive. I see it. Is that...a Caspian tern?" one of them exclaimed. "Unusual to see them so far north, no?"

Megan smiled under her binoculars. Moments like this told her she'd done the right thing coming to Lost Harbor. These passengers—mostly elderly retirees with a passion for nature—were her kindred spirits. Where else could an entire boatful of people—okay, so she only had five customers today, but the season was still early—sigh in unison at the rare sighting?

The *Forget Me Not* was now close enough to Bird Rock so that she could clearly make out the Caspian tern's ruffled plumage.

"Ruby, come on out here, I want you to see this." She beckoned to her daughter. Ruby came skipping out of the wheelhouse in her brown rubber boots and her polka dot slicker and once again Megan experienced that overwhelming sensation of being exactly where she was supposed to be.

Ruby loved Alaska. She loved Misty Bay and the glacial peaks of Lost Souls Wilderness arrayed on the other side of the bay. She never got seasick the way Megan sometimes did. The cold didn't bother her. She never got bored on the water. When things got slow, she curled up in the wheelhouse with a backpack full of math books.

*I made the right choice coming here. Just look at that face!*

Smiling, Megan held out her hand to Ruby, whose face glowed as she darted across the deck.

And then everything happened at once.

Another boat roared between them and Bird Rock. A cloud of cawing birds flapped into the air. The wake of the passing boat rippled toward them in a curl of white. Ruby's boot hit a patch of water and she wheeled her arms to keep her balance. Megan flung herself across the deck to grab Ruby's arm. Even though her daughter was laughing hysterically, Megan's imagination had already conjured up the image of Ruby launching over the railing into the ocean.

"Hey!" she yelled at the boat. Through the spray misting the air between the two vessels, she recognized the culprit. *Of course.* The F/V *Jack Hammer.* Fishing charter to the wealthy. Her nemesis. Destroyer of peace. Ruiner of everything.

Standing on the back of the deck, a dark-haired man in sunglasses and full waders raised a gloved hand in apology.

*Lucas Holt.*

The first time they'd met, he'd rudely called her an "ignoramus" and lectured her about a "Boating Basics" class. Things hadn't gotten any better since then.

Had she really just been thinking that Lost Harbor was exactly where she was supposed to be? It would have been absolutely perfect except for one person—the man pretending to be sorry for nearly capsizing them.

"I don't accept your apology!" she shouted after the boat. Its stern seemed to mock her, the giant twin engines thumbing their noses at her. Had Lucas intended to mess with her Caspian tern sighting? She wouldn't put it past him, even though he probably had no idea how exciting it was to see one.

Scratch that. Of course he knew. Lucas had grown up here and knew quite a bit about the wildlife. As he'd put it to her once —"the birds help me find the fish. The fish help me find the money. So yeah, I've learned what I need to know about birds."

God, she hated him.

"Mama!" Ruby tugged her arm out of Megan's grip. "You're squishing me."

"Sorry, sweetie. I thought you were about to go over the side."

"I'm wearing my float vest."

"Of course you are." Megan wouldn't let Ruby step foot on any boat without a PFD. "But that water would turn you into an ice cube in about twenty seconds."

"The Caspian tern is gone." The disappointment in her passengers' voice made her heart sink. There went half her tips. All thanks to Lucas Holt and his irresponsible boating practices.

"We can hang out here for a little bit and see if he comes back." Megan glanced back at Ben, who was busy navigating the wake of the *Jack Hammer*.

*Jack Hammer*. Was there ever such a stupid name for a boat? It had been named by Lucas' father, Jack "the Hammer" Holt—someone arrogant enough to name a boat after himself.

Maybe arrogance ran in the family.

"But we have lunch reservations," said one of the tourists.

"Oh, that's not a problem. Lunch is included." She waved her hand at the cooler that sat against the wheelhouse. "Juice boxes and a selection of healthy sandwiches."

The passengers glanced amongst themselves. "Yes, but our reservations are for all-you-can-eat King Crab legs."

"Right. Of course." She caught Ben's eye and jerked her head in the direction of the harbor. If she had her wish, she'd head the other way, toward the point, where she'd once spotted a Wandering Tattler and an orca had surfaced about three yards away.

But not everyone had her stamina when it came to wildlife viewing. Some people actually had lives, and lunch reservations.

Captain Kid, looking relieved, swung the wheel so the *Forget Me Not* headed for the harbor. He probably had lunch plans too.

Well, so did she. She planned to eat sandwiches out of a cooler with Ruby. Because at this rate, that was all she could afford. Unless business started to pick up, she wouldn't even be able to fuel the *Forget Me Not*. It would become the *Fuel Me Not*.

"Why are you laughing, Mama?" Ruby tugged at her hand. "It's that weird laugh when you're thinking something mean. You aren't mad at Lucas, are you? I didn't go overboard."

"No, but you could have. Thanks for reminding me. I'm going to talk to him as soon as we get back to the harbor."

Ruby tilted her head up, her wide dark eyes sparkling. "Mama, he's actually pretty nice. You just don't believe it."

"Maybe he's nice to you, which I appreciate. But not to me. I'm going to talk to him, and then depending on what he says, report him to the harbormaster."

"You already did that."

So she had—and the sound of the harbormaster's laughter still echoed on certain late nights when she relived the whole saga of her and Lucas.

"And I'll do it again. Someone's got to speak up."

Ruby shrugged, losing interest. "I'm hungry, Mama."

The *Forget Me Not* hit a swell and its aluminum frame vibrated with the impact. Megan grabbed the railing with one hand and Ruby with the other. Her binoculars bumped against her chest. "We'll eat as soon as we tie up."

"Pizza?" Ruby asked hopefully.

"Sandwiches. Lots of sandwiches."

# CHAPTER TWO

The *Forget Me Not*, carefully following the five-mile-per-hour no-wake rule, glided through the harbor toward the slip Megan rented. Before she'd come to Lost Harbor, she'd never imagined all the costs associated with running a boat. She hadn't needed to, since she'd been hired as a naturalist guide. But just after she'd arrived, when she was still getting her bearings, everything had changed.

With only a few weeks left in the season—it was late August —the owner had gotten into a huge fight with her life partner, packed up all her belongings in her RV and offered the business to Megan.

Megan had, of course, discussed it with her ex-husband, Dev. Although she had primary custody of Ruby, Dev was still very involved in Ruby's life. She and Dev had met in grad school— she'd been studying ornithology, he'd been studying business. Their marriage had been the only impulsive thing Dev had ever done. Megan, on the other hand, specialized in "impulsive."

Just look at the way she'd fled to this faraway Alaska outpost.

Even though their marriage had only lasted a few months,

Megan appreciated many things about Dev. He was financially responsible. He didn't do drama. He loved Ruby. He respected their agreements.

They'd never gone to court to settle custody issues. Instead they relied on a professional mediator back in San Francisco. Poor Eliza Burke had the patience of a hundred saints.

Her move to Alaska had required three sessions with Eliza.

"I get why you want to leave the Bay Area," he'd grumbled after they'd hammered out a plan. "But why does it have to be Alaska?"

"We need a change."

*She* needed a change. And he knew the reason perfectly well, though they never talked about it.

"If Ruby doesn't like it, she can always come stay with me."

"That's the thing—it was her idea. That's why I considered it in the first place. Talk to her yourself, you'll see!"

In the end, Dev had given his consent and offered financial help. He still thought it was insane, but Ruby had talked him into it. He was such a sucker when it came to Ruby.

Not that she was any better. As they passed Last Chance Pizza, with its deck overlooking the harbor, Ruby made a pleading face at Megan.

She rolled her eyes in a gesture Ruby knew how to read perfectly well. *Fine. You win.* Pizza with Zoe, the owner of the restaurant, was no hardship, after all. Zoe was Megan's closest friend in Lost Harbor, the only one who'd accepted her immediately. She'd tried to win over the other "harbor rats"—people who worked on the boardwalk—with cupcakes and kindness, but it was a slow process.

They cruised past more businesses along the boardwalk that ran the length of the harbor. Ice cream shops, local crafts stores, restaurants, fishing charter offices, bear-viewing outfits.

When Dev had done his analysis of the business environment of Lost Harbor, Alaska, he'd been very impressed. "They do an excellent job catering to the tourist traffic. The fishing charters in particular do very well. Can you transform the *Forget Me Not* into—"

"No."

"But the ROI would likely be exponentially—"

"*No.* I'm not here to fish. I want to use my almost-degree in a way that allows me to spend time with my daughter. It's perfect, Dev."

"Fine. But I estimate you have about a twenty-one percent chance of making a profit."

"Really? That actually gives me hope, Dev. Thanks. I figured it was more like negative five percent."

"That might be more accurate," he admitted.

She hated to say it, but Dev was probably right. Her main problem was that the cost of fuel kept rising. Or maybe it was that boat repairs were expensive and the *Forget Me Not* had more leaks than a salad spinner.

Or that she couldn't steer a boat and be a guide at the same time, and therefore had to hire Captain Kid. Or that she couldn't afford her own office and therefore had to rent a virtual closet in the back of the Jack Hammer Fishing Charters office. The receptionist, Carla, only answered the Forget Me Not Nature Tours phone line when she wasn't busy. Plenty of potential bookings went straight to voicemail.

Or maybe her biggest problem was that her marketing efforts screamed "science geek." Or that...but why keep torturing herself? Sure she had challenges, but what new business owner didn't? The summer season had just begun—her first full summer running nature tours out of Lost Harbor. It wasn't over yet. She could still make this work.

Miracles could happen.

The *Forget Me Not* bumped against the side of the float,

which had a long strip of carpet fastened to it to cushion the impact. She jumped out and grabbed the bow line. As soon as the *Forget Me Not* settled into place, she wound the line around a cleat. Ruby had followed her off the boat and was doing the same thing to the aft line.

*Aft line.* She'd never even put those two words together until she'd come to Lost Harbor.

She offered Ruby a high five. Her daughter slammed her palm a little too hard, as she always did. Captain Kid came out of the wheelhouse and unlatched the gate on the starboard side. Together, they all helped the passengers off the boat and onto the float. The guests said things like, "Lovely trip," "Too bad about that Caspian tern," and "Where's the nearest restroom?"

She was in the midst of pointing it out when Lucas Holt strode past. He'd shucked his waders and wore work pants tucked into rubber boots, along with an obviously hand-knit sweater the color of smoke.

It smelled like smoke, too—like wood smoke curling through crystal clear air on a winter's night. She had a quick image of him kneeling next to a campfire, blowing on the flames, while she snuggled under a blanket to keep warm.

She shook it off. It was just a fantasy, because she and Lucas Holt would never find themselves camping together, anywhere. She'd rather run into Lost Souls Wilderness across the bay and take her chances with the bears.

Usually Lucas ignored her and her passengers. They weren't his speed; they didn't bring coolers of beer on the boat or boast about the size of their last catch. But this time he paused and cast a charming smile across her little crew of elderly naturalists.

"Sorry about the close call out there. I'm training a new guy. He still has a few things to learn. I hope no one got wet because of that bonehead move."

Lucas had dark hair and dark stubble and dark eyes and no

wonder she secretly called him Lucifer. But he was good-looking; she had to admit that.

Not that it mattered. Character was what counted. Not looks.

"You're seriously going to blame your crew?" she asked.

A hint of irritation crossed his face. She hated the way he always looked at her—as if she was a frivolous birdbrain hippie chick. She had part of a PhD, for pete's sake. But that seemed to mean nothing to him, even though she'd mentioned it more than once.

"Just explaining what happened. He got a little carried away. He won't do it again."

"I hope not because I have witnesses. And I'd really prefer not to go the harbormaster again."

His dark eyebrows quirked together. "On the one hand, I doubt that's true, because I'm sure it gives you a special kind of joy to report on me. On the other hand, maybe it is true because I hear it didn't go so well the last time."

She gritted her teeth together. Unfortunately, he had a point. After her third trip to the harbormaster's office, she'd decided there had to be better ways to handle her feud with Lucas.

Sadly, she hadn't figured them out yet.

"I am not easily deterred," she said stoutly. "Especially when it comes to Ruby's safety."

Lucas smiled down at Ruby, who glowed back at him. Darn him. That smile changed things in an unfortunate way. If he ever smiled at her like that...

She sighed. Luckily, there was no chance of such a thing.

# CHAPTER THREE

Lucas kept his gaze fixed on Ruby. At least one of the Miller women didn't think he was an irredeemable piece of crap. "Are you okay, kid? I saw you slip-slide around that deck like a pro."

"I'm fine." The little girl's skin glowed gold in the reflected light from the water. Her skin was darker than her mother's, which had made him give some thought to who her father might be. And where. And what the mother-daughter duo's story was. They'd appeared in Lost Harbor late last summer and no one had expected them to stay long. But here they still were. Still plugging those bird-watching tours. Still reporting him to Bob.

He'd first run into Megan shortly after his father's death, when he was still reeling. He'd been a complete dick to her. He'd been a dick to pretty much everyone at that point, but that was no excuse. Later, he'd wanted to repair the damage he'd caused, but it was too late. Their adversarial path had been set.

Besides, it was kind of fun sparring with the pretty newcomer. Kept things interesting around here.

"Someday you'll have to come out on a real craft," he told Ruby. "Something that can go faster than a go-cart."

"Really? Can I?" Her face lit up as if he'd just told her Santa was coming down the boat ramp.

"Any time—"

"Over my dead body," Megan interrupted. "Sorry, Ruby. It's not a safe situation."

He snorted. If she had any idea how many times he'd snuck onto her boat and patched a leak that her baby captain hadn't noticed, she'd lose her shit completely. "The *Jack Hammer* has a perfect safety record."

"Not a single drunk venture capitalist has ever gone overboard?"

"Not unless they deserved it."

A whisper of a smile sketched across her lips. And yes, of course he'd noticed her lips. They were full and lush, with an up-curve that disappeared when he came along. "You probably pay the Coast Guard to ignore all your infractions."

"Now there's an idea. Does it work? Because I think I spotted a problem with—" He gestured toward the water.

"Shhhht!" She jolted toward him, her eyes cutting toward the small group of senior citizens waiting on the ramp. In a rapid undertone, she told him, "That's been resolved and there's no need to mention it. It's very unfair that you would even bring it up but I guess I should expect nothing less from you."

He had no idea what she was referring to. Great. Now she thought he'd intended to bust her for some infraction in front of her passengers. No wonder she hated him.

"I was talking about the baby sea otter hanging out on the breakwater." He raised his voice so the passengers could hear. "Did you all get a look at the little guy?"

She blinked at him, clearly trying to reorient herself. Man, he enjoyed surprising her. She so clearly looked down on him that catching her off guard was very satisfying.

"Oh. No. He was gone when we passed. We nearly, uh—

anyway..." She turned to her passengers, who were listening to their back and forth with expressions of fascination. "Lunch reservations, right? Captain Crabbie's is that-away. I recommend the salmon chowder if the crab legs are a little too creepy for you. I always think they look like giant spiders." She waved her hand at the boardwalk while Lucas tried not to laugh. Captain Crabbie's should definitely not hire Megan to do their marketing.

The seniors launched into their goodbyes and thank yous.

"Wait," Lucas said when there was a pause in the chatter. "I have something for you all. By way of apology."

He dug in the pocket of his work pants for his phone, then scrolled through his photos. He presented it to the closest passenger, a lanky man in a herringbone cap who peered at it through wire-rimmed glasses.

"Well, look at that," the man marveled. "Fantastic shot of our Caspian tern. Did you take this?"

"I did. We spotted him on our way out to the fishing grounds. Got a video too. Anyone who wants a copy, just make sure Megan has your email address. You're welcome to it."

The joy on the faces surrounding him made his gut twist. These retirees were roughly his father's age. But he'd never get to see a smile on old Jack's face again. Not that his father had been a big smiler to begin with, unless he landed the biggest halibut of the day, or when he cracked open his first Shipyard ale.

The elders ambled away toward their lunch, and he turned to find Megan staring at him with narrowed eyes, hands on her hips. She wore her usual gear of rain pants and a fleece overshirt. Tiny diamonds of moisture were scattered across her hair, which was twisted into a thick braid. Its color landed somewhere between teak and mahogany, a fine woodsy brown. Other than her eyes, the blue of forget-me-nots, she had a vividly expressive Marisa Tomei vibe.

"That was nice," she accused.

"Sorry?"

"What's your angle? Are you trying to steal my clients?"

"That wouldn't be very sporting. You have few enough as it is."

A flush burned in her cheeks, and he wished he could take that back. He knew her business was struggling; everyone on the boardwalk knew it.

"Look, I spotted the tern and knew you'd be excited, bird nerd that you are. So I took a photo. If you don't want it, no worries. I can just delete it—"

"No!" She literally jumped across the ramp at him, like a panther from a tree. "Don't you dare delete it. My email address is Megan at Forget Me Not dot net."

He punched in her address and sent the photo.

So he had her email address now. He could have gotten it before, but now she'd *given* it to him. Imagine the trouble he could cause with that.

"Is it okay if I add you to the list of boardwalk volunteers?" he asked innocently, hand poised over his phone. "There's a dog poop cleanup day coming up."

"Yes! Yes!" Ruby jumped up and down. "I want to clean up dog poop! Mama, can we get a dog, please?"

Megan gave him another look of death. "No dogs. Lucas knows that. He's just mentioning dogs because he's...well...I'm sure there's a good word for it."

Honestly, teasing her was almost too easy. And yet, still very enjoyable. "It's okay, Ruby, you can play with Fidget any time you want."

"Where is Fidget? Didn't he go fishing with you today?"

"Nope, I gave him the day off. Barking at fish can really wear a dog out." After Jack Holt's death, no one else had stepped up to take care of his old Irish setter. One more responsibility landing splat on Lucas' shoulders.

"I want to see him bark at fish!"

"And you will, when you come out on the *Jack Hammer* with us. Just pick your time, we'd love to have you onboard. You'd be a big help. You can handle filet knives, right?"

When Megan blanched, Lucas decided his work here was done. A good deed, mixed with some jokes and a few jabs, just to keep things even.

Megan's phone pinged. "That's so crazy, it took that long for an email? We're standing about six inches from each other."

He spanned the space between them with one hand, though he was careful not to touch her. Honestly, he was slightly afraid of how actual contact with Megan Miller might affect him.

She jerked a bit, as if she too was afraid of potential contact.

"Sorry, city girl. That's the way things are here in the wild. We have to chop our own wood and emails take up to a minute to get here. Crazy, right?"

She rolled her eyes at him, then put her hand on Ruby's shoulder. "I know I should thank you for the Caspian tern photo."

He tilted his head in exaggerated expectation.

"I...I'm grateful."

He looked at Ruby. "Help her out here, kid. What's that thing you say when you're grateful?"

But instead of playing along with him, she crossed her arms over her chest. "I'm not falling for that."

He burst out laughing. "Smart kid." Sometimes he forgot how smart. Rumor had it she was some kind of math prodigy. It was easy to forget when he saw her running around the harbor boardwalk like any other kid.

Megan gave him an unfriendly look, along with a "move along" gesture. "Thank you so much for the photo, now have a nice day. Happy now?"

He tucked his phone back into his pocket, wondering once

again what it would take to start fresh with Megan. She wasn't exactly the most popular person in town. She'd shown up in Lost Harbor like a whirlwind trying to change things that had existed for decades. Not that all her crusades were bad—he'd supported her push for recycle bins and bike racks on the boardwalk. But he'd put his foot down when she lobbied for extra slip surcharges to pay for waste oil removal. She didn't understand how hard it was for fishermen simply to make a living. Adding too many fees and extra charges would put some of them out of business.

"I'm heading in the direction of Captain Crabbie's if you need a guide," he told the crew of seniors. He offered one exhausted-looking woman his arm; she leaned on it gratefully. With a wink he added, "I'll give you my card in case you ever want something more exciting than bird-watching."

At a leisurely pace, they moved toward the ramp that led to the boardwalk. Behind him, he could sense Megan fuming.

What was he doing, poking at her like this? Her nature cruises didn't affect his business. They were no skin off his nose. He was back in Lost Harbor for one reason only, and it wasn't to spar with an admittedly cute bird nerd. It wasn't even for the fishing. It was for his father. Even in death, the bastard couldn't leave him alone.

No one else in the family was stepping up to deal with everything Jack Holt had left behind—the business, his mother, the homestead, the decades' worth of junk stored there. Only Lucas had put his life on hold and come back to Lost Harbor.

Just lately he'd been wrestling with something else. How had a lifelong ocean lover and fisherman like Jack Holt drowned in the harbor next to his own boat? It had been ruled an accident, but something felt wrong.

Which reminded him that he had an appointment with Lost Harbor's only detective. He already knew what she was going to say. To accept the ruling and get on with his life.

Too bad he hated anyone telling him what to do—another gift from the old Jack Hammer.

# CHAPTER FOUR

Megan kept a tight grip on Ruby's shoulder as they wended their way through the lunch crowd at Last Chance Pizza. She'd discovered, since arriving in Lost Harbor, that she didn't much like crowds. Living mostly in cities, she'd never noticed it because it was always there in the background. But the relief of being on the water, with nothing but the vast arch of sky overhead and open ocean in all directions, had opened her eyes: she didn't like crowds.

Most especially after what had happened at the university exactly a year ago.

*Don't think about that. Moving on. Moving on.*

She forced her thoughts into another direction.

What if Forget Me Not Nature Tours went bust? Would she have to move back to a city to get work? Could she handle the crowds? She didn't know, which was one more reason to make sure that didn't happen. She didn't want to go back. Couldn't go back.

Zoe spotted them and waved them toward a table in the back. Even though the little restaurant was mobbed, she showed no signs of stress. She still moved at the leisurely pace of someone who only did exactly what they wanted to do. Zoe did not like to be rushed, and if anyone ever tried it, they might find themselves out on the boardwalk with no chance of pizza.

Most people liked to hang out at the front of the restaurant where the brick oven dominated the space. But Ruby always loved the back because the large picture windows looked out on the alleyway that ran behind all the boardwalk businesses. It was like a secret village that only the locals got to see.

Zoe's place sat between a shop that sold native Alaskan crafts and a fish-cleaning station. Several such stations were scattered throughout the harbor for use by the public, but this one—and a few others—was reserved for the charters. Here, the deckhands cleaned and filleted the halibut and other fish that their customers had caught. They packed them into insulated containers and handed the booty back for transport to the "Lower Forty-Eight."

It was bloody, squishy work and Ruby loved watching the workers in their rubber aprons twirling their knives so expertly. Sometimes Lucas joined them, and Megan had to admit, she took a few peeks herself when that happened.

"I snagged a couple of leftover slices for you, you want?" Zoe appeared at their table with two paper plates loaded with cheese-oozing pizza.

"Ooh, yes." Megan accepted them eagerly and set them down between her and Ruby. "I know I should be eating those turkey-on-wheat sandwiches my clients completely ignored, but this looks a lot better. Can you sit?"

"No, there might be a riot if I take too much time. But I had to come say hi. I haven't seen you two in ages. Been busy?"

"Sure," Megan said, not really wanting to get into her lack of customers.

Zoe lifted one eyebrow. "That bad, huh?"

Megan bit into the pizza so she didn't have to answer.

"Hey, it's okay. Takes time. Did you put your name in for the show?"

"The ahh??" she asked through a mouthful of cheese. She held up a hand, asking for a pause, and chewed as quickly as she could. "The what?"

"That travel show everyone watches. I don't even know what it's called because TV just annoys me."

"Wait...are you talking about *Trekking*?"

"Yes, that's the one. Apparently they're coming here to Lost Harbor and they're looking for subjects to film. Shoot. Whatever. They want to follow people around with cameras for a day. They asked me and of course I said 'hell no.' I have enough business. Any more and my head would explode."

Megan suppressed the automatic rise of envy. "No one told me about it."

"Really? I think they wanted to profile one of our local fishing boats. I mean, it wouldn't be Lost Harbor without one. I'm pretty sure they talked to Lucas. Why wouldn't they? He's the most photogenic of the bunch, that's for sure."

Megan's envy turned to something more like bitterness. "Of course they would want Lucas. He's the perfect choice. I can't even argue with that. He grew up here. He's gorgeous. He can turn on the charm when he wants to."

Zoe lifted an eyebrow at her. As a part-Italian, part-Greek woman, she prided herself on her unapologetically thick eyebrows. She could express so much with those eyebrows: skepticism, curiosity, disapproval, excitement. "Did you just call Lucas Holt gorgeous? My ears must have glitched for a minute."

"Oh stop. I never said he wasn't attractive. I said he was a jerk. Don't confuse the issue here."

Zoe exchanged a knowing glance with Ruby. Megan found it infuriating and swiped her hand between the two of them as if she could erase that moment from existence. "Ruby, eat your pizza. You pestered me enough for it."

"I don't pester," Ruby said with dignity as she lifted her pizza closer to her mouth. "I plead."

And just like that, all of Megan's irritation melted away. God, she loved her daughter. More than seemed humanly possible sometimes. "I stand corrected. Now eat."

Ruby obediently guided the pointy end of the pizza into her mouth. She had her own technique for eating everything, pizza included. She had a three-corners approach; she liked to rotate bites at each corner, creating more and more sides to the pizza.

"I should have mentioned the show to you earlier," Zoe told Megan. A customer was trying to get her attention but she ignored the man. "I should have figured you'd get overlooked."

"Because no one likes me."

"Because you're new," Zoe corrected. "No one ever thinks newbies will stick around."

"Last winter doesn't count?"

"Sorry, no. One winter is a kind of bare minimum base level commitment. Anyone can last one winter. It's all a big adventure when it's just one."

It definitely had been an adventure, and to be completely honest, Megan and Ruby had spent several months of it in the Bay area. "Well, I'm sorry, but Ruby needed to see her father and—"

Zoe put up a floury hand to stop her. "Believe me, I don't care how long you've been here. I'm just glad you are."

"Really?" Megan blinked at her gratefully. Establishing herself in Lost Harbor had been tough—still was. Mostly she'd encountered skepticism and even some hostility. "I think you might be the only one."

"Ignore the doubters. We still wouldn't have recycle bins if you hadn't shown up. And Lucas would have no one to argue with." Zoe flashed her a wink, then sighed as someone back near the brick oven called for her. "I'd better get back to work. I'm training my twin sisters."

Megan craned her neck to catch a glimpse of two dark-haired girls covered in flour and laughing hysterically. "Haven't met them yet. How old are they?"

They're sixteen and they've aged *me* about twenty years this week."

Megan smiled affectionately at her friend. "You should come by for dinner and let us feed you for once."

"I'll do that. Hey, if I could get you a meeting with the show producer, would you want that? You could try to convince him that their viewers would rather see birders than halibut-hunters."

"Could you really do that?"

"I can try. He left me his card." A shout of alarm came from the front of the restaurant as a puff of smoke burst from the brick oven. "Can't I step away for a damn second without them setting fire to the place? I'll talk to you later."

Not even smoke could get her to rush. With no hint of hurry, she strolled back to her station like a queen surrounded by her subjects.

Megan watched her with envy. As far as she could tell, Zoe didn't have an anxious bone in her body. She used to be that way too—carefree and impulsive, adventurous. But that was before Ruby had arrived. And definitely before the—

*Don't think about that.*

Settling in one place had become important to her, and she'd come closer to peace here than anywhere else. She glanced toward the next-door crafts studio. The owner was watering the flowerpots on the back deck. Behind him glittered the silver-washed blue of Misty Bay. The bay and the jagged ridge of snowy peaks on the other side—Lost Souls Wilderness—had a way of taking her breath away when she wasn't prepared. All that extravagant beauty just minding its own business while the harbor workers went about their mundane tasks.

Sometimes she'd glance up while doing something basic like filling up her car and just laugh at the outlandish glory splashed across the bay like an artist's backdrop. It was almost too spectacular for her eyes to take in.

Pulling her gaze away from the flowerpots next door, she switched to the neighbor on the other side of the pizza shop.

And there her glance landed on a different kind of work of art.

Lucas Holt cleaning fish. Lucas Holt *without a shirt* as he cleaned fish. The sun was beating down on his bare back. Holy halibut, did he have to be so bronzed and muscly? His head was bent over the white plastic folding table with the hose mounted to it. His rubber-gloved hands moved quickly and efficiently, cutting, rinsing, tossing bits to the waiting seagulls. He frowned as he worked; she got the impression that his thoughts were far away.

He was probably thinking about how much more money he was going to make when he starred in *Trekking*.

The worst part was that her parents watched every episode of *Trekking*. Maybe they'd finally accept her choice to live in Alaska if they saw her on TV.

But no, they'd be watching Lucas instead of her, and so would every travel hound in America. Would he take his shirt off for the show? Maybe he was practicing for his starring moment.

On impulse, she propped open the window and called out to him. "Hey Holt, don't you know *Trekking* is a family show? Your cheap tricks won't work."

He glanced up in surprise, his hands stilling. "Spying, Megan? Or just enjoying the scenery?"

Her cheeks warmed. "I'm just giving you fair warning. I want that spot on *Trekking* and I'm going to work my ass off to get it."

"Guess I'll have to step up my game."

"You will. I'm a very competitive person, you know."

"I picked up on that." He pulled out a handful of fish guts and dropped it in a five-gallon bucket. "Sorry to say they already scheduled a shoot with me. So you'd better get your ass in gear."

"You shouldn't refer to my ass."

"You referred to it already."

"That's different. It's mine. I can refer to it all I want. Like, kiss my ass, for instance."

He laughed, gazing at her from the lower deck like a Romeo in oilskins. The sun glided across his bare chest picking out dips and ridges like an artist. "You trying to light a fire under my ass?" He paused. "I can refer to my own ass, right? You don't have a problem with that?"

She had a problem with everything he did, to be honest. Perhaps because he always surprised her and that made her nervous. "I have no problem with that. Except it's not going to work. I'm going to grab that spot if it kills me."

Ruby crouched next to her, a warm little bundle at her side. Megan startled. She'd momentarily forgotten about her own daughter. Why was she talking about "asses" within earshot of Ruby? "If what kills you, Mama? Hi Lucas!"

"Hi there." Lucas waved his fillet knife. "How's the pizza?"

"You should come have some with us."

Megan nearly panicked at the thought of Lucas sitting down with them. *No no no.* But of course she shouldn't have worried.

"That's nice of you, Ruby, but I'm all tanked up." He brought a handful of fish guts halfway to his mouth and pretended to dive in for a voracious bite, like a pirate.

"Ewww." Ruby laughed and squealed, and so did a few nearby patrons. Megan caught the sound of a camera clicking. Photogenic Lucas Holt was going to appear on someone's Instagram.

Well, he was probably used to it. All the fishing charter customers took tons of photos. She'd even noticed a photo of a much-younger Lucas on the bulletin board in the harbormaster's office—apparently he'd caught a record halibut when he was a teenager. Making headlines even as a kid.

She couldn't exactly compete with that, could she?

"Come on, Ruby, let's finish our pizza and let the fish surgeon finish his operation."

"Fish surgeon. Not bad, Bird Nerd."

Megan gritted her teeth and dropped the window closed. With Lucas, she always tried to get the last word and yet so rarely succeeded. He was almost as good with the verbal jabs as he was with his fillet knife.

"Mama, what did you mean 'if it kills you'?" Ruby wore a worried look as she scooted across the wooden bench back to their plates.

"Oh, it's just a silly expression. It's an exaggerated way of saying I really want something."

"Want what?"

"To win. To beat Lucas." She laughed at how competitive that sounded. "No, what I really want is the opportunity to be on a TV show that could be very helpful to the *Forget Me Not*."

She had to keep her priorities straight here. Beating Lucas wasn't the point. Keeping her business afloat was.

"Couldn't you both be on the TV show?"

"I don't know. It's possible, but Zoe said they wanted to profile one boat. If they only pick one, it will probably be the *Jack Hammer*." She was so used to being overshadowed by Lucas and his charter business. He had the most desirable slip, the prime advertising spot on the Chamber of Commerce brochure, the most prominently located office on the boardwalk. It made sense; everyone knew the *Jack Hammer* and no one cared about nature tours. But sometimes she got discouraged. "I think that's a great solution, sweetie. I'll see what I can do. Now what do you say we go to the beach and walk off this pizza?"

"I wish we had a dog to walk," Ruby said mournfully as they clambered down the scrubby path that led to the shoreline. "Or at least Fidget."

Megan suppressed a sigh. If it wasn't Lucas, it was Lucas' dog. If it wasn't Lucas' dog, it was his boat. Lost Harbor was obviously Lucas Holt territory, and where did that leave her?

# CHAPTER FIVE

Lucas met with the detective the next morning. Maya Badger had been a year ahead of him in high school, and they'd actually dated for about three months—a time they never talked about anymore. She'd always been smart but quiet, and he never would have pegged her for a future police officer.

Showed what he knew, because she'd joined the tiny police department right out of school and worked her way up to lead—and only—detective at a rapid pace. Her quiet manner worked in her favor. She knew how to drain the drama out of a situation and get suspects to spill incriminating secrets.

But so far, she hadn't been able to get Lucas to drop his quest to find out if there was more to his father's death than the official ruling of "accident."

Maya showed up at the *Jack Hammer* as he was setting out a bowl of food for Fidget, whose nose was already twitching with delight. "Morning, Officer. Nice and sunny today."

"Let's do ourselves a favor and skip the weather portion of the conversation," she said dryly.

He shrugged and brushed his hands on his pants. "If no one

in Lost Harbor talked about the weather there'd be a lot of silence."

"No, there wouldn't. There'd be endless drama filling the gap. I'm pro weather convos because they don't generally go off the rails. But right now I don't have time."

"Do you at least have time for some coffee?"

He already had a pot brewing in his little onboard galley.

"Got decaf?"

"For you, Officer..." He gave up. "No. Sorry, I don't think I have any decaf on board. I might have an ancient mint tea bag from circa 2003."

"Pass. Thanks." She tucked a strand of hair into her bun. Maya was one of a handful of African-Americans who had attended his high school, maybe five in a class of a hundred graduating seniors. He'd often wondered what that had been like for her, but even when they were dating they'd never talked about that. "So. Mr. Hammer Junior."

He winced. "Thank God that's not an actual nickname."

"I could work on that. Spread the word in a few key spots around town." She fixed him with a mildly threatening look. He'd always appreciated her sneaky sense of humor.

"Now that's just mean. Am I really causing that much trouble?" He sank down onto the cushioned starboard seat and rested one arm along the gunwales. She didn't sit, but kept her boots braced apart on the deck as the Jack Hammer gently rose and fell.

"Here's the thing, hotshot. I investigated your dad's death *personally*. I mean, of course I did because who else was going to? It's my job."

"And you did a good job. I know you did. I'm not casting doubt on that. You know that, right?"

"Not really. If you believed that, you wouldn't be wasting your time the way you are. I mean, I heard you wanted to interview the coroner. He *drowned*, Lucas. He fell off his boat and drowned. He was extremely drunk. He was often drunk. You know all this."

The sentences came at him like jabs of a knife. "I know this," he agreed tightly. No one knew it better than him.

"So why'd you start up with this ten months later? Maybe I just answered my own question. You're following in your dad's footsteps. Jack Holt never let go of anything in his life, did he?"

"He let go of me."

That came out starker then he'd intended. Her face softened. "He had to. You left Alaska. He still talked about you, though."

His throat tight, he nodded. Fuck, why did talking about his dad get him so worked up? They'd fought until they were each bloody and bruised—sometimes literally. They'd fought until the rest of the family fled or put on headphones or blasted the radio. One of the things they'd fought about was the *Jack Hammer*. Lucas had never wanted to take over the damn thing. He'd left so he didn't have to. Started his own business. Made a decent amount of money. And yet here he was, after all that, running the *Jack Hammer*. Fuck, what kind of idiot was he anyway?

"Did you ever think that maybe you'd be better off talking to a counselor than trying to solve something that doesn't need solving?"

"Funny thing is, I have, Officer."

"You don't have to call me that all the time."

"Detective?"

"That either."

"I can't just call you Maya. You're an officer of the law. That's requires some respect. You earned a title, right?"

The corners of her mouth lifted in a pleased expression. "When you put it that way, sure, I'll take the title. Officer Badger."

"That's both appropriate and oddly adorable," he murmured,

then winced. "Adorable" didn't seem to go very well with the "respect" part. "Sorry."

"Don't sweat it. Anyway, back to my main point. People are grumbling. They don't like being interrogated by a civilian. It's awkward."

"I'm just asking questions. I don't want to put anyone on the spot. I'm just trying to piece together a timeline of that night. Who he talked to, who he was drinking with, who he was feuding with."

"Your father had a dozen feuds going at a time." With a huff of frustration, she pulled a black leather bound notebook from her pocket and scribbled on a page. She tore it off and handed it to him. "Talk to Nate Prudhoe. He was the first firefighter on the scene. First to examine your dad. If you don't believe me, maybe you'll believe him."

Her exasperation gave him a stab of guilt. "This isn't personal, Officer Badger. I mean, it is personal in that it's my father. But not when it comes to you. I know you did a thorough investigation. I just can't—"

"What? Can't what?"

"Can't get his voice out of my head," he admitted. "I never thought he'd go that way. Not yet, anyway. Falling out of his own boat—drowning—it's too sudden. That's not how it was supposed to end."

"This isn't a movie, Lucas. Things end when they end."

He winced at her bluntness. "I'm guessing you don't do a lot of notifications of loved ones?"

"I'm about 'tough love,' you know that. You're grieving, Lucas. I see that. But you're starting to rub people the wrong way. Not just me, not just my boss, but other people around town."

Lucas felt that familiar "Hammer" stubbornness settling into his bones. When that happened, there was no budging a member of the Holt family.

"Maybe you should give me a list of those people. Maybe there's a reason they don't like me asking questions."

With a giant roll of her eyes, Maya flicked the piece of paper she'd given him. "Not happening. You talk to Nate, then you stand down."

He knew Nate. They'd played hockey together. It would be good to catch up with him. "How about this? I won't bug anyone. I'll simply listen. Observe. Drink a few too many mugs of beer at the Olde Salt Saloon. If I pick something up, I'll—"

"Come to me."

"Come to you," he agreed reluctantly. "I don't like taking up your time, though."

"You won't. Because there won't be anything. Because there's no mystery here. No crime. No foul play. It was an *accident*."

He gave her a neutral nod as she stepped over the railing onto the ramp. "Thanks for stopping by, Officer Badger. If you need any halibut for your freezer, give me a call."

"Can't stand halibut. Nasty flabby-ass bottom feeders. See you around, Lucas. Be good."

"Yes ma'am."

# CHAPTER SIX

After Maya left, Lucas set to work on the right-hand eight-cylin-
der, thirteen-thousand horsepower MAN marine engine, which
had been misfiring more than he liked. He unscrewed the casing
and set it carefully to the side. His father had taught him how to
fix engines starting around the age of eight. Jack Holt would
crack open a beer and bask in the sun while Lucas took an
outboard apart and put it back together again.

Occasionally he'd grab a part and toss it overboard.

"Now do it without that. Jerry-rig it. You're out on the water,
engine fails, what do you do?"

"Call the Coast Guard?"

"Sure, but the nearest Coastie's all the way around Far Point
and the wind's picking up. You gotta get that engine going."

"We have two engines. I'd just use the other one and go half
as fast." It seemed like a brilliant idea to him.

"I said a storm was coming." That irritable voice, the crunch
of a hand tightening on a beer can...

Lucas ignored the signs. "So I'd go into a cove or something
until the storm was over."

"Do you have to argue about every fucking thing? Fix the damn engine." Lucas ducked as something went flying past his head.

"Hey, that was my lunch from Mom!"

"Yeah well, you can go crying to her when the job is done."

---

"HEY! Holt. We're heading to the Olde Salt for a quick one."

Lucas jerked his head up, the memory of his father darting away like an eel slipping underwater. Three of his father's friends clustered next to the *Jack Hammer*. In their fishing boots, flannel shirts and unruly beards, they were a motley crew. "It's not even nine yet."

"By the time we get there, doors will be open."

Good God. Why was he even surprised? Many fishermen liked to drink, especially the older generation. Jack Holt had probably spent a million hours in the Olde Salt Saloon over the course of his life.

But he didn't want to go against Officer Badger's orders quite so soon.

"Sorry, guys, I just got into this engine. Save a spot for me."

One of the fishermen—Lenny—peered into the cabin. "Looking good in there. Jack would hardly believe his eyes."

"Yeah, I've done some upgrades."

He'd cleaned and ripped out the moldy old seat cushions. Painted. Installed some new brass fittings. Mostly cosmetic fixes, but enough to attract a more modern clientele.

Old Crow, whose hair was still as black as ever, shaded his eyes and scanned the interior. "Hardly looks like Jack's boat anymore. Not even his suitcases are left."

"Suitcases?"

"Yeah, he was sleeping on his boat a lot before he drowned.

Kept hauling suitcases down here. Guess your mom must have grabbed 'em."

"Guess so." *Suitcases?* What the hell? Why was he just now hearing about this? Could that be a clue of some kind?

He should have invited the fishermen onto the *Jack Hammer* months ago.

"Catch you in a bit," he told them as they headed off for their morning pick-me-up.

Suitcases. What could that signify? Mom had never mentioned anything about any suitcases, but he knew his father had been sleeping on the boat. Everyone had told him about that, including Mom.

Was he meeting someone here? Carrying on an affair? Smuggling contraband? Developing dementia?

It might mean nothing. But he didn't remember seeing any suitcases when he'd first stepped onto the *Jack Hammer*. So it could be significant.

Would Officer Badger be unhappy that he had a possible new lead? Probably.

Was he going to see where it went? Definitely.

Something bumped against the bow of the *Jack Hammer*. He sighed. He knew exactly what it was, because the same thing happened every week or so. He climbed out of his boat and strode to the tie-up ahead of him. The stern of the damn *Forget Me Not* was kissing the bow of the *Jack Hammer*, the barest brush of wood against fiberglass.

Grumbling, he unfastened the line from the cleat and drew the boat tighter against the ramp. It wasn't completely Megan's fault. Their boats both needed bigger spaces, but an influx of wealthy sports fishermen had made summer slips hard to come by. But still—she needed to be more careful about tying up her boat.

He tightened the lines and coiled the end neatly next to the cleat. Then he went back onto the *Jack Hammer* and found one of his business cards. He wrote a note on the back and wedged it between the line and the cleat.

This time when he went back to work on his engine, he couldn't suppress his smile. He could already picture the face she'd make when she saw his note, her *woof* of exasperation.

*Forget how to knot?* He'd written. *Private lessons available.*

He'd be lucky if she didn't try to dump him overboard after that. This feud was pretty ridiculous. But also kind of fun.

# CHAPTER SEVEN

Padricny of Megan's friends ever came to Lost Harbor for a visit, they'd probably think she'd lost her mind. The cabin she rented barely had running water, and you had to wait a good fifteen minutes for the on-demand water heater to make enough hot water for a shower. For washing dishes, often she saved time by heating water on the stove.

The little cabin had one bedroom, which she and Ruby shared. It had no landline, and the power went out at least once a month. Even though it had a propane heater and a wood stove, during the cold months she and Ruby had bundled up in layers of wool and silk underwear. And still they'd noticed every little cold draft that snuck through the cracks in the walls, which dated from the 1940s.

But she loved it despite all those flaws.

It had one feature that made up for all those drawbacks: a view. Perched on a ridge a thousand feet above sea level, the cabin's hundred-and-eighty degree view was better than TV. On clear days they could see all the way to the open ocean on the other side of the point. She and Ruby loved to count the glaciers and peaks of Lost Souls Wilderness just across the bay. They could even see the long arm of the Lost Harbor breakwater curling protectively around its flock of boats.

From here, the name Lost Harbor made perfect sense. Sailing in from the ocean, the first explorers would have seen spectacular mountains and glaciers and vast endless wilderness before they noticed the notch in the coastline where boats could shelter. Maybe they kept losing track of it, as the legends said.

And then there were the clouds. Megan could watch for hours as clouds paraded across the sky and cast shadows on Misty Bay. On stormy days they loomed dark like a horde of elephants stampeding through a gap in the mountain range. Sometimes clouds drifted like dandelion fluff lost in a dream. On certain days banks of thick fog would roll in, or whimsical wisps of mist, which explained the name Misty Bay.

The bay was always changing, and if Megan had an ounce of artistic talent, she would set up an easel and never move.

Instead, she usually kicked up her feet in a lounge chair and never moved.

She and Ruby had bought planters and filled them with oregano and rosemary. An old apple crate made a side table between the two plastic Adirondack chairs she'd rescued from the dump.

While Ruby buried herself in a new math book that Dev had sent, Megan took her mug of tea and laptop to the deck. Even though the tourist season had begun, the air still hadn't warmed up enough to qualify as summer. She still needed a cardigan and fuzzy socks, not to mention her hot tea.

She set her laptop onto the apple crate and dropped into the chair with a sigh. Her to-do list lurked inside her computer like a troll. Check for new bookings. Answer inquiries. Update website. Pay bills. Ask for extensions on bills. Consider advertising options. Explain to her father why she was throwing away her almost-degree on nature tours.

She ignored all that and tilted her face to the sky. The air still held the memory of winter, but a tender warmth was just beginning to break through, like a green shoot through snow. And it was so pure, as if the glaciers had washed it clean as it passed across Lost Souls Wilderness.

Her phone rang. *Zoe.* One of the very few people she'd consider talking to at this moment.

"The *Trekking* producer wants to see you in action before he commits, but he's open to considering you."

"Really?" She sat straight up and planted her feet on the deck. "That's incredible, thank you."

"Actually, you should thank Lucas. He told the producers they should give you a look."

A funny feeling settled into Megan's stomach. She didn't want to owe Lucas anything. He'd just lord it over her. "How do you know that?"

"The producer told me. He also told me that he thinks audiences will find it boring."

Megan winced. That stung. "Have you ever heard of the concept of sugarcoating?"

"I have. I'm not a fan. I'm giving you good information here. You have a shot to get on TV, but you have to make it interesting."

"Science *is* interesting! It's everything. It's all around us. Birds are fascinating, they're like little dinosaurs flying around."

"Yes, but this is a travel show, not Bill Nye the Science Guy. It's TV, it's visual. And a bunch of elderly tourists staring through binoculars is not visually compelling. You need a gimmick."

"A gimmick. What kind of gimmick?"

"Well, you have Ruby. A mother-daughter team running boat tours, that's appealing."

"No, I'm not putting Ruby on TV. Dev would hate that. He's always going on about privacy issues."

"Well, you have to do something, because—" Another call flashed on Megan's screen.

"Crap, it's Dev. I have to take it. We signed an agreement never to ignore each other's calls."

"See that, in a nutshell, that's why I never want a husband. I reserve the right to ignore calls."

Megan laughed. "I'll call you later, Zoe. Thanks, I really appreciate it."

She switched to the other call. "Hi Dev."

"Hi. I have a free week coming up, I need directions. Why is it called Lost Harbor? Is it hard to find?"

She couldn't hide her shock. "Wait, *what*? You're coming here?"

"Making the arrangements now. I did hope you'd give up on that silly boat by now, but you're still there."

"Thanks for that vote of confidence."

"No harm meant." Dev still had a trace of a British accent from being raised in India. "You know what I mean."

She did, of course. After the university incident, she'd needed to escape, to get as far away as possible. "I honestly didn't expect to stay this long either. But Ruby really loves it."

"Then I need to see this place."

"You won't like it. It's chilly and not very exciting."

"*I'm* certainly not going to live there."

"Of course you aren't," she said fervently. Did that sound a little too enthusiastic? "I mean, you could if you wanted to, I suppose."

"I got your point, no worries." His dry tone reassured her. In many ways, they'd had the perfect breakup. As a couple, they'd driven each other equally crazy, and neither had wanted to hang onto the relationship any longer than the other. The only catch was Ruby, and they both worked very hard to do the best thing for her—with Eliza Burke the mediator's help.

"I've been researching some programs for gifted students that might be right for Ruby. Perhaps even for this fall."

"So soon? She's only eight!"

"She's a prodigy, Megan." She heard the pride in his voice, and while she shared it, it also made her nervous. "She needs to have the best teachers available. No matter how scenic Alaska, there probably isn't a PhD to be found in that little town of yours."

*There's me*, she wanted to say. But that wasn't a solution, even though she'd been home-schooling Ruby up to now. Her degree was in ornithology, not math, and she hadn't even completed it. Ruby had already surpassed her in calculus. "She's also a kid who wants to have fun. Dev, just wait until you see her here. She loves the ocean, she loves all the harbor doings, she loves the characters here."

"That's why I'm coming, so I can see for myself. But Megan, we're responsible for her development. We can't just hide her away in the wilderness and forget that IQ of hers."

Megan took the phone away from her face and glared at it. She counted to five, then spoke into it again. "An IQ is just a number. Ruby is a person. We're responsible for all parts of her, not just her brain."

"Of course, but her brain is paramount. I'll see you soon."

After he ended the call in his usual abrupt way, Megan nearly hurled the phone off the deck. Dev was so highhanded. Of course Ruby's gift for math was important. But was it the *most* important? What kind of special program did he want to send her to? Would it require leaving Lost Harbor? Would she be on her own? That, Megan would never agree to. She and Ruby stayed together, no matter what.

If Dev insisted on sending her to some advanced program

somewhere, Megan would be right by her side. *Forget Me Not* forgotten.

But maybe Dev would see right away how happy Ruby was here. She'd make everything perfect for him. It generally was perfect, except for one person.

Maybe she'd get really lucky and Lucas would be out of town during her ex's visit.

Ruby came out on the deck, her math book open to a page covered with charts.

"How's it going there, sweetie?"

"Good," she said absently and climbed into the other chair. Completely engrossed, she didn't look up from the book.

Damn. Maybe Dev was right. Ruby had a mind for math and she deserved the best education they could give her.

"Honey, I just talked to your dad. He's coming for a visit."

"Okay."

"He wants to send you to a program for math whizzes."

"Okay."

"He thinks we should sell the boat for scrap."

"Okay."

Megan sighed. When Ruby was deep in her studies, nothing could distract her. Megan used to be like that too, until life had interrupted with all its twists and turns. Now she got distracted by all kinds of irrelevant things—like Lucas without a shirt.

Lucas winking at her from the lower deck. Lucas lobbing verbal volleys at her while the sun gleamed on his chiseled muscles.

Why had he recommended her boat to the *Trekking* producer? What was in it for him? As long as she'd known him, he'd been a grouchy bear to her.

She'd never forget the first moment they met. She'd been docking the *Forget Me Not* on one of her very first solo trips.

Admittedly, it wasn't her best effort. A new boat was tied up in the spot next to hers, and it surprised her.

It was a slick charter boat with fishing poles aggressively bristling from it. Even the sight of it unnerved her.

She'd come in too fast, bounced off the float like an enormous pinball, and then jammed into reverse. Too late. She'd bumped against its stern hard enough to jolt it.

On the deck, a man had jumped to his feet. He was holding something in his hands, but she couldn't see what. Everything was a blur—his dark scowl, his broad shoulders, his protective posture.

"Hey! Watch it!"

"Sorry!"

Wrestling with the helm, she'd successfully brought the *Forget Me Not* snug against the float, dropped the fenders over the side and jumped out to tie it up. But Lucas was way ahead of her. He snagged the line off the bow and whipped it around the cleat in the kind of smooth motion that meant he'd grown up doing it.

"Where's Carmen? Why's she letting an ignoramus drive her boat?"

Every bone of her body had snapped straight. How dare he speak to her with so much scorn dripping from his voice? "It's my boat now. Carmen's gone."

"Did you run her over?"

"No! She left. I'm taking over. I *did* take over. Forget Me Not Nature Tours is mine now."

He'd stared at her for a long moment, then given a harsh bark of laughter. "Where the hell did she find you? Let me guess, California."

"You have something against California?"

"Ha. So I was right."

She waved him off. "The fact that I'm from San Francisco is irrelevant. I have a degree in—"

But he was already turning away. "I don't need to hear your resume. I doubt you'll be around long enough for it to matter. But if you really want to study something, try the Boat Basics class at the high school. They do an excellent job teaching the kids."

That was the first time he got the last word.

She'd fumed for a good hour or two as she'd hosed off the decks of the *Forget Me Not*. What. An. Ass. She'd just barely bumped his boat. He didn't need to be such a dick about it. *Jack Hammer,* his boat was called. Seemed about right.

The next time she saw Zoe she'd asked about the captain of the *Jack Hammer*. That was when she learned that his name was Lucas Holt—son of Jack Holt, who had drowned shortly before Megan had arrived in Lost Harbor. Lucas had hauled out the boat for repairs—that was why she'd never seen the *Jack Hammer* before. Zoe also told her that Lucas was a local legend as a rescue volunteer and had saved more lost boaters than anyone.

With her sympathy activated by the news about his father, she'd decided to be nice to Lucas. She'd brought him a coffee the next day as an apology for bumping his boat.

He told her he was trying to quit coffee.

She'd offered her condolences on the loss of his father. "Did you know him?" he'd asked.

"No."

"He was a mean bastard and he would have ripped you a new one."

"Amazing how genetics works," she'd murmured.

"What was that?"

"Nothing important."

"No, I heard you. Just wondered if you'd be willing to say it again, a little louder."

She'd snatched the coffee back. "I retract my condolences."

"And my heart breaks all over again."

And that was the second time he got the last word.

Clearly he wanted nothing to do with her and her niceness. The only time he smiled around her was when Ruby was at her side. The rest of the time, he either ignored her or mocked her or publicly disagreed with her suggestions for the harbor and the boardwalk.

Fate kept throwing them together—the only office space she could find was at the back of the *Jack Hammer* office. The only slip available was right up against the *Jack Hammer*. Etcetera, etcetera.

So she'd followed his lead and switched to giving back as good as she got. It was empowering, really. Energizing. It felt good, fighting with him. Sometimes she even got the last word and a kind of fizzy joy would follow her the rest of the day.

Maybe...she jolted to her feet as a thought occurred to her. Maybe Lucas was pulling a bait-and-switch. A double-blind bait-and-switch. He knew the producers thought a nature cruise was too boring. By suggesting they give her a shot, Lucas got to look like the good guy. She would still get rejected, but he'd come out smelling like a rose.

Oh hell no. If Lucas thought he had this in the bag, he'd better get ready to eat his words. To grovel at her feet. Because she was about to shock them all.

She snatched up her phone and called Zoe.

"I have an idea about the *Trekking* audition. But I might need your help."

# CHAPTER EIGHT

The day of Lucas' *Trekking* shoot did not start off well. His mother was in a mood. Even the Holt Homestead, which consisted of a hundred acres of land, three houses and six cabins, wasn't big enough for both of them sometimes.

Janet Holt, whose primary passion in life was crafting, had recently bought a Tibetan yak with the idea of shearing it for wool. Yaks were supposed to like the Alaska climate—just like the Himalayas. But the yak didn't get along with her cows, so she'd had to build a separate enclosure, and still the yak liked to secretly nip at the cows. Milk production was down.

He didn't say it out loud, but to him it was no surprise to find one more feud on Holt property. Or in Lost Harbor in general, for that matter. Feuds came with the territory.

After ranting in her mud boots for a good half hour about the yak's passive-aggressive ways, she launched into her complaints about Lucas. He knew them by heart by now.

*Why was it taking him so long to go through his father's junk pile?*

Because Jack Holt had accumulated tools and machinery and

supplies for sixty years before he died. All of it was stored on the property in case he needed it one day.

*Why didn't Lucas just move into the big house so they could rent out the other ones?*

He was paying rent, a fact which she conveniently ignored.

*Why didn't he sell his consulting business and stop threatening to leave Alaska?*

He wasn't ready to sell, and it wouldn't be so simple in any case.

*Why didn't he sell the Jack Hammer? They could all go on a cruise to Florida with that money.*

He'd rather dive under an iceberg than go on a cruise to Florida.

*And why did he keep dating tourists who never stayed longer than a few nights?*

Easy one. Because they never stayed longer than a few nights.

It definitely wasn't the right moment to ask about what happened to the suitcases on the *Jack Hammer*.

*She's grieving,* he had to keep reminding himself. He knew the strange ways that grief could appear. He'd reacted much the same way himself. For the first few months, he'd barely been civil to anyone. He would have been better off under that iceberg.

Eventually he got his mother calmed down and drove his truck into town.

He stopped by the fire station first to talk to Nate, the first responder on the scene of his father's drowning. He found his old hockey buddy hosing off one of the fire engines out back.

He'd always liked hanging out with Nate, with his broken nose and laughing gray eyes. But in this case, he got nowhere.

"I'm sorry, man, but he'd been dead at least half an hour before I got there. He was right there, next to the *Jack Hammer*. Current was pushing him against the side. I don't think there's any mystery there. I found an empty bottle of Scotch rolling around the deck."

"What about a suitcase?"

"A suitcase? Might have been. I didn't inventory everything on the boat. I was focused on your dad, and had to call for backup to get him into the paramedic van."

Nate gave his shoulder a sympathetic squeeze. He'd always been a kind soul. "I'm really sorry. I liked your dad. Had more than a few drinks with him at the Olde Salt."

"What about the call to the station, the 911 call? Anything there?"

"A panicky call from Boris Clancy? Nah. He was riding his bike on the boardwalk and spotted the body. Badger interviewed him. He didn't have much to say."

"He never does." Boris Clancy was one of the harbor's most eccentric characters. He carried his pet chicken in a basket on his bike and avoided eye contact at all costs.

"You know, there is one person he talks to. I mean, if you think he might have more to offer."

"Yeah? Who's that?"

"The new girl, the cute one with the nature tour. He likes her. I've seen her chatting with him."

He meant Megan. A shot of ... something, maybe possessiveness?... surprised Lucas. Why would he feel anything of the sort about Megan? He shoved the stupid reaction aside.

"Thanks, man. Appreciate it."

"Anything I can do to help, let me know."

Was it a lead? Hard to say, really. He'd never had a conversation with Boris because the man always fled at the sight of him.

---

AFTER THAT, he met the producer and camera crew of

*Trekking* at the top of the ramp. The tide was almost dead low, so the ramp tilted at a vertiginous angle. The camera operator eyed it nervously.

"We're getting a few shots from up here first," the producer, Tony LaRousse, explained. He wore a thick down parka and tight black jeans. He was a twenty-something black guy with a mellow, seen-it-all vibe. "Not sure we have enough liability waivers to cover that ramp."

Two kids carried a kayak past them, holding it over their heads as they loped down the ramp.

"You get used to it," Lucas explained with a smirk.

"Sure. We'll work on that. So which boat is yours?"

Lucas pointed out the *Jack Hammer*, with its bold, hyper-macho profile.

"Damn. It's like the 'fuck you' of boats," said Tony.

"Yeah, I guess it is. It's got more horsepower than most of the other charters. It can go farther, faster, so we can get to the deep water holes and back in time for dinner."

"The deep water. Where's that?"

"Around Far Point's the best fishing. Currents come in from the ocean, collide with other currents from the bay. You can find a huge variety of fish out there. With halibut, you want a depth of two to three hundred feet. So we have a few secret spots we take people to. I can pretty much guarantee you'll catch something."

"Let's hope so, because we have to get this into editing soon. Crazy production schedule."

"We'll make sure you get some good footage—" He trailed off as everyone's gazes turned away from him and toward the water.

"Now that's what I'm talking about," murmured the camera operator as he focused on something. "That's how you get the eyeballs."

"Keep shooting. We'll worry about the releases later," ordered Tony.

Over the steady hum of an engine—it sounded like the *Forget Me Not*—he could hear the beat of dance music. A party boat? Lost Harbor didn't have party boats. Everyone here operated very serious fishing-focused operations. Lucas swung around to see what was going on.

The *Forget Me Not* cruised slowly through the harbor. Music pumped from the wheelhouse. On the deck, a sexy woman grooved to the beat. She wore a bikini top and cutoff shorts and rubber boots and looked sexy as hell. Her flowing brown hair tumbled over her shoulders. From under white-framed sunglasses, she grinned at Lucas and the camera crew.

Holy shit. *Megan Miller?*

He'd only ever seen her in fishing clothes. Baggy rubberized rain pants, waders, flannel overshirts.

Boots.

She wore the same boots as usual, but somehow the effect was completely different with bare legs.

Damn, she was sexy. Her waist curved inward in a dainty little notch. Her hips flared out—he caught a teasing glimpse of hipbone. The delectable mounds of her breasts nestled inside the cups of her orange bikini top. He imagined his hands there instead, touching that supple skin with its scattering of freckles.

"Who are they?"

*They?* Lucas dragged his gaze away from Megan and saw that Zoe was there too. She was going for the sexy look too, in a belly shirt and form-fitting workout leggings. He usually only saw her behind the counter at her pizza shop, and hadn't realized what a va-va-voom figure she had.

But as voluptuous as Zoe was, he couldn't keep his gaze from straying back to Megan. She always presented herself as the nature-loving bird-nerd science geek. How had he missed the fact that she was also a radiantly sexy woman? Or maybe he *had* noticed, but had chosen to overlook it for his own peace of mind.

Someone turned the music up and Megan and Zoe started to dance. Megan beckoned to the crew on the ramp. "Wanna go for a ride? We've got room!"

The producer and the camera operator looked at the ramp again, then shrugged. "I'll risk it if you will," said the cameraman. "Wouldn't mind mixing up the footage with something besides fish."

"I like it. An all-female crew running a boat in Alaska. That's a killer angle. Let's go."

Lucas wanted to point out that Ben captained the *Forget Me Not*, but then he realized that wasn't true. Trixie Tran, who ran the best ice cream shop on the boardwalk, was at the wheel. He couldn't see what she was wearing, but no doubt it was something equally sexy. Hell, Trixie had probably come up with this idea. She was the biggest flirt on the boardwalk—and he said that with all the affection in the world, since Trixie was a gem.

From the deck of the *Forget Me Not*, Megan caught his eye and blew him a mocking kiss.

He shot her a middle finger which he quickly turned into a thumb's up.

She drew her finger across her throat and pointed at him.

He pointed two fingers at his own eyes, then at her—the classic gesture for "watch your back."

She turned her back on him with a saucy little flounce of her ass.

He decided he wasn't going to win this one, and executed an elaborate bow, like some kind of courtier at Versailles.

She did a highly annoying in-your-face victory dance.

Fine. He'd give her this one. Let her think she'd won. Wasn't he the one who'd suggested the *Forget Me Not* to the producers? He sure didn't need the publicity. But Megan's dwindling business bothered him. She worked so hard, and her kid was so cute. And Lost Harbor would be a lot duller without her.

Especially now that he'd seen what she hid under her workaday fishing clothes. The problem now would be how to get that vision out of his mind.

Maybe it was time to do a reset on things with Megan.

"I'm going to get the *Jack Hammer* ready for action," he said, voice gruffer than usual. "Meet you on the float when you're done."

# CHAPTER NINE

Megan's plan had left out one crucial detail: Alaska was definitely not the right place to be out on the water in skimpy clothing. They'd barely reached the breakwater before they all had to put their jackets on. As soon as they left the harbor, the wind chilled them to the bone. Gamely, they kept the music going, and served slices of Zoe's pizza to the TV crew. Trixie entertained the camera crew with stories of growing up in Lost Harbor. The producer filmed that part, and got a great zoom shot of the lost baby otter, but as soon as Megan explained the true nature of Forget Me Not Nature Tours, his eyes glazed over.

"I'm sorry, but when people think of Alaska, they want to see extreme weather conditions and gigantic crab legs. Everything bigger and wilder."

"We saw a Wandering Tattler the other day. Do you know how rare that is?"

"No idea. Look, I appreciate the effort, and an all-female crew is definitely worth a mention."

"We're not always all-female. My regular captain is a man. Well, more like a boy," she admitted.

"Ah. Well, no matter, we'll certainly include you for at least three seconds. And we'll put your website on the page for the show. That's about all I can offer."

Even though it was better than nothing, Megan's throat tightened with a sense of despair. She could feel this opportunity— this chance to make a living in Lost Harbor—slipping away.

"I understand. Thanks for coming out with us." She signaled to Trixie to turn the boat around. The *Forget Me Not* lumbered in a wide arc to head back to port. "Can I ask what charter outfit you're going to feature? Is it the *Jack Hammer?*"

She couldn't help it. Just when she thought she'd gotten one up on Lucas, he was going to walk away with the prize after all. And it didn't even mean anything to him, that was the worst part. Everything always flowed his way. He was the king of his world and all she wanted was a tiny piece of it.

"Most likely, yes. It's at the top of our list at the moment. Charismatic captain, tragic backstory. High-powered boat."

"Tragic backstory? You mean his father?"

"That's part of it, yes. He left behind his million dollar consulting firm to come back here and take over his dead father's business. He was worried about his mother. That's pretty compelling."

Oh God, now she felt like a jerk for harboring ill will towards Lucas. What was that saying about being kind because you never know what kind of battle someone is fighting?

But how was she supposed to know if he never exchanged a friendly word with her?

She staggered as something bumped the boat. A vibration ran through the wooden planks, almost like an electric shock.

"What the hell..." said Tony, grabbing onto the railing. "What was that?"

"I don't know." She'd never felt anything like it. The water had a normal amount of chop, its surface broken by only a few lines of creamy froth. Had they struck a rock? Had Trixie taken them over a sandbar by mistake?

An ominous quiet gripped the *Forget Me Not*.

"You, with the camera," shouted Zoe. "Get out there and point at the water off the starboard side. There!" She gestured as the camera man didn't budge. "Start rolling. Now!"

All that practice bossing her pizza peons around did the trick. The camera operator hurried to the deck and slung the camera onto his shoulder.

"There!" called Zoe.

Everyone looked where she was pointing. A slippery flank of polished black flesh broke the surface of the water. At a deliberate, hypnotic pace, it cut through the waves like a fillet knife through butter, as if water and fish were two sides of the same substance. Not fish—orca.

Megan automatically switched into nature tour mode. "You're looking at an orca, commonly known as a killer whale, but there's no need to worry. Orcas aren't interested in attacking people or boats."

She caught Zoe's eye as her friend shook her head frantically. Right—this was *Trekking*. Cue the drama, the life-threatening conflict.

"That is, fishermen in these parts know to keep a wary eye out for these powerful predators," she said in a hushed voice. "One snap of an orca's jaws and an entire catch could be lost. They've been known to snatch seals right off the ice. Even though they're technically dolphins, they're called 'killer whales' for a reason. They're apex predators who hunt in packs, almost like wolves. If you come face to face with an orca and he mistakes you for a sea lion, your only hope is that he's not particularly hungry or angry. Or hangry."

A muffled snort came from Zoe's direction. Too far?

"Will they attack humans?" The cameraman took a step back.

"Not in the wild. There have been incidents in captivity, but never in the wild. Orcas are truly fascinating. They're picky eaters, so if one goes after you it's only because he's mistaken you for something else. He will abandon the hunt as soon as he realizes his mistake. Orca pods are complex communities with deep family bonds. They've existed on this planet far longer than we have, about eleven million years."

They all watched the orca's smooth body slide through the water. The white mark on his neck disappeared under the water.

"Why don't they eat humans?" asked the producer, sounding almost disappointed.

"Unknown. The Tlingit have a legend that explains it. A wood carver created the first killer whale and sent it off to get revenge on his brothers, who had abandoned him. But then he felt so terrible about what he'd done that he ordered the orca never to harm a human."

Glancing at their faces, she realized that instead of amping up the drama, she'd done the opposite. She really sucked at this.

"I should mention that one of the hazards of boating in Misty Bay is the risk of a whale surfacing under your boat. It's been known to happen in these very waters."

The producer's eyes brightened. "So are we literally in danger at this very moment as we wait for the orca to surface?"

Probably not, to be honest. Orcas were highly intelligent and knew they weren't a good food source. But she could fudge it.

"Until we know where he is, who knows what could happen next?" She waved a hand toward the forested bluffs a few hundred yards away. "We're nearing Lost Souls Wilderness, and the locals say strange things happen around Lost Souls."

A few breathless beats passed while they shaded their eyes and gazed at the water around them. A breeze ruffled the surface and a cormorant swooped past them on black, hooked wings. No sign of the orca.

A small fish—probably a grayling—broke the surface and disappeared again. The orca had most likely moved on if the grayling felt safe enough to do that. But Megan kept that information to herself.

With a sigh, the cameraman shifted his focus to the majestic sight of Lost Souls Wilderness. "What can you tell us about that area? Why is it called Lost Souls?"

Megan glanced at Zoe. "Want to field this one?"

Zoe seamlessly took over in the same suspenseful tone she'd been using. "Alaska is brutally tough territory. Many of the early explorers died in that wilderness. Countless mariners and fishermen have been lost to the sea. Loss is a constant here, and the name reflects that."

"But there are other stories," Megan added.

"Such as?" Tony spoke in a tense voice as the cameraman scanned the harsh bluffs and deeply wooded ravines across the bay.

"Well, there's a local legend about a native tribe that disappeared into the glacier and never came back."

The camera swung toward her. She glanced at Zoe and Trixie, who were both frowning and shaking their heads. Oops, was she not supposed to talk about that tall tale?

She scrambled to correct her mistake. "But mostly, it has a metaphorical meaning."

"How's that?"

How was that, exactly?

"A lot of people find their way to Alaska because they're... looking for something."

"They're lost souls, so to speak," said Zoe. The camera swung to her. She smiled and picked up a slice of pizza for a nibble.

"That's right. They feel like lost souls and somehow they find something here that speaks to them. Like, in Zoe's case, pizza."

Zoe batted her eyelashes over the slice of pizza.

Trixie joined in next. "I've seen it happen many times. People come into my ice cream shop—Soul Satisfaction Ice Cream, isn't that appropriate?—It's right on the boardwalk and we have both indoor seating and a few picnic tables outside—they come in looking lost and lonely and by the time they leave they're thoroughly satisfied and riding a soul-sugar high."

Megan bit her lip to keep from laughing.

"So, now we're onto the product placement portion," Tony said dryly.

"We have sorbet too," Trixie chirped. "Our blueberries are picked locally."

"Okay then, camera off. Nice try. The orca, though, that was good. You got lucky, Megan. Looks like you'll be getting more than three seconds of airtime."

# CHAPTER TEN

All in all, Megan was in an excellent mood by the time she trudged up the ramp to the boardwalk. She'd left Ruby with Hunter, a boy whose family ran the Wild North kayak rental business. She found them playing cards on the floor of the office. Lucas' dog, Fidget, lay just outside, his chin resting on his paws.

"Are you dog-sitting, Rubes?"

She bent to scratch the dog's head. He barely opened one eye, then drifted back to his nap.

"Lucas said he'd buy me an ice cream cone if I took Fidget for a walk. We took him to the beach but now he's tired."

"I know the feeling. Did you already get your ice cream?"

"No, he isn't back yet." She lay down a queen of spades and scooped up a handful of cards.

"Then I'll buy you one. Come on. The *Forget Me Not* just had a huge day and I want to celebrate. I'll buy you both a cone."

"First I have to win." Ruby glared ferociously at Hunter. "I'm going to win, you know. The odds are now seven to six in my favor."

Was it a good thing that her math whiz kid was learning how to calculate odds like a Vegas bookmaker?

Ah well, she was in too good a mood to worry about it. She sat with her back against the shingled outer wall of the office and scratched Fidget's head. The warm sunshine pressed her eyelids down, as if she were a child being soothed to sleep by an infinitely loving parent.

*Lost souls ... wounded souls ...searching for something ... was there something to all that?* Her imagination drifted through the people she knew in this little harbor. Zoe's family had come here from Boston when she was a kid. Trixie had grown up here, but her family was from Thailand. They'd probably come here looking for an opportunity. Not much more to it than that. Or was there?

Visitors really make an effort to reach Lost Harbor, Alaska. It was way off the beaten path, almost an afterthought at the end of a long highway, as if the founders had traveled so far they didn't want to go back when they'd reached the end of the peninsula. Maybe the first explorers literally were lost. That would explain the name they'd given the wilderness across the bay. And what about the story of the native tribe that had vanished into the glacier? Why hadn't Zoe and Trixie wanted to share that story?

"My dog has no damn loyalty." The deep male voice, rich with amusement, startled her awake. "First you steal my shot at stardom, now you're taking Fidget?"

Lucas loomed over her. At first she couldn't quite open her eyes against the sunlight haloing his form. She held up a hand to block the sun, but he noticed and shifted so it wasn't necessary.

Those thoughtful little actions of his made it very hard to hate him.

"Just keeping him company while his master gallivants about."

"Gallivant. I need to do more of that."

Fidget climbed to his feet, his whole body quivering with excitement. Megan sympathized with that reaction. Her pulse skipped a few beats as she gazed up at the compact mountain of man above her.

She didn't like feeling at a disadvantage like that and tried to scramble to her feet. He reached a hand down to help her. The warm clasp of his grip, the rough slide of his calloused palm against hers, didn't help the fluttery heart situation at all.

"Want to come gallivant with me?" he murmured as she reached a standing position. "You probably want to celebrate. I heard you wowed the *Trekking* guys with your feminine wiles."

"No, with an orca," she corrected.

"Right. A whale, not a wile."

She laughed. "Technically, they're dolphins."

He glanced behind her at the two kids, who were now arguing over something that had just happened in their game. How could you argue over War? Somehow they'd found a way.

Crap—was she setting a bad example for her child by battling with Lucas as much as she did?

She should fix that. Right now. What better moment, when the sun was warming her face and melting all her defenses? "I can celebrate for a bit, as long as these two are okay."

"You kids okay for a few minutes?" he asked them.

The two children barely looked up at the grownups.

"I'll take that as a yes."

"We'll be back in a jiff, Ruby," Megan told her daughter. "I'll bring you a treat, okay?"

"I already owe her an ice cream." For the briefest moment, Lucas' hand rested on the small of her back as he guided her across the worn planks of the boardwalk. He dropped it almost before she noticed it was there. But the imprint of that slight pressure persisted even as they strolled past a display rack of sweaters.

"I know. It's not necessary, though. She loves walking Fidget.

She'd probably give *you* an ice cream cone just for the opportunity."

"She's never had a dog of her own?"

"Nope. We've always moved around a lot, for research projects and such. Once she came home from school with a goldfish and I had to outwait the darn thing before I could accept a teaching assistant job. I didn't want to move with a fishbowl. Luckily, they have short lifespans. I should have known she'd love it here. Fish everywhere you look."

She waved at the nearest charter office, Hooked on Halibut Charters. Two deckhands were hooking the day's catch to a hanging scale for the official weigh-in. A cluster of tourists were documenting the event with iPhones and video cameras.

"You don't like fish?"

"They're not my specialty. Birds are so much more interesting. I've always loved birds, ever since I was Ruby's age. Did you know that birds develop different dialects depending on where they're living? The White-crowned Sparrows we see here have a slightly different call than the same species down in midcoast California."

"Is that where you're from?"

Why was he asking all these personal questions? He'd never done anything like that before. And where was the impatient scowl he usually directed at her? Something was up with Lucas Holt.

"My family mostly lives in Arizona," she said cautiously. "But I went to grad school in the San Francisco area."

"What brought you to Lost Harbor?" They'd reached one of the few coffee shops on the boardwalk. At a table on the terrace, two fishermen were deep in a game of chess. The board was painted onto the table, along with many victors' initials. Tradition held that if you won, you could write your initials on the prefab concrete.

She caught a quick look of sadness crossing Lucas' face, and realized that all those "JHs" must be his father's initials.

One more reminder of how deep his roots here went—and how nonexistent hers were.

# CHAPTER ELEVEN

They stepped into the cool interior of the coffee shop. It had the feel of a retro apothecary. Jars of loose-leaf teas filled the mahogany shelves that lined the walls. A classic Italian espresso machine gleamed black and gold on the counter. A standup bar ran the length of the front wall. Perfect for people-watching on the boardwalk.

Lucas ordered a coffee and gestured for her to make her choice.

Slightly wary, she ordered a cappuccino. What was this all about? Why the sudden friendliness from someone who'd been dismissive of her since day one? Was this some kind of chess move in the ongoing feud that was their relationship?

If it was, she'd just watch it play out and respond accordingly. Or maybe she'd throw him off with an equal amount of friendliness.

"Thanks for putting in a good word with the *Trekking* producers," she said cheerfully as they carried their mugs to the standup bar. "You didn't have to do that. I appreciate it."

"I'm not the asshole I behaved like at first." He pushed a

small ceramic tub of sugar toward her. How did he know she liked a lot of sugar in her coffee?

"Isn't that what assholes always say?" She added a smile to her words. Did she think he was an asshole? Maybe she had—maybe she still did—but he was more complicated than a simple insult like that.

"My dad always boasted about being an asshole." He shrugged, then immediately hid behind his coffee mug.

Impulsively, she put a hand on his forearm. The steely strength lurking under his sleeve sent a shock through her. "I am sorry about your father."

Clearly embarrassed, he put down his mug with a click. "You said that when we first met. I'm not in the market for sympathy, unless it's over the piles of junk I have to deal with."

Hadn't they had this conversation already? "Fine. You don't want me to be nice. I got that message before. Then what are we doing here?" She gestured at the coffee shop. The girl behind the counter had disappeared into the back somewhere, probably sifting teas into jars.

"Peace treaty," he said. "I was an ass to you the first time we met, and I've felt bad about it ever since. I was fresh off my dad's death but that doesn't justify it." One side of his mouth quirked upwards. "Kinda wish we could start over. Like when you first bumped into my boat."

"Fine. We can start over. Here, let's do a reenactment." She took a yellow packet of Splenda and plopped it on the counter. "This is the *Forget Me Not*. Here's the *Jack Hammer*." She selected a brown packet of raw cane sugar for his boat.

"Raw. Is that in honor of my raw animal magnetism?"

"I was thinking more along the lines of your uncivilized manners." Again, she smiled to make sure he didn't take offense.

"Got it." He seemed unfazed by her teasing. She liked that about him. He usually let her barbs roll off him. Sometimes it got annoying, but overall she appreciated it. She didn't have to hold back with him. "So this is like one of those Civil War battles, with sugar packets instead of uniforms?"

"Exactly. So there's you, tied up at the float right next to my slip, where I'd never seen a boat before."

"The *Hammer* needed some repairs. It wasn't some kind of sneak attack."

She ignored him and tapped the Splenda packet. "And here's me, obeying every speed limit, following all the rules, returning from a hard day's work of chick counting."

"In what world is 'chick counting' work?"

She ignored his double entendre. "In the ornithology world. We need to track population growth and breeding rates, obviously."

"My bad. Sounds exhausting. Proceed."

She steered the packet of Splenda across the counter toward the packet of sugar. "Imagine my surprise when there's an aggro fishing boat where I'm supposed to tie up."

"Aggro?"

"Aggro," she said firmly. "That boat is designed to bully. It's the kind of boat that would stuff you in a locker. The kind of boat that can deadlift a Volvo. The kind of boat that kisses its own biceps. The kind of boat—"

"I get the point." Lucas was laughing, and it was a glorious sight to see. She noticed a dimple flashing through his dark late-day stubble. "You're saying my boat is an asshole."

"Your word, not mine. And here's the dainty old *Forget Me Not*, which is the closest thing a boat can come to a rocking chair, drifting innocently through the harbor, practically knitting as she goes."

"And when she reached the ramp, she executes a perfect maneuver to land as softly as a duck feather next to the *Jack*

*Hammer*." Now he was getting into the spirit of things. "What happens after your magnificent docking job?"

"First, you applaud."

He did so, clapping and bowing down to the Splenda package.

"Then I step out of the boat and introduce myself. Hi, I'm Megan Miller. I recently moved to Lost Harbor. I'm happy to meet my new harbor neighbor."

"And I say..." He cleared his throat. "Harbor neighbors aren't a thing. But welcome to Lost Harbor, Megan. I'm Lucas Holt. If you need anything, give me a call. Always happy to help out. Here's my number. I don't sleep much so feel free to call anytime." He handed her a napkin.

"Oh. Thank you, what a nice gesture. I'm sure I'll be fine because even though I'm new to the world of boats, I love a good challenge and how hard could it be?"

His smile went a bit rigid. "Wishing you the best of luck, of course, Megan, but may I point out that such a cavalier attitude is risky to you and those around you? Especially your harbor neighbors?"

"I thought that wasn't a thing."

"You introduced the concept so apparently now it is."

"So it's a thing only when it suits you."

"Just trying to speak your quirky California lingo. It's like a different language."

Megan paused for a breath before launching her next lob, but then caught his eye. They stared at each other for a moment, then both burst into laughter.

"So apparently no matter how things start out, we're destined to end up squabbling," she said, wiping away a tear of laughter.

"I guess some things are just meant to be."

But now all the tension of a moment ago had melted away and something very different took its place. A warmth—something sunny and electric and knee-melting. She became very aware of how close his arm was to hers. How hard and muscled and solid he felt next to her. Lucas was the kind of man who would be a bulwark against anything the world threw at him. The kind of man who took risks like heading into stormy waters to rescue people.

She edged her arm away from his on the counter. This new feeling unnerved her. Just when she'd gotten used to their battles, now he wanted to change things up? To what end?

"By the way, I took an entire course on boat safety before I came to Alaska. I passed the final test with a perfect score."

He tilted his head at her with a quizzical glance. "Grad students know how to study, not a big shock."

"It was a practical exam. The entire course was hands-on. I would never have taken this job and put my daughter on a boat if I didn't know what I was doing."

His dark eyes held her gaze. This close—had she ever been this close to him before?—she noticed the flecks of jade mixed in with the deep brown. One more surprise about Lucas Holt.

"Why did you come here?" he asked. Asking such a normal question seemed to make him uncomfortable. He took an awkward sip of his coffee. "If you don't mind me asking."

"A lot of reasons." The primary reason flashed like a siren, but she didn't want to get into that one. *Don't think about that.* "Mostly for Ruby. She can live in her head a lot, and I worried that if we stayed in the city she'd never form a relationship with nature."

His dimple flashed again. "Relationship with nature, huh?"

With a shrug, she stirred more sugar into her coffee. "Do I sound like a hippie? Look, when I studied ornithology I spent more time on my computer than I did in the field. Everything we do is online or on our phones. I started to wonder if Ruby would think the whole world can be found in a book or on a screen." She sipped the coffee. "Even if we go back to San Francisco now, she'll always have this time in Lost Harbor to remember. She'll never forget the ocean mist on her face or the tug of a halibut on the end of your line."

"Best feeling, isn't it?" He gave a quick quirk of a smile. "It's like the ocean tapping you on the shoulder to tell you a secret."

It took her a moment to put that almost-poetic description together with the rugged fisherman standing next to her. "Wow, that's an interesting way to put it. I like that. So it's not just about money to you."

"Fishing charters? Not exactly. I made a lot more money with my investment business back in Colorado. I still do, even though I've cut back on my client list."

"Colorado's about as far away from the ocean as you can get."

"Yes it is."

He didn't elaborate, but she'd gotten this far, so she decided to push onwards. "Did you miss the ocean?"

"Colorado has mountains. Rivers. Lots of nature."

"That's ... not an answer to my question."

A muscle in his jaw ticked as he studied the coffee swirling in his mug. "Know how I learned to swim?"

"How?"

"My father tossed me overboard when I was a toddler. It's one of my first memories, and I'll never forget it. The cold just... engulfed me. It was dark and terrifying and I opened my mouth to cry but water rushed in. I knew my dad wanted something out of me. Maybe for me to die. Either be strong or die. Something. But I couldn't think or move or do anything—or maybe I did, I'm sure I must have. That survival instinct is so primal. All I remember is that I got lifted up toward the surface by some kind of current."

He paused. Megan didn't want to breathe a word that might interrupt his flow. His story fascinated her.

"I've always wondered what kind of current would have propelled me straight up like that. Maybe I just remember it wrong. Anyway, I bobbed up to the surface and splashed around until I caught my breath. My dad reached over the side and offered me his hand. But I didn't trust him anymore. I dog-paddled to the ladder and clung to it. I couldn't climb because I was shivering so hard at that point. In the end he pulled it up with me hanging on for dear life."

Megan shivered from the chill the story gave her. "Were you okay?"

"I spent a couple days in bed under a pile of blankets. The water here will give you hypothermia in a couple of minutes. I survived, obviously. And I never trusted my father again. But the ocean..."

He glanced out the window, across the boardwalk and the road to the restless waters of Misty Bay.

"Yeah, I did miss the ocean," he finally said. "I guess it's part of me by now. No matter where I go."

# CHAPTER TWELVE

Why the hell had he told Megan Miller that story about his father? He couldn't remember ever telling it to anyone else. The closest he'd ever come was when he'd told Maya Badger, back in high school, that his father redefined "throw him into the deep end and see if he can swim." He'd never shared the details or anything about how it had affected him.

But now when he glanced at Megan, he took in her softened expression with a sense of...tenderness, almost. Sweet of her to care, but it didn't matter.

"Don't get that sappy look on your face. I've been over it for about thirty years."

She blinked at him, her long eyelashes dropping over her wide blue-gray eyes. If he had to find a word to describe Megan's usual expression, it would be "hopeful." Or maybe "naive." Or even "annoyingly optimistic." She'd blown into Lost Harbor like a spring breeze with all her ideas about reducing waste and cleaning up the harbor. Not that they were *bad* ideas, per se. He respected her idealism and energy.

But she didn't seem to get the flip side of her proposals—that she believed they'd been doing things all wrong before she arrived. The community of Lost Harbor had persisted through nearly a hundred Alaska winters. People here knew how to survive.

"I don't have a sappy look. I'm never sappy except when it comes to YouTube kitten videos, and you are the opposite of a kitten video."

He snorted. "You're sappy about everything. You're sappy about my dog. You're sappy about a random bird with a broken wing. You're sappy about a soda can getting thrown into the ocean."

"That's not sappiness. That's fury." Her eyes sparked and the sprinkle of freckles across her nose seemed to glow. Everything about Megan was warm and glowing and tempting, like a fire on a cold night. "Do you know what those sharp edges can do to a sea otter if it tries to stick its nose inside?"

He pointed at her face. "Sappy."

"Argh, just when I start to think you're a human being after all, you turn right back into Lucifer."

"Lucifer?"

"Oh, just a secret nickname I have for you." A rosy flush covered her cheeks. "Sorry, you weren't supposed to know about that."

To be honest, he kind of liked the fact that she had a secret nickname for him. It meant that he took up space in her thoughts —even if it wasn't flattering. "Maybe I need a nickname for you too."

"No, you really don't," she said quickly. "You already call me 'city girl' and 'bird nerd' and that's more than enough."

"But that's so generic. There are millions of city girls, but there's only one Megan Miller." He scrutinized her through narrowed eyes, various names running through his mind. The problem was, none of them were especially insulting. M'n M, for her initials? Flower child, for her eco-minded crusades? Hippie-chick?

"I've got it." He plucked the yellow package of sweetener from the counter, the one that had represented the *Forget Me Not*. "How about Splenda?"

"*Splenda?* What kind of nickname is that?"

"A terrible one," he admitted. "I'm sorry, but I can't come up with anything truly Megan-bashing. I guess you're off the hook when it comes to a nickname. I'll just stick with 'short-timer.'"

A stricken look came across her face. Oh hell—he'd managed to land on the one that actually hurt, when it was the last thing he'd intended.

But before he could take it back, she propped her elbow on the counter and faced him. "What's this all about, Lucas? You said you wanted a peace treaty. Why?"

He hauled in a breath and shifted his focus away from the fall of her silky hair over her shoulder. "I need your help," he admitted.

Her eyes widened. "Something to do with the slip assignments?"

"No, nothing like that."

"You want to pass some clients my way?" she asked hopefully.

"I'll consider that, but no, it's not related to boats or fishing or anything like that. It's about Boris Clancy."

For a moment she stared at him blankly. "Boris? The old fisherman with the pet chicken who rides in his bike basket?"

"Yes. He's...a little off, as you know. When he gets an idea in his head, he won't let it go. And he decided long ago that he hates me."

"Well, no comment about that. He's always been friendly to me."

"Exactly. He must like you."

"I'm often catnip for mentally challenged men. It's been a theme my whole life," she said ruefully.

He would guess that she was catnip for more men than she knew. But there was no need to get into that. "It sounds like he trusts you."

"Okay, so?" Her forehead creased in confusion, her face turned to his like a flower. For a moment he flashed on the sight of her in a bikini, dancing on the deck of her boat. That sweet curve of her waist taunted him. He shoved the image aside.

"He was in the harbor the night my father died. He was the one who called 911 when he saw him in the water. But there's no way he'll talk to me."

"Your father's drowning was...an accident, wasn't it?" Her tentative tone made him impatient. He didn't like pussyfooting around basic facts.

"His death was ruled an accident, yes. But I'm not a hundred percent convinced that it was."

After a long moment of scrutinizing his face, her eyes lit with understanding. "That's what you're doing back here. You want to find out more about your father's death."

"Not at first, it wasn't. I came back for other reasons. Find someone to take over the *Jack Hammer*. Deal with the literal tons of junk my father left behind. I need to make sure my mother's okay. But now...yeah. I need to be completely sure there was nothing sketchy about his death. Beyond his usual sketchiness," he added. "And don't get that sappy look, because you didn't know him."

"Stop calling me sappy or I won't help you," she snapped.

He pretended to zip his mouth shut. "Done."

"I have to say, that was oddly satisfying." Her smile seemed to sink into his bones like sunshine. "So you want to ask Boris some questions about what he saw that night?"

"That would be great, but I know he won't talk to me. Maybe we could meet with him together."

"I don't know. I actually know why he hates you, and it's not something he's going to get over."

That was a surprise. She and Boris must talk about all kinds of things. "What is it? Maybe I can fix it. I can be pretty charming when I want to be." He bestowed his most seductive smile on her, the one his latest girlfriend had told him was equivalent to a panty-melting neutron bomb.

Megan reacted to it, all right, but her panties stayed right where they were. She frowned at him with disapproval. "Charm isn't going to cut it. He hates you because Fidget attacked Ruffles once."

"Ruffles?"

"His chicken. His last chicken," she corrected. "Ruffles passed away in March and it was a very hard time for Boris. His new hen is called Anushka."

Lucas drew in a long breath. How had he stepped into this rabbit hole? "You know all about his chickens?"

"He likes to talk about them. It's harmless."

"So you both love birds. No wonder you've bonded."

"You like birds too, don't give me crap about that. I could tell from your photo of the Caspian tern. There was a lot of love in that shot."

Was she teasing him? He couldn't tell. "I've always wondered what tern stew would taste like. Anyway, moving on," he said quickly before she could get too riled up. "If I compliment his chicken, will he talk to me?"

"You can try." She shrugged one shoulder, drawing his gaze to the line of her collarbone, firm under her freckled flesh. "You have both recently experienced a tragic loss."

"You're comparing my father to his chicken?"

She pulled an apologetic face. "Sorry. That chicken was his daily companion."

"Whereas I fought with my father my whole life." Maybe poor Boris had it worse. He wondered if Ruffles' death haunted Boris the way his father's haunted him.

"Anyway, it was a very tough time for him," Megan said. "The fact that Fidget attacked Ruffles really weighs on him. He kind of blames your whole family because no one ever apologized."

"He wants an official Holt family apology? He'll get it. Is that enough? Will he talk to me if I apologize?"

"I have no idea, but it might be worth a try. Or, if you like, I can try to bring up the topic."

"Great." He liked that plan, since it didn't involve bonding over dead chickens.

"Wait." She rested a hand on his arm. Tanned and capable, its light weight sent warmth through his veins. "What do I get out of this peace treaty? There has to be a quid for the quo in here somewhere."

"Name your quid. Anything you like. Dinner sometime?" That slipped out before he even realized it. *Dinner?* That sounded disturbingly as if he'd just asked her out. He hadn't intended to do that. Going out with Megan would bring all kinds of complications. Not that he even wanted to date her. Or maybe he did, because the words had come out of his mouth without any forethought.

But it would be a bad idea. He only dated tourists who were just passing through. He didn't like to be talked about. If he and Megan got together, after all their battles, it would be topic number one for the entire summer.

But how could he take it back without insulting her?

"You and Ruby, of course," he added smoothly. "Ice cream cones for all."

Her eyebrow arched ironically, as if she'd understood his entire silent thought process. "Nice save. Don't worry, I have no need to go to dinner with you, with or without Ruby."

Ouch. That stung, to be honest. Why did he keep misstepping with this woman? "A favor to be named later, then. Unless there's something now that you'd like?"

She twisted her mouth to the side as she considered. "I'll take the favor to be named later. I'm sure you'll be useful at some point."

"Thanks," he said dryly. "That's the sort of ringing endorsement a guy just can't get enough of."

She laughed, and their eyes met and held. A sweet kind of energy flowed between them, drawing him to her like a current. His breath hitched. He felt himself harden painfully.

So he *was* attracted to her. He'd suspected it, denied it, but right now, he couldn't lie to himself. He had it bad for Megan Miller, bird nerd and city girl.

She cleared her throat, breaking the moment. "I'll text you after I feel things out with Boris."

"Good. Sounds good. You have my number?"

"Somewhere." She sounded just as rattled as he felt. At least it cut both ways. "And you have my email address."

"Yup." He grabbed his mug, gathered hers as well, and took them both to the bin for dirty dishes. With his back to her, he had a chance to wrestle his erection under control. When he turned around again, he took the time to steel himself against her mouthwatering curves and teasing smile. "Let's go," he said gruffly.

He knew he sounded rude, like the Lucas Holt who had spoken to her with such hostility when she first bumped his boat. It was probably better that way. And a whole hell of a lot safer.

# CHAPTER THIRTEEN

Sweet mother of pearl, what the heck had she said or done? Just when things were finally settling into friendly mode with Lucas, he'd shut down. Didn't he understand that his icy attitude was exactly what scared someone like Boris? Boris was a sensitive soul. Lucas' dark and frowning demeanor would frighten him.

A kind word and a smile would go a long way—especially his outrageously charming smile—but would Lucas remember that or would he revert to his old self? She'd better talk to Boris on her own first.

While Lucas paid for their coffees—she didn't protest, since she'd apparently forgotten her wallet on the *Forget Me Not*—she wandered out onto the boardwalk. A brisk wind cut across from the ocean side and she wished she had her fleece with her. A tourist on a rented beach cruiser bike veered past her. She felt a moment of pride—those bike rentals had been her idea.

She was dodging a kid on a skateboard when she heard Ruby calling her. "Mama! Mama!"

Turning back to the harbor side of the boardwalk, she spotted her daughter racing through the crowds. In her shorts and sneakers, with a t-shirt that read "*Forget Me Not Nature Tours. Unforgettable adventures,* she darted past strolling pedestrians and a raven perched on the railing. Megan's entire heart turned to sunshine at the sight of her little girl. *She's so happy here. I have to make this work.*

And then—Ruby tripped over a crack between two boards and suddenly she was flying headfirst through the air, launching like a rocket right toward a planter of petunias.

Megan darted forward, nearly tripping herself as she raced toward her daughter. Her panic gave her wings; she felt as if she could run a hundred miles an hour or fold time like a tesseract if she had to.

But before she could reach Ruby, a hand plucked her from the air and snatched her upright. *Lucas.* Ruby clung to his arm, completely rattled. "Are...what...Mama?"

Megan landed next to her—it felt literally as if she'd flown there from the terrace with the chessboard—and crouched next to her. "Are you okay?"

"Yeah. I think so. The ground was right under my face and then it wasn't." She wrinkled her nose and looked up at Lucas, who still had a hand on her upper arm. "How'd you do that?"

"Easy. I couldn't have you ruining those purple petunias." He winked at her little girl. Even though he made light of it, Megan saw the same panic in his eyes that she'd just experienced.

"Thank you, Lucas." Her heart was still racing. "I could already see the scraped knees and bloody elbows." She turned to Ruby. "This is why you don't run on the boardwalk, Ruby. How many times do I have to tell you?"

"But—"

"No buts. You saw what just almost happened. No 'buts'. " She held up her hand in a "solemn vow" gesture. "Promise not to run on the boardwalk anymore. Or I'll find you a babysitter who never leaves the cabin."

Ruby held up her hand to match Megan's. "I promise, but we tried to call you from Hunter's and you didn't answer."

Megan grabbed her phone from her back pocket and saw that she'd missed three calls from Ruby. She'd been so distracted by Lucas and their conversation that she hadn't even noticed her phone buzzing. A new worry took hold. "Is there an emergency? What's wrong?"

"It's..." Still trying to catch her breath, she scrambled for the right words. "It's Dad."

Megan went cold. "What about him? Is he okay?"

"He's *here*."

Ruby flung her arm to gesture behind her. And there was Dev, strolling down the boardwalk, looking completely out of place in his superfine wool overcoat. It set off his deep bronze skin and horn-rimmed glasses, as if he'd wandered out of a commercial for thousand-dollar Swiss watches.

Vaguely, she was aware of Lucas shifting his focus toward Dev as well. Of all people to be the first to encounter her ex, why did it have to be Lucas? Why not an actual friend, like Zoe? Or Boris with his chicken?

"Dev! You didn't tell me you were coming today. Why didn't you give me a heads up? I would have picked you up at the airport." Babbling. She was babbling.

"There's an airport?"

"Of course there's an—How did you get here if it wasn't by plane?"

"Helicopter. It dropped me off at some kind of toy airstrip."

"That's the airport."

"The pride of Lost Harbor," added Lucas. He stuck out his hand. "Lucas Holt. I take it you're this fine young lady's father?"

"Yes, that's my claim to fame. Dev Siddhwarma."

"My name is Ruby Vashti Miller Siddhwarma," said Ruby

proudly. "You should try to say it, but you might have to practice."

"Ruby Vashti Muller Siddhwarma," said Lucas promptly. "Oops, I got the Miller wrong."

Everyone laughed. Bless Lucas for making this encounter a little less awkward than she'd feared.

"Well done," said Dev, offering his hand. A businessman to the core, he never missed an opportunity to schmooze a new acquaintance. "Are you a local here?"

"Born and raised." Lucas gestured toward the bristling masts of the harbor. "Family fishing charter business. I should really get back to it."

For some strange reason, Megan didn't want him to leave. With Lucas here, she felt anchored to Lost Harbor, whereas Dev had a way of making her feel frivolous and insubstantial. He always saw her passions and plans as whims that would blow over.

"Good to meet you. Maybe I'll book a trip on that charter of yours."

"We're pretty busy this time of year." Lucas shot Megan a noncommittal glance, as if he was trying to figure out where she stood on the Dev-goes-fishing-with-Lucas idea.

She appreciated his thoughtfulness. But maybe it would be a relief to get Dev out of her hair for a while.

"You do owe me a favor," she pointed out.

"Good point. Name the day, we'll make it happen. Welcome to Lost Harbor, Dev." He nodded to the three of them and headed off down the boardwalk to the *Jack Hammer* office.

Ruby straightened her t-shirt, which had gotten twisted during her near-fall into the petunias. "What should we show him first, Mama? How about the beach with the starfish? Or the ice cream shop? Or the baby otter?"

Dev laughed at her enthusiasm, while Megan snuck a glance at the departing rear end of Lucas Holt.

She hid her sigh at the terrible timing of Dev's arrival. Had Lucas maybe-nearly-possibly invited her to dinner?

Nothing ruined a moment like an ex-husband showing up.

# CHAPTER FOURTEEN

Lucas employed three deckhands who worked on rotating shifts, an office manager who handled billing and shipping, and a receptionist who took bookings and posted occasional photos on social media. Right now, every single one of his employees was getting on his nerves.

He hadn't been this irritable since he'd first come back to Lost Harbor.

Bad time for a staff meeting.

He leaned against the reception desk in the Jack Hammer Fishing Charters boardwalk office and massaged his left temple. A tiny jack hammer of his own was pounding away in there.

He blamed Megan. Or her ex-husband. Or both. He eyed the tiny closet-size area that she rented from him for her office space. It was dark and empty. She was probably off somewhere with her ex.

"Thanks for coming in, everyone. The summer's about to really get going and things are gonna get busy. I wanted to get us all on the same page before the craziness hits. Any issues? Any recommendations? I brought donuts so speak freely." He gestured at the box he'd grabbed at Safeway on the way in.

Everyone answered at once.

"When are we going to be on TV?"

"Can we get copies of the show?"

"Did they keep that part where I caught the Irish Lord, cuz that was gnarly as shit."

Lucas held up his hand to stop the din. He wasn't even hungover and yet his head throbbed.

Seeing Megan with her ex had done something to him. It had activated some primitive caveman instinct that made no sense. He wasn't dating Megan. Her rich, smooth-as-butter ex-husband could move to Lost Harbor and it would make no difference to him. *Should* make no difference to him.

So why was he so riled up? He was an idiot, that was why.

Also, he really cared about Ruby. She was a great kid; Fidget loved her and Fidget was never wrong.

Maybe he needed to find out how Fidget felt about Dev. Right now his old hound was dozing at Lucas' boots. Actually, more like *on* his boots.

When Mr. Business Degree held staff meetings, did his dog lie across his feet?

He shook himself back to his current job. "I don't know shit about the *Trekking* show. As soon as I do, you will."

"Viewing party at the Olde Salt!" Carla Baker, the receptionist, who worked for him mostly because she liked spending summers on the boardwalk, snapped her fingers through the air. "Leave all the planning to me."

"If you want to do that, I won't stop you. I also won't be there, but party on, kids."

His deckhands all looked relieved by that announcement. No one wanted their boss to catch them partying too hard. He'd already bailed one of them out of jail after a late-night brawl. He regularly talked to them about putting some of their pay into a savings account rather than blowing it all within two days. He even offered to do it for them. He'd opened a mutual fund account for each of them and every time he paid them, he asked how much they wanted to keep and how much they wanted to invest.

So far, his contributions were keeping the damn things open. But maybe they'd see the light someday.

"Couple things from the harbormaster," he told the crew. "First, he and the Coast Guard wanted to pass along their thanks for the outstanding job we did on that kayak rescue last week. So thanks, guys. Great work."

A kayaker had gotten caught in the day breeze and become too exhausted to paddle any farther. He'd actually passed out in the cockpit of the kayak. Ralphie, the deckhand on duty, had spotted the kayak drifting toward Widow Reef. The Coast Guard had asked Lucas to handle the rescue.

The retrieval had gone smoothly, and Lucas had spent a long time with the poor kid afterwards, explaining how easy it was to get fooled by the Alaska waters. *It could happen to anyone. That's why we look out for each other out here.*

He led the staff in a round of applause for themselves, then checked his notes.

"Next item. That orphaned baby otter you've probably noticed on the breakwater. They're saying that it's bonded with that marker buoy just off the end. Thinks it's his mother. Fish and Wildlife is trying to decide what to do, but in the meantime give it a wide berth. You are allowed to take photos, but don't get within thirty yards of it."

"Tell that to the *Forget Me Not*," said Peggy Boyle, one of the deckhands. "They've been taking their passengers right up close."

"I'm sure Fish and Wildlife is talking to them." He could

imagine how excited Ruby must be about the otter. He wished he could take her out there himself.

*No.* He and Megan had shared a brief moment of peace treaty, but that didn't mean they were going to get involved in each other's lives.

"Speaking of the *Forget Me Not,* Megan called and said you offered her ex-husband a charter. I told her I'd get back to her, because seriously?" Carla pushed back the sleeves of her *Jack Hammer* hoodie. "I thought she was on crack or something."

He gritted his teeth. Right. The favor. He was hoping they'd forgotten about his offer. "Squeeze him in somewhere."

"Really? But you and Megan..." Under his narrow-eyed stare, Carla elaborately zipped her lips. "Never mind."

"Go on." He gestured for her to continue.

"Everyone knows you and Megan hate each other. Oh!" She snapped her fingers. "That's why you're taking her ex out. It's part of an evil scheme to make an alliance behind her back. Oh, you are good, Lucas Holt. Your dad knew how to carry on a feud, but this is next level."

"Excuse me?" He snorted in disgust. "This isn't *Survivor.* I don't hate Megan, she doesn't hate me, and I'm not scheming. I have no need to scheme. She's not even a competitor. I don't even know how she keeps that business going."

"I heard she might have to fold," said Beth, the business manager, who knew all the boardwalk gossip. "I'm surprised she didn't give up over the winter, to be honest."

"That's because you don't know her," Lucas muttered.

His staff shot him a range of confused glances.

"That's sad if they go under," said Ralphie, who always got the biggest tips because of his sunny friendliness. "Megan's a straight hottie."

Carla gave him a wounded look. She and Ralphie had hooked up briefly, and she still pined for him.

Exactly why Lucas stuck to tourists. Good reminder.

"Her ex-husband is a wealthy and very good-looking businessman, and he has a British accent, so I doubt she'd give some raggedy fisherman a second look," Peggy told Ralphie.

Lucas clenched his jaw tight. His deckhand made a good point, and it applied to him too. Not that he was interested in pursuing Megan. He'd already very much decided definitely not to.

"We're getting off track here. What other *Jack Hammer* business do you guys have?"

The newest deckhand, Peggy's younger brother Dale, raised his hand. "Can we get a different brand of hand soap on the boat? I think I'm allergic." He rotated his hand, showing it from all angles. A red rash swept up his hands to his forearm.

"Beth, please research non-allergenic soaps and pick a good one for the boat."

"Yes Lucas. Does everyone like lemon?"

"Lavender is nice," said Ralphie thoughtfully.

Still angry, Carla glared at him. "Nothing takes out the fish smell like lemon. Everyone knows that."

"What's wrong with fish smell?" Peggy sniffed her hand. "We catch fish, come on."

"Everyone will be fine with whatever scent you choose," he said firmly, before another argument could get going. "Are we done?"

Carla raised a pen in the air. "Quick question. Do you want Megan's ex-husband on one of your trips or *not* on one of your trips?"

Goddamn it. Even when Megan wasn't here, she was causing a ruckus in his life. "One of mine," he growled.

He ignored the knowing smirk on Carla's face as she wrote that down in the booking ledger.

After the staff meeting, he had another hour before he had to get ready for a private trip someone had booked to one of the island lodges in the bay. They didn't want to fish, they just wanted transport—in style.

He filled the time with a few calls for his *other* business. When he'd gotten the news that his father had died, he'd put his investment consulting business in sleep mode. That didn't mean he'd shut it down. Consulting was completely portable. With Internet and phone service, he could work from anywhere. Some of his clients had no idea that he was now operating from a little town in Alaska instead of a big city in Colorado.

When he'd left Lost Harbor, he'd wanted to leave his rugged homestead upbringing behind, so he'd chosen business school. He'd worked his way through an accelerated program and graduated close to the top of his class. He'd gotten a job at a big firm in Denver, at which point his ingrained independence had asserted itself. He'd quit after a couple of years and started his own business, Holt and Associates Investments. "Associates" being the occasional freelancer he hired for things like creating prospectuses.

Holt and Associates had grown and thrived; he'd had his first million dollar year two years ago. He'd told no one about that benchmark. Not his mother, not his father, not his brother and sister.

No one knew that he'd been walking around with a fat bank account for the past two years. He didn't want anyone in Lost Harbor to know. To them, he was the son of Jack Holt, legendary waterfront character, and that was about the end of it. Fine by him. His life wasn't here. His future wasn't here.

If they knew he had money, they'd look at him differently. They might recruit him to run for city council or some shit. Instead, he made anonymous donations to the Mariners' Fund and the Lost Souls Clean Energy Initiative.

If Megan knew about those donations, she might actually approve of him. But what would be the fun in that?

After rearranging a few things in a client's portfolio—a fund focusing on tech looked promising—he checked in with his mother.

"How's the yak?"

"You know something about that yak?" she said in a conspiratorial whisper. "I think he might be your father reincarnated."

"Uh...say what now?"

"He's just as stubborn and just as horny. I caught him going after the milk cow and they aren't even the same species. And sometimes I catch him looking at me and I think—that's Jack."

"Mom. That's impossible."

"Why? You don't believe in reincarnation? You should see this yak's beard. I swear it's just like Jack's."

"That yak is what, three years old or so? Dad died eight months ago."

"Well, I don't know how it all works. Maybe Jack kicked out another soul that was already in the yak. I wouldn't put it past him."

Lucas tilted his head back in silent laughter. Hey, what did he know? Maybe his mother had a point. "Well, you want to call a yak exorcist? What do you want here?"

"There's no need to mock me. Why don't you come have a little chat with him?"

"A chat with the yak?"

"It's surprisingly relaxing."

"That's okay, Mom. Sounds like a private moment between husband and wife. And yak." He hung up before he laughed out loud. If Lost Harbor had one thing in abundance, it was eccentric characters.

He included his whole family in that category.

# CHAPTER FIFTEEN

Megan hadn't gotten the opportunity to show a visitor around Lost Harbor yet. Her parents hadn't been brave enough to visit—also, they highly disapproved of her being so far away. Taking Dev around town made her look at the place with fresh eyes.

Especially when she had to defend it from all his criticisms.

"It's tiny. How many people live here, like five thousand or so?"

"Five thousand and thirty at last count. But how many people do you even know when you live in a big city? Not five thousand!"

"But...five restaurants?"

"We have at least ten good restaurants in the summer. There's nothing wrong with making your own food, you know. People have gardens, they preserve their own food, pick their own berries, smoke their own fish..."

Dev's look of horror made her laugh.

"You don't have to do those things, but it's good for Ruby to be exposed to such a different way of life."

"That doesn't mean she should *live* here. You can't home-school her much longer, Megan. She needs school. Show me the best school."

"There's only one school," she admitted.

They drove to MacMurray Elementary, which was closed for the summer. A digital sign at the entrance said as much—except that "summer" was spelled "sumer."

"They're not very good at spellchecking that sign." She sighed. "But it's a respectable school. Ruby and I toured it in April when we got back. Ruby, what did you think?"

In the back seat, Ruby was working on a puzzle Dev had brought her—an eight-sided Rubik's Cube.

"It looked boring," she said absently.

Megan winced. Well, she wouldn't want Ruby to lie.

"Obviously she'd have extra work. Online classes and so forth. Maybe she could attend school for half the day and do home studies the rest of the time."

Dev sighed heavily and ruffled his black hair with one hand. Then immediately patted it back into place, because he despised the mussed look. "What's the appeal of this place? I just don't get it. For a getaway, sure. A short getaway. You see the mountains, you catch a fish, you check out the local artists gallery, you buy some birch syrup, and you get the bloody hell out."

"Doesn't it feel peaceful here?" She heard the pleading tone in her voice. Even though she had custody, they both had to agree on something so important. "The bay, the glaciers, all the birds... it's so beautiful, and every day is different. The clouds are different, the moods of the ocean change—"

"Oceans don't have moods. I thought you were a scientist."

"It's a figure of speech. But actually, thanks for that reminder that I am a scientist and that's one reason I'd like to stay here. I've come up with a few ideas that I could research here and turn into a solid dissertation and finally finish my degree."

"By taking tourists on bird-watching tours?"

"That's a way to make a living *and* do science *and* be with Ruby. It's perfect, I just wish you could see that." They drove past a wetlands marsh where sandhill cranes stalked invisible prey on their stilt legs. Dev barely noticed the magnificent creatures, who always reminded Megan of women in bustles. Dev never noticed things around him, unless they were clients and/or women. "Why don't you come with me on the tour today, Dev?"

"Lord no, you know how boring I find bird-watching."

"You will not be bored, I promise. Being out on the water around here is always exciting. They're calling for two-foot seas and a medium chop today." She recited the marine forecast proudly. She loved listening to the weather reports in Lost Harbor. The prosaic words conjured such vivid images of white-caps and twenty-foot tides.

"I'm afraid you might toss me over."

"That's not funny. Eliza would be very disappointed if I did that," she added.

He chuckled. "Cute. Sorry, I'm going to pass on the nature tour. Besides, I'm going fishing, remember? You set it up."

"Right. Of course. Are you sure you wouldn't rather come with me? Fishing can get bloody."

Truthfully, she regretted calling in that favor on Dev's behalf. What if Lucas sabotaged her efforts to get Dev to warm up to Lost Harbor? Not that he'd do it on purpose...or maybe he would.

Maybe he'd be happy if she left Lost Harbor. No more sharing office space and fending off the *Forget Me Not*.

So far she'd seen many Lucases—gruff, grieving, impatient, unpredictable, generous, confusing—but the most recent one had been surprisingly caring.

Maybe she should have a little trust.

At their next stop—a bakery to appeal to Dev's outrageous sweet tooth—she went to the bathroom and texted Lucas.

She'd never texted him before and it felt weirdly intimate.

*This is Megan. About that fishing trip with Dev. It's very important to me that he have a good time.*

It took an excruciatingly long time for the telltale three dots to appear, and then his answer.

*I'll wear my best perfume.*

She snorted out loud. Lucas could be really funny when he wasn't being...Lucas. Or maybe that was the real Lucas. Or maybe he was just a complex being with many different qualities and layers.

*Just treat him like a real client, that's all I ask. Btw, I spoke to Boris this am. I brought him coffee and some mealworms. Holding up my end.*

He sent her back a thumbs-up. And then—

*Mealworms? Is that real or autocorrect?*

*For his chicken.* Didn't everyone know that chickens loved mealworms?

*Do they love fish guts? Got plenty of those.*

*They're not picky.*

Someone knocked on the bathroom door, and she jumped. "Just a minute." Suddenly she felt like a teenager busted for talking on the phone after midnight. But the truth was, she'd rather be here in the bathroom texting with Lucas than out there defending her life to Dev.

*Do you have any exes you have to get along with?* she texted on impulse.

Again came a long pause before the three dots appeared. *2 high school girlfriends still live here. One runs the fueling station with her husband. The* Jack Hammer *needs a lot of fuel. So yes I have to get along with her.*

A smile tugged at her lips. She really enjoyed Lucas' dry sense of humor. It could really sneak up on you. It would probably pass right over Dev's head. Dev wasn't attuned to nuance. He liked things bold and obvious.

*Think of Dev as my fuel provider. That's how important this is.*

*I see what's going on. You don't trust me. You think I might take him out to the deep water and dig up all your secrets.*

Her *what?* That possibility had never occurred to her. *Secrets?* Why would Lucas care about her secrets? She didn't even have any, except...

Except for that terrible afternoon at the university...*don't think about that. Don't think about that. Don't think about that.*

Another knock sounded at the door, more impatient this time. Better get back out there and deal with Dev.

*Gotta go,* she texted Lucas. *Please make sure Dev has fun.*

She washed her hands and hurried back to her ex. He was, of course, flirting with the cute barista. That familiar sense of mortification swept through her. Not once had Dev ever made her feel like she was enough, just her. He would flirt with the bread rolls if there were no pretty girls around.

"Let's go, Lucas is waiting," she told him.

"Ooh, you're fishing with Lucas?" The barista wrapped up a fudge brownie to go. "Give him this for me, would you? He'll know who it's from."

Cursing all men, especially the ones with dark hair and a wry sense of humor and a subtle air of vulnerability, she snatched up the brownie and headed for the car.

If Dev's appearance was good for anything, it was to remind her that she should think very, very carefully before getting involved with another man. Ever.

# CHAPTER SIXTEEN

Lucas had been joking about digging up Megan's secrets. Or at least he'd thought of it as a joke. But as soon as they reached one of his favorite halibut holes—two hundred feet deep with a nearby underwater ledge—curiosity got the best of him.

How had this smooth-talker ended up with someone as genuine and authentic as Megan? And how had he let her go?

He gave the controls to Ralphie and got Dev settled into the cushioned swivel chair with his best Okuma SST halibut rod. He baited the round hook with herring, attached a lead weight, and gestured for Dev to toss the line overboard. "Wait until the weight hits bottom, then close the reel. Have you done much fishing before?"

"I went fly-fishing once. I never got the feel of it. Waste of an afternoon, except that I signed a big client that day."

"Yeah, fishing's good for that kind of thing. It's relaxing. Kind of a bonding experience."

Dev's coppery forehead wrinkled. "Don't worry, I'm not here for the bonding."

"Got it. No bonding allowed."

Something tugged at Dev's line. He reeled it in too roughly and whatever it was disappeared.

"Keep a nice even pace on that reel," Lucas instructed. "It's easy for the hook to get dislodged if you yank too soon. Let the halibut eat the bait first. Every once in a while, pull on the line and let the weight fall back to the ocean floor. That releases the scent of the bait, which draws the halibut."

Dev gave a curt nod. Oh great, one of those guys who didn't appreciate instruction. Lucas had met all too many of them. He decided to scratch the interrogation section of the fishing trip and just enjoy being out on the water.

The sun struck a million crystal lights on the faceted surfaces of the waves. A gaggle of Arctic terns floated nearby. A whiff of seaweed drifted past his nostrils; probably one of those rafts of kelp that had gotten uprooted in the last storm. It mingled with the smell of baitfish in a nostalgically nauseating way.

The gentle rocking of the *Jack Hammer* lulled him into a sense of security that was smashed by Dev's next question.

"Are you interested in Megan?"

Okay then. Getting right to the point. "Why would you ask that?"

"I saw you together on the boardwalk. I know Megan very well. We weren't married for long, but we're intertwined because of Ruby. I got the sense that she likes you."

He had no interest in this line of discussion. "She's been pretty clear about disliking me."

"No, that's not what I saw. She likes you. It's okay, I'm not fighting you for her. We only got married for Ruby. Bad idea all around. No regrets on the divorce."

"That's...good."

He looked around for some kind of distraction, but there was no escape from this conversation. "We share office space. That's more or less it."

"See, that's what I wanted to know. If you're not interested in her, I'll hold my tongue. But if you are, there's something you should know. Something I'm sure she hasn't told you because she doesn't talk about it. But she should."

This sounded like the textbook definition of invading someone's privacy. It felt wrong—beyond wrong. And yet he was only human—and therefore curious.

"Whatever it is, shouldn't she tell me herself, if she wants to?" he managed.

"She should. But she probably won't. She dragged Ruby here to Alaska for a reason. I understand that. But she's alone here and I don't like it. At least one person ought to know the truth. So that's why I'm asking—are you interested in her?"

Lucas wrestled with how to answer. "Interested" seemed simultaneously too bland and too risky. He glanced back toward the wheelhouse. Was Ralphie listening to this conversation? He didn't want any word of it spreading around. But Ralphie was talking to someone on the two-way handheld. Maybe checking in with Carla back at home base. And the engine noise, even at this low idle, would mask their conversation.

"We have a...something...going on. Not exactly sure what it is," he admitted. "But we're not 'involved.'"

Dev nodded a few times, as if that matched up with his suspicions. "Not yet," he offered.

Lucas shrugged. He couldn't predict the future. He definitely couldn't predict anything having to do with Megan.

"All things considered then, I feel I should tell you something before you go any further."

Lucas glanced longingly at the sixty-pound Dacron line extending into the water. This would be the perfect time for a halibut to make its presence known. Or anything really, even a clump of seaweed. This conversation was making him extremely uncomfortable. "Megan's business is her own."

"She was the victim of a workplace shooting."

"*What?*" Lucas jerked his head around. "What are you talking about?"

"Just before she moved to Alaska, she was working part time in the admissions office of the university where we met. An expelled student came in with an automatic weapon and started firing. Several were injured, but fortunately there were no deaths."

"Was Megan hurt?"

"Not physically. But she struggled with insomnia and panic attacks afterwards. She went on medication for a time. She may still be on it, I'm not sure."

Now that definitely sounded like personal information that was none of his business. "She seems to have recovered pretty well. I've never seen her have a panic attack."

"Let's hope she doesn't, especially at the wheel of a boat with passengers aboard. Or Ruby."

Lucas glanced at him sharply. What was Dev's true purpose here? Was he trying to cast doubt on Megan's ability to run a boat?

Frankly, he already had doubts about her boat skills. Ever since Megan had arrived, he'd questioned whether she knew what she was doing. With this new information...well, he didn't yet know how it fit in.

"You want me to keep an eye on her," he finally said. "That's why you're telling me this."

"Yes." Dev nodded and tugged at the line. "Felt a bite."

"Don't react too soon. Gentle now."

Alertly, they both watched the line slide through the water. "Nothing," Dev finally said. "Perhaps we should change locations."

"I'll check the depth-finder."

Lucas went into the wheelhouse to consult his Lidar and his

deckhand. "Got a good feeling," Ralphie said. With one ankle propped over his knee, he aimlessly picked his nails with a fishhook. "No sense in moving yet. It's nice here. Feel that day breeze? It's gonna start pushing us around soon."

"Sure. Hope the fish start biting because..." He shrugged. Badmouthing a client didn't sit right. "Find us some fish, that's all."

"Want me to take a turn with the client?"

"Nah. Don't want to interrupt your manicure."

Ralphie laughed good-naturedly and scratched his head with the same fish hook. "Good the TV crew isn't here now. I'd go viral."

As soon as Lucas rejoined him, Dev picked up where he'd left off. "You obviously know what you're doing on the water. I look at Megan and I think, is this some kind of post-traumatic stress reaction, is that why she wants to be out here with nothing but birds and fish? And I suppose that's understandable, but I need to think of my daughter. So I'm asking you, man to man, just keep an eye on her. Even if you're nothing more than colleagues, or fellow boat-owners, or whatever it is."

"Harbor neighbors," Lucas murmured.

"I'll even pay you."

Stunned into silence, Lucas didn't answer at first. The quiver of the boat deck under his feet told him the day breeze was picking up, just as Ralphie had said. It happened every afternoon, a brisk onshore wind sweeping through Misty Bay and making the waves dance.

Why was he thinking about the day breeze when this man had just seriously insulted him?

"Pay me for what, exactly?" he asked in a dangerously soft voice. "To spy for you?"

Dev seemed to sense that he'd overstepped. "More like...be a kind of bodyguard. To watch over Megan for her own protection.

And for Ruby's. You seem to have a good rapport with my daughter."

Lucas fought to get a grip on his anger. As much as he'd clashed with Megan, he knew how much she loved Ruby. He'd never consider her some kind of risk to her daughter, but that was what Dev was implying. A panic attack at the helm of a boat would be dangerous. But he'd been watching her operate her business, and she was never reckless or careless.

And yet—it was true that he didn't know Megan very well. She'd definitely never mentioned anything about a shooting or panic attacks.

"I won't take your money," he finally told Dev. "But I keep an eye on everything having to do with the boats in our harbor. Not just me, everyone does. And then there's the Coast Guard."

"That doesn't reassure me."

He thought of another thing. "The nature tours require calm conditions. Megan doesn't generally take her boat out unless the seas are under two feet. Maybe you should just trust her to know what's best."

Inwardly, he rolled his eyes at his own hypocrisy. How much trust had he afforded Megan? He'd written her off as a flighty Lower 48 wannabe without getting to know her.

"I trust Megan, but PTSD is unpredictable." Dev fished out a business card from his jeans pocket. "Here. My private number's on the back. If anything seems like a red flag, call me. This is for Ruby," he emphasized again.

Just then, a firm yank on the line made him jerk around. He pushed the card at Lucas and turned to the rod, which was now arching deeply from the weight of a fish snagged at the end.

Ralphie ran out from the wheelhouse to lend a hand. The next adrenaline-packed minutes were a blur of reeling, yelling, staggering across the deck and making way for the enormous hundred-pound halibut that eventually flopped onto the floorboards.

"Nice one." Ralphie exchanged a high-five with Dev, who wore a shell-shocked look.

"I caught that thing," he said in awe. "That's simply...bizarre."

"Never caught a fish before?"

"Not one like that. What happens to it now?" He backed away from the thrashing halibut.

Lucas was kind of enjoying his discomfort. "We'll pack it in ice until we get back to the harbor, where Ralphie here will gut it, clean it, fillet it and pack it into a shippable container for you."

"And then what?"

"You take it home with you. Or I supposed you could mail it. I recommend next-day air."

Dev stared at the fish again, looking so queasy Lucas almost felt sorry for him. Except that the dude had tried to hire him to spy on Megan.

"So a massive container of fish is going to show up on my doorstep and I'm supposed to...what, cook it? Eat it?"

Lucas exchanged an amused glance with Ralphie. This was probably the oddest reaction to a newly landed fish that Lucas had ever witnessed. "That's generally what happens, although we don't usually follow up with our clients after they go home."

Dev wiped his hands on the seat of his jeans and studied the captured halibut as if it was a problem he was determined to solve. Lucas recognized Ruby in that look. "I don't suppose you have any recipes you can share?"

Lucas bit back a laugh. "We'll set you up. No worries about that. Ralphie, take it away." As Ralphie bent to extract the hook from the halibut's mouth, Lucas clapped Dev on the shoulder. "You up for more? Or you want to head back?"

"More. The next one's for Megan and Ruby."

Lucas gave him a thumbs-up and strode into the wheelhouse. He opened up the throttle and pointed the bow in the direction of Deep Hollow, his go-to spot for rockfish. He happened to know that Ruby loved rockfish much more than halibut.

Dev's business card rustled in his pocket. It felt like his conscience pricking him with needles. If Megan knew about his conversation with Dev, she'd be livid. He didn't have to know her very well to understand that.

He should tell her what Dev was up to. She'd probably appreciate the heads up. Yes, that was what he'd do at the next opportunity. "Megan, I think you should know that your ex-husband is telling people that you have PTSD and wants to hire a spy."

But then he'd have to reveal that he knew about the shooting and the PTSD, something Megan clearly didn't want to share.

Better to pretend he still knew nothing about it. And maybe keep an eye out for trouble. Which he always did anyway.

# CHAPTER SEVENTEEN

After three more days of awkwardness, Megan drove Dev to the tiny Lost Harbor airport. She'd never been so relieved to see someone off before. Never before had his patronizing ways been so obvious. Was it because she'd been running her own business for months now? Had the *Forget Me Not* at least given her that?

All in all, she considered the visit successful. Dev's main purpose had been to give Ruby an online math aptitude test he'd discovered. Once that was done, the two of them had spent several happy hours beachcombing. They'd found a starfish as big as a manhole cover and a washed-up jellyfish that Ruby was determined to rescue.

The expression on Dev's face as he'd tried to prod the jellyfish onto a towel for transport—priceless. He really was the ultimate city boy.

"I'm glad you came, Dev. Ruby really had fun showing you around. We're going to make a photo album of all those rocks you found on the beach."

"So I'll see her next month, yeah?"

"Yeah." It went against the grain to send Ruby away during

the heart of the Alaska summer. But Dev had enrolled Ruby in an excellent math day camp at the local university. She was excited about it, so Megan didn't object. It would only be for three weeks. She'd manage.

Oh, who was she kidding? She'd be a mess. But she'd survive, as she always did during Ruby's absences. Ice cream, lots of random projects, and intense housecleaning usually helped.

"About the *Forget Me Not*. Does the business need a bailout?"

"Absolutely not," she said quickly.

Dev really knew how to dent her self-confidence. A *bailout?*

He'd already offered her some extra money beyond his regular monthly child care amount, but she'd refused. She didn't want to give him any ammunition to think she wasn't taking care of things here.

"The *Trekking* show is airing tonight and the extra exposure is really going to help."

"Here's hoping." Dev held up two crossed fingers, then bent to kiss her on the cheek. "Offer's open. If there's anything I know how to do properly, it's rescue troubled businesses."

"Good for you," she said through gritted teeth. *Troubled business?* Why couldn't he just mind his *own* business? But, of course, her business would always be intertwined with his, because of Ruby. "Are you going to watch the show?"

"I'll have my assistant record it."

*And thus ends the latest chapter in the co-parenting adventures of Megan Miller,* she thought as she drove her truck back from the airport. She'd left Ruby at the beach with Hunter and his mother. They were collecting driftwood for a fire and Megan hadn't wanted to drag her away from the fun. Ruby didn't like extended goodbyes. Airports made her restless and snappy. Megan often wondered if it was because so many of their family partings happened at airports. She probably had bad flashbacks every time she stepped into one.

Megan could relate to bad flashbacks. Good thing she had complete control over hers.

Her phone rang. Captain Kid was on the line. "Big viewing party tonight at the movie theater," he told her. "Spread the word. They're putting it up on the big screen."

The "movie theater" was little more than an old warehouse with a projection screen and rows of seats from an old school bus.

"I was thinking I'd watch at home with Ruby."

"Ruby can come. That's why they're having it at the theater. Family friendly."

"Okay, maybe." She wondered if Lucas was going to be there. She hadn't seen much of him since the fishing trip with Dev. "I need to make sure our website is up to snuff in case we get a rush of new bookings."

"Ya never know."

He didn't sound especially hopeful. It didn't matter much to him, since he could get work on any fishing boat he wanted. The only reason he'd chosen the *Forget Me Not* was that he wanted to stay close to home instead of leaving for weeks at a time.

She parked in the gravel lot of Seafarer's Beach, where a bronze statue honoring all the lost fishermen gazed wistfully out to sea. Long driftwood logs separated the parking area from the beach. Beach peas and lupines added touches of color—radiant purple and cheerful green. She sidestepped between two logs and shaded her eyes against the sunshine. In the hazy sparkle of ocean light, she had trouble identifying the people on the beach. Dog-walkers, kids making castles in the dark sand, teenagers flirting with the icy surf.

The sand in Misty Bay wasn't anything like the fine stuff she'd lain on during her honeymoon in Mexico. The sand here was a close cousin to mud, with a weighty density to it. Clams lurked under the surface, their homes revealed by tiny air holes. It had a spongy feel underfoot and squished pleasantly between the toes.

Finally she spotted Ruby, who had her arms wrapped around the neck of a handsome Irish setter. Fidget, it looked like. A sneaky thrill shot through her. Was Lucas here too?

And why was that possibility making her pulse pick up a beat?

She spotted Lucas a little distance away from Ruby. He gripped a stick in one hand. With a dramatic windup, he winged it down the beach. Fidget chased after it in long galloping leaps. Ruby shrieked and clapped her hands with glee.

"Go Fidget, go!" she called to the dog. He pounced on the stick, then raced back toward Lucas. Then paused, torn between the excited little girl to his left or his beloved owner to his right.

Megan laughed at the poor dog's dilemma. Who could resist Ruby? Or Lucas, for that matter? And then Fidget did something that really surprised her. He ran straight for Megan and dropped the stick at her feet.

"Why Fidget, for me? What a sweet gesture. How'd you even know I was here?" She crouched down and gingerly picked up the slobbery stick. "You probably know a lot more than you're letting on, don't you?"

He fixed dark, soulful eyes on her and pawed at the sand. She tossed the stick for him and he swirled away in a rooster tail of wet sand.

Lucas jogged up the beach toward her. His pants were rolled up halfway to his knees and wet sand clung to his bare feet. For some reason she found the sight of his long, muscular calves inordinately sexy.

"Didn't see you up there," he called as he approached.

"I was spying." Her cheerful joke drew a strange reaction from him. His slight smile dropped into a more neutral expression. "It's a mother thing. I like to watch my kid when she doesn't know it. Gives me endless joy."

"Fair enough." He handed her Ruby's little purple backpack. "Her friend had to take off and I happened to be walking Fidget, so I volunteered to hang out until you got back."

"Thanks. That probably made her day." Ruby was now tussling with Fidget for the stick. "I'm glad Fidget's around, otherwise we'd probably have to get a dog of our own."

"No space for a dog?" His slate-blue t-shirt had a streak of wet sand across it. Maybe Fidget had jumped up on him? The damp patches clung to his muscles. What would happen if she ran her hands under his shirt and touched that hard flesh?

*Focus. Don't get distracted by this inconvenient attraction.*

"It's not that. We could find room for a dog bed. But I don't feel right about getting a dog when I don't know how long we'll be here."

One dark eyebrow lifted. "Oh?"

"Hey, it can't be a surprise that the *Forget Me Not* isn't exactly setting the nature-tour world on fire." She attempted a smile but it didn't last long. "We'll see. The summer's young."

"Yes, but it's over fast up here. Starts getting cold in August."

"Which is when the fall migration starts. That could be one of my busiest times." One could always hope, although last fall hadn't brought her much extra business. But this season, she had a secret weapon. *Trekking.* "Everything could change after the show hits the air. Are you going to the viewing party tonight?"

She tugged her lower lip between her teeth, wishing she could take that back. It sounded too much like an invitation.

And of course he pounced on it, dark eyes flashing a hint of jade. "Should I?"

"Well, I'm sure you're going to be the star of the show. Don't you want to see how many closeups you got? While surrounded by most of Lost Harbor?" She laughed at his suddenly horrified expression. "Or maybe you'd rather do your taxes or scrub mold off grout. Very understandable."

"I don't know. There's always the chance of seeing you in that bikini again."

Oh God. She'd forgotten about that part. All of Lost Harbor was about to see her in her swimsuit. Not her most attractive bikini either, because that one didn't fit her anymore. No, she'd worn the faded polka dot top with the failing elastic. How much side boob had they caught? Had she lost her mind that day? "You know, come to think of it, I'm feeling a little under the weather. I'll skip the group viewing and watch by myself with a giant bottle of vodka."

"Oh no you don't. If I can take it, so can you." He reached for her hand and took it into his warm grip. "We're in this together."

"You were wearing all your clothes," she reminded him. His hand felt so good against hers, so reassuring. She let her hand linger in his longer than she should, long enough so tingles spread up her arm and her knees turned to water. How good would it feel to lean against him? To tuck her head into the notch just there, under his collarbone?

She came to her senses and released his hand as Ruby came running up to them. "Something's wrong with Fidget," she gasped. "He stopped playing and now he's limping."

Closer to shore, Fidget lay on his side in a woebegone heap.

Lucas bolted across the sand toward his dog. Megan and Ruby ran after him, catching up as he dropped next to the miserable-looking pup. "What happened, Fidge?" Gently he picked up each paw in turn. "Glass," he finally said. "A shard of glass right in the pad. Ouch. Okay, buddy, this has to come out. I'm not gonna lie, it might hurt."

"Does he understand you?" asked Ruby.

"He understands something. Tone of voice mostly. We've been here before. He got a snout full of porcupine quills last year and stepped into a hornet's nest before that. Magnet for trouble, aren't you, big guy?"

Fidget watched him with a trusting expression that brought tears to Megan's eyes. How could she hate a man whose dog loved him so much?

Face it, she hadn't "hated" Lucas in a while. If she ever really had.

"How can I help?" she asked him.

"I need to keep him steady while I work on his paw. I'm going to bring him into my lap and maybe you could just, maybe scratch his ears. That always soothes him."

He sat on his rear on the sand and cradled Fidget close to his body, between his powerful thighs. That position gave the dog no room to maneuver or escape.

"Ruby, back up please. If he struggles I don't want you getting a toenail in the face." His tone was light, but it held enough authority that Ruby scuttled backward a healthy distance.

"Is he going to be okay?" she asked anxiously.

"Stand by," murmured Lucas. He nodded to Megan, who gingerly reached for Fidget's silky-soft head. To do so, she had to be very close to Lucas, closer than she'd ever been. Hyper aware of his magnetic presence, she kept her focus on the dog.

"It's okay, Fidget," she whispered. "Lucas will take care of you." She scratched the spot between his ears that Ruby had discovered always made his tail thump. It did so now, slapping against the sand.

"Good thing my pocket knife has tweezers," Lucas said absently as he touched the tool to Fidget's paw. It bristled with attachments like a metal porcupine. "It's probably the handiest part of this tool. Do you know how many splinters I've gotten out with this thing?"

"What else does it have?" Ruby crouched a few feet away,

spellbound by the whole process.

"Anything you can think of. Nail clippers. Several sizes of knives, of course. A corkscrew. It's a magical all-purpose tool, and I think you need one, Ruby."

"I *do*?"

Megan shook her head in warning. "Her dad would never go for that, sorry."

"Oh. Of course." His hand tightened on the knife. "My bad. Okay, everyone, here comes the glass. It might be a little bloody."

He slid the shard from the cushioned pad of Fidget's paw. The dog yelped and quivered wildly in Lucas' lap. Blood trickled onto the sand.

"You got it!" yelled Ruby.

"We got it!"

Megan noted the generous use of "we." She hadn't done much besides try to keep her cool so close to Lucas.

"You okay, Megan?" He was looking at her with a funny expression, as if the sight of blood might make her faint.

"Of course. All I did was pet this good boy's head." She scratched his fur again. "You did all the work."

"Can you take this?" He handed her the pocket knife. "I'm going to dip his paw in the ocean. Saltwater's good for stopping infection. Be right back." He rose to his feet, his muscular thighs flexing, Fidget in his arms.

Holding the knife, still warm and sweaty from Lucas' hand, Megan heaved a sigh of relief.

"Poor Fidget," said Ruby.

Okay. Sure. Poor Fidget.

Stepping on glass, bad. Being carried into the ocean by Lucas Holt, not quite so bad.

Damn it. She really needed to go back to hating Lucas instead of lusting after him. Was there a Hate Potion Number 9 she could take?

# CHAPTER EIGHTEEN

After washing off Fidget's paw, Lucas carried him to the bed of his truck and laid him gently down on the plaid wool blanket he kept back there. Fidget would probably limp for a couple of days but he'd be fine.

Not so much things with him and Megan. Something had shifted between them while he tended to Fidget. For one thing, he now had the fragrance of her hair lodged in his memory. Light, like orange blossom. But also spicy, like cinnamon. He'd inhaled a few times just to pin down the scent. And now he wanted more chances to sample it.

She'd been so solid during the whole incident. She hadn't flinched once while Fidget whined and squirmed. There had been no sign of a panic attack or a flashback to another traumatic event. Was that because a workplace shooting bore no resemblance to a dog with glass in his paw? Or was it because Dev was full of shit?

He needed more information.

As soon as he got home and settled Fidget into his dog bed with an extra treat, he logged onto his computer.

He googled Megan Miller and shooting. Even putting those words together made him cringe. Hell, even googling her felt out of bounds.

Several references populated his screen. He opened the first article, from the *Central Coast University Weekly*.

*Expelled Student Opens Fire in Admissions Office*, read the headline.

So it was true. Jesus. He scanned the body of the article and discovered that every single detail matched what Dev had told him. Several injuries, no deaths, the former student arrested. And among the witnesses—Megan Miller. The article even included a quote from her. "I never thought that all these filing cabinets would save our lives, but they did. We used them as a shield and it worked. We could hear the bullets hitting the metal. It was such a terrifying sound, I'll never forget it. We thought we were going to die. We were all holding hands and trying to stay as still as we could."

That sounded like a recipe for trauma to him. Did she still hear that sound of bullets hitting filing cabinets? Did she get freaked out by gunshots? Especially during hunting season, it wasn't an uncommon sound.

Even some boat captains carried guns but that was pretty rare. Lucas didn't allow guns on the *Jack Hammer*. To him, guns and boats didn't mix, but that might be due to his father's habit of getting drunk and then threatening to play target practice with seagulls. Luckily, after the first beer he'd never remembered the combination of his gun safe.

Lucas read further in the article.

The admissions officer speculated that the gunman had been experiencing burnout. "He was a star student, very gifted. But then he started struggling academically. His whole life had been focused on getting into a good university. Once he was here, he had trouble adjusting."

Thoughtfully, Lucas shut down his laptop. So what Dev had told him was true. Megan had survived a workplace shooting and said herself that she'd never forget it.

But did that mean she was so traumatized that she needed a babysitter? Or a bodyguard? Or a spy...or whatever it was that Dev had wanted him to do?

Fidget shifted on his bed and uttered a low whining groan. His paw twitched. The poor pup was probably reliving the pain of stepping on glass. Lucas brought him a bowl of water and set it next to his head so he wouldn't have to move when he woke up.

"You okay on your own here, big guy?" He stroked his dog's furry head. A whistle of wind rattled the windows. He glanced around the raftered great room with its hooked rugs and walls hung with hand-sewn quilts. His mother was just about out of space to display her crafting creations. The next rug would have to become a dog bed.

This wasn't the decor he would choose. Back in Denver he had a brand spanking new condo with polished floors that he never covered up with rugs. He also had a healthy income that didn't require managing deckhands, buying bait, or schmoozing with clients over coolers of beer.

He had a whole life of his own back in Denver. That life had everything he wanted. Freedom, independence, autonomy. No one needed anything from him and he didn't need anything from anyone else.

Here in Lost Harbor, everyone needed him. An aging dog was just the tip of the iceberg. His mother needed him, the homestead needed him, his crew needed him, the harbormaster, random unconscious kayakers, even the goddamn ghost of his father.

But what did *he* need? What was he doing here?

The memory of the cinnamon scent of Megan's hair floated past, as if carried on a breeze through the window, from down the ridge to the heart of town, where the movie theater was probably already filling up with people.

He got to his feet and followed it down the hill.

---

THE LOST HARBOR Theater had a raucous party atmosphere —probably thanks to all the "harbor rats" who'd downed a few shots beforehand and were laughing and chatting up a storm. Lucas had gotten there too late to find a seat, so he leaned against the back wall and tried to ignore the fact that it was sticky. Had some teenager about to make out stuck his gum back there?

He scanned the crowd, not sure if he was looking for his crew or the show producers, until he spotted Megan and Ruby a few rows from the back. Then he knew that, of course, he'd been looking for them.

Damn it.

Megan had twisted her hair into a knot held in place by a yellow pencil. Dainty little wisps clung to the back of her neck. She was talking to someone next to her—Boris, he realized. Without his chicken, for once. Would the poor man be able to function without his pal Anushka? Probably—thanks to Megan, who was listening to him patiently.

That was the thing about Megan. She treated everyone with the same generosity, even if they were...a little off in some way.

The delicate curve of her neck, exposed by her hair style, made his mouth water. What would her flesh feel like against his tongue? Would her pulse flutter wildly under that soft skin?

He shook himself out of his reverie and fixed his gaze on Ruby instead. With her black hair in two sleek pigtails, she was sitting on her heels and knees on the seat, rocking it back and forth to make it squeak. Megan, without looking her way, put a hand on her shoulder to make her stop. Instead, the stubborn child simply slowed her rocking.

Someone pushed through the swinging door that offered entrance from the outer lobby to the main theater space. It had to be someone not local because every Lost Harbor resident knew to be careful with that door. It was lighter than it looked, so if it got pushed too hard it banged against the wall with a loud retort.

That was exactly what happened. *Bang.* Megan jerked at the sound. Not just a slight jolt but a full-body shudder. Her arm automatically went around Ruby, shielding her with her body.

From the sound made by a door opening.

Jesus, she really did have some PTSD. At least a little bit.

Right away, she must have realized that she was reacting to a memory instead of reality. She played it off by patting Ruby on the shoulder and dropping a kiss on her head. Lucas could see the effort it took for her to relax and sit back as if nothing had happened.

Boris was still ranting away; he hadn't noticed either the bang of the door or Megan's reaction.

If only he could expel Boris from his spot next to Megan and take her into his arms, the way she had with Ruby. The urge to protect her, to soothe her, was so strong he had to physically fight it. He planted his boots on the floor and stood firm.

Where was this strong reaction coming from? Maybe it was just the natural protective instinct built into every human being. He had it—that's why he'd joined so many rescue operations in Lost Harbor, starting from the age of sixteen. He'd nearly made a career of it, but left home instead. He knew very well that he'd been born with a strong protective urge. It didn't mean anything about Megan in particular.

Or did it?

The person who'd opened the door strode down the aisle.

Tony, the *Trekking* producer. "Sorry about the door," he called to the crowd. "Who's ready for a fun show?"

Applause accompanied him to the front of the theater. He faced the audience and tucked his tight dreadlocks behind his ears. "I want to thank y'all for being great hosts and great TV subjects. This is just a rough cut, and we don't usually do this because we don't have time, but I asked my boss if I could because you guys were so stellar and I wanted a reason to come back to Alaska. She said 'yes' so here we are. The finished show will air next week. Hope you enjoy it, and thanks for all the fish."

A chuckle swept through the crowd as the lights came down. The familiar *Trekking* theme song and opening sequence played across the screen.

"At *Trekking*, we travel to the ends of the world so you don't have to leave your couch. Prepare for the adventure of a lifetime. Tonight, we explore the remote and stunning ocean harbor of Lost Harbor, Alaska. To reach Lost Harbor, we had to drive through several mountain passes to the very tip of a land mass that shelters the magnificent Misty Bay. On the far side of the bay looms the forbidding Lost Souls Wilderness with its icy peaks and ancient glaciers. On this side, the enchanting fishing outpost of Lost Harbor."

The crowd erupted in cheers, then quickly hushed so everyone could hear.

"In this town of five thousand souls, life is centered around the tides and the seasons...but most of all, the fish. And in one case, the birds."

A shot of Megan in her bikini posing with binoculars flashed onto the screen. "Meet Megan Miller, who wants visitors to know that there's more to life than the next big catch."

The camera closed in on Megan speaking earnestly to the camera. "I wish people here would get just as excited about an auk sighting as they do about a run of king salmon." The images switched to beautiful shots of Misty Bay and the glaciers and flocks of birds over Bird Rock. She continued, "With birding, you get the thrill of the hunt without actually killing anything ... We monitor the bird populations, which is very important during this time of threat to our environment."

The camera zoomed in on Lost Souls Glacier, wedged in a valley between two steep mountain peaks. "Have you noticed the effects of climate change around here?"

Uh oh. This was Megan's second favorite topic after birds. It was also the topic that got her in trouble with the old timers.

"Oh, absolutely. That glacier you're looking at is shrinking every year. A lot of people say Alaska is the canary in the coalmine when it comes to global warming. Not only are the glaciers shrinking but permafrost is thawing and there's less sea ice than there used to be. All of the species that live here or who migrate here in the summer are being forced to adapt. Some won't be able to. See all those glorious spruce trees?"

The camera panned across a grove of spruce standing guard over a stark granite cliff.

"They're probably doomed. This entire peninsula will shift from spruce to birch, probably within twenty years. I honestly don't think people realize how quickly everything's changing. They're burying their heads in the mudflats, so to speak." Her tone shifted, as if she'd suddenly realized how dire she sounded.

"So if you want to see this magnificent scenery in person, you should come soon!"

And there was Megan again, on camera, with a big grin and a thumbs up.

A hostile murmur swept through the audience. Oh shit. Of all subjects to talk about, why couldn't she have picked something less controversial—like her damn Caspian tern?

The narrator's voice took over again. "Megan Miller has been studying the birds here for almost a year. Lucas Holt grew up in

Lost Harbor and owns and operates the family-run *Jack Hammer Fishing Charters*. Suffice it to say, he and Megan Miller don't see eye to eye on much."

Lucas saw his own face fill the screen now. He squinted to reduce the weirdness of seeing himself like that. Sunglasses, waders, a t-shirt, a tan. He stood on the deck of his boat, legs braced against the slow rollers coming in from the open ocean.

"A lot of people come here from other states and don't understand the unique challenges of living in Alaska. My grandparents were homesteaders here, before there was even a store. They survived by trapping, fishing, raising their own food. It was an exceptionally hard life. It's still hard in many ways. Fishing is considered one of the most dangerous professions on earth. If you make a mistake, it has a good chance of being fatal. Props to the fishermen who go out in all conditions—ice storms, thirty-foot waves—just to make a living and take care of their families."

A murmur of approval rose from the audience. Lucas cringed at the way his comments were edited to contrast with Megan's. She hadn't intended to offend anyone, of course. She just didn't realize how resistant people were to change. Or to *acknowledging* change.

"What do you want people to know about Lost Harbor? What was it like to grow up here?"

Onscreen Lucas hesitated, looking across the water as if for inspiration. "Hard and beautiful," he finally said. "It's hard work, surviving the winter without going crazy. I always say if you can survive in Alaska you can survive anywhere. I stand by that."

"What would you say to those warning about changes to the ecology here?"

"Everything changes. We'll survive. We'll adapt. We have so far."

Applause broke out in the crowd. Lucas wiped a hand across his forehead; it came away sweaty. Shit, they'd edited his comments to make it look like he disagreed with Megan. But he didn't, not really. The glaciers *were* shrinking. Things were changing. Anyone with eyes could see that.

At that point the scene on camera switched to him and Megan together. They were standing on the boardwalk. Both of them stood with their hands on their hips, confronting each other. What had they been talking about? He couldn't remember, but probably not climate change. Maybe they'd been arguing about whose turn it was to replace the toilet paper in the office.

The narrator's voiceover didn't mention toilet paper.

"Even if Lost Harbor survives the changes in the climate, it might have a harder time surviving the arguments over it."

Megan waved her finger in Lucas' face. Ah—now he remembered. They'd been arguing about whether the ice cream shop served mango sorbet. It had seemed very important at the time. Neither of them ever wanted to lose an argument.

Eventually he'd taken her by the arm and hauled her over to the ice cream shop to prove he was right.

He wasn't. So he'd bought her an ice cream cone as an apology. He'd bought himself one because he needed it after all that arguing.

The next shot showed the two of them licking at their cones as they strolled down the boardwalk.

"Of course in a small town like this," said the narrator, "people learn to resolve their differences—over ice cream, if possible."

Amused snickers rose from the audience. "Get a room," someone called out. The laughter increased. Lucas looked again at the shot, which the producers had slowed way down to increase its impact. Megan looked sexy as hell in slo-mo. Her cutoff jeans and rubber boots showed off her shapely legs. She wore a long-sleeved top that shouldn't have been attractive but somehow it was. Her breasts rose and fell as she walked.

She looked up at him, laughing at something. With a sidelong smile, he tilted his head to meet her gaze, and the chemistry could have sizzled a hole through the screen.

Holy shit. *Chemistry with Megan.* And it had taken a TV show to make him truly see just how strong it ran.

He slipped out of the theater into the lobby. There was only one way to handle this. He was going to pretend he hadn't seen the show. He was especially going to pretend he'd never seen those shots of him and Megan.

He'd hang onto the shot of Megan in a bikini, however. He couldn't forget that unless he got himself a lobotomy.

# CHAPTER NINETEEN

All of her hard work trying to make headway with the Lost
Harbor community—gone in a snap. All that stuff about climate
change—she hadn't even thought it would make it into the show!
She'd just been casually chatting at that point. It had never
occurred to her that they'd put boring rants about the environment in the show.

What a fiasco.

And somehow it made it even worse that Lucas came across
so well on camera. Not only was he photogenic and utterly
gorgeous in his sunglasses and waders, but he spoke well. Not like
he was trying to prove something, but like he was telling a story.
He was easy to look at *and* to listen to.

While she came across as a ranter. A hippie-chick ranter in a
bikini.

She should have stayed miles away from the *Trekking*
production.

She could tell the difference as soon as she drove out to the
boardwalk after dropping Ruby at the library. No one stopped to
chat with her about the weather. No one gave her any friendly

nods as she hauled a bucket of soapy fresh water down to the *Forget Me Not*. She needed to give the dashboard a good scrubbing and somehow the ocean water never got things clean enough for her liking.

From the overlook on the boardwalk, with its view of the boat ramps, she saw that the berth next to the *Forget Me Not* was empty. The *Jack Hammer* must already be out on the water. At least she wouldn't have the humiliation of watching Lucas gloat. She was actually surprised that his boat was out; the forecast called for a rare summer storm.

As she reached the top of the ramp, she paused to survey the bay. Only a slight breeze ruffled the surface. Maybe the forecast had changed. That happened a lot around here.

A text from Zoe came in. *You okay there, girl?*

*Yes. No big deal. I'm used to being shunned.*

*It's not that bad. You're only the second top topic of the morning.*

*After what, dare I ask?*

*Carla smashed into Ralphie's truck after the viewing last night. Maybe on purpose.*

Oh good. Drama. Maybe they'd all forget about the *Trekking* show. Or maybe, for once—would it kill them to actually listen to her? She sighed heavily. Fat chance of that.

*Stay strong, lady. Don't worry about the old crabs around here.*

At least she hadn't lost her only friend in Lost Harbor.

When she reached her slip, she found a police officer standing next to the *Forget Me Not*, writing something in a notebook.

Right away, her heart went into triple speed. The last time she'd been in the presence of a police officer was right after the shooting.

"Can I help you?" she asked through the flutters in her throat.

The officer, a black woman around her age, fixed her with a

stern stare. "I'm Officer Badger. Are you Megan Miller?"

"I am. This is my boat, the *Forget Me Not*. I'm in my proper slip and I'm paid up through the summer and all my licenses are current and I'm not sure if maybe someone said otherwise but—"

The officer held up her hand to stop her nervous flow of words. "Have you noticed anything unusual on your boat?"

"Well, I just got here, so I can't really say." She walked to the edge of the ramp and gave her boat a thorough scan. "Everything looks normal. Why?"

"We got a call this morning from someone worried on your behalf. He thought we might want to swing by and make sure no one does anything stupid. How about I wait here while you check over your boat?"

A chill shot through her, from her head down to her toes. "Something stupid, like what?"

"Oh, could be anything. Fishermen get pretty creative when they're feuding."

"I'm not feuding with anyone. Well, Lucas Holt, but I don't think..." She sucked in a breath. "He wouldn't—"

Officer Badger laughed. "I've known Lucas since high school. He's actually the one who called to give me a heads-up there was rumbling in the ranks. I don't think you have to worry about him."

"Right. Of course not." Flushing with embarrassment, she put down her bucket of water and climbed onboard. Not only had she almost accused Lucas, but he was actually looking out for her. When would she ever get a read on that man?

She started up the engine. It gave a spluttering cough before it settled into its purring idle. "It always does that," she called to the officer, who nodded with little surprise. It was a rare boat engine that didn't have some kind of quirk.

"Everything seems normal." She shrugged as she came back out on deck. She reached into the cooler. "I appreciate the drop-in. Would you like a cupcake?"

"Now that definitely isn't normal." Officer Badger smiled as she accepted it. "You're upping the game around here."

"I use whatever advantage I can get. I always offer my passengers cupcakes but I usually end up with extra. Too many special diets these days."

"I hear that. Me, I eat it all, except fish. Too slimy for me. Just don't tell the guys around here or I'll never hear the end of it." As Megan smiled, the officer handed her a business card. "Call me if anything comes up."

"Thank you. I will. Oh, Officer," she added as the woman turned away. "Just curious. What was Lucas like in high school?"

Officer Badger nibbled the icing of the cupcake as she contemplated the question. "One of the good ones," she finally said. "A lot more sensitive than he looks. But don't tell him I said that or he'll never forgive me."

Once Officer Badger was gone, Megan brought the bucket of soap suds onboard. She tried to focus on her cleaning task, but the encounter had unsettled her. Even though the woman was perfectly nice, she still wore a uniform and carried a firearm holstered on her belt. Megan had tried hard not to look at it, but could sense its shiny menace.

*Totally different gun, totally different situation,* she told herself. *You can't freak out every time you see a gun.*

She drew in a few deep breaths as she'd learned to do to fight anxiety. It helped, but not quite enough. Her heart still raced, and her throat tightened. The other boats—the hulking tenders, the sleek sports boats, even the more refined sailboats—seemed too close, almost threatening. The constant *thrum* of boats passing in and out of the harbor grated on her nerves.

She needed some peace and quiet.

If Lucas had gone out, she probably had time for a quick run before the storm hit. *If* it hit. It could have easily changed course when it hit the Lost Souls Wilderness peninsula.

Ruby was at an all-day art class at the library. Her next tour booking was later in the day, but she was considering canceling it due to the forecast. She had a little time to herself, for once, so why not take advantage of it?

After casting off the lines, she steered the *Forget Me Not* toward the mouth of the harbor.

She dialed Captain Kid on her cell as she steered with one hand. "Hey, I'm taking a little pleasure cruise out to Bird Rock. I want to check on that tern we spotted. Maybe I can see a nest or some chicks. Anything new on the weather front?"

Terrible connection. All she heard of his response was the word "squall."

"Did you say 'squall'?"

The phone crackled in response.

"I can't hear you, Ben. If you can hear me, go ahead and cancel this afternoon's trip if there's a squall in the forecast. I think there's only three people booked for it. I won't be long, an hour max. Talk to you later."

By the time she stopped talking the connection had dropped out completely. As she glided past the fuel station at the mouth of the harbor, she noticed that their wind socks were going crazy.

She hadn't seen them whipping around like that since winter.

Should she go back to her slip? A sea otter glided past her, floating on his back as he gnawed on a mussel. He seemed unworried about anything other than extracting every bit of nutrition from his catch.

If a bad storm was coming, the otters would sense it, wouldn't they? She tuned her radio to the marine channel.

"Marine warning for northern Misty Bay, seas of fifteen to twenty feet and winds up to sixty knots," the forecaster intoned. "Small craft advisory posted for Aurora Bay to Tenpenny Creek."

Megan relaxed as she rounded the tip of the breakwater that formed the harbor. Lost Harbor was in the southern part of the bay. She should be fine as long as she didn't go toward Tenpenny Creek. She opened up the throttle. The bow of the *Forget Me Not* lifted eagerly. A mist of spray splashed across the windshield and she laughed with joy.

All her anxiety vanished. Out here on the bay, with nothing but ocean and air and wild creatures, everything made sense. All her worries fled as if chased away by the rising wind. Out here, there was absolutely no chance that a terrifying figure brandishing a weapon would suddenly appear before her.

Except in her memory.

When those images came back to her, she couldn't always stop them.

He'd worn a gas mask. People didn't mention it much, but that little detail was the thing that surfaced in her nightmares the most. He hadn't looked *human*. When he'd first walked in, she'd wondered for a wild moment if they were being invaded by aliens. And the sounds hadn't made any sense at first. *Pop-pop, splat.* Roar. Scream.

She focused her gaze across the bay, on Lost Souls Glacier, picking out each crevice filled with blue light. That was the glacier she'd told the crew about, the one in the local legend about a lost tribe. The story had always piqued her imagination. Was it based on a real event or was it pure fabrication? Maybe it was a warning. *Strange things happen around Lost Souls.*

A hissing sound brought her back to the here and now.

The flat bottom of her boat thumped against the surface of the water. The strange sound was coming from her right; she looked that way just in time to see a wave curling several feet above the side of her boat, like a dragon ready to strike. *Holy shit.* That thing could swamp her if it broke broadside. She swung the wheel hard to starboard so she could hit the wave head on. Or more precisely—so it could hit her.

*Slam.*

# CHAPTER TWENTY

The *Forget Me Not* crested the wave, lost power for a second, then plunged into the valley between one wave and the next. A shudder traveled through her boat; she could feel it in her feet, in the controls, in the rattle of gear.

Jesus. *She'd lost her steering for a second.* The rudder had been out of the water, that was why. These waves were too big for the *Forget Me Not*.

The storm had hit. Fast, powerful, inescapable.

Another wave crashed across the bow and sent gray water rushing over the windshield. The splash and roar of it, the whine of the engine, all added to the din—as if she'd plunged at full throttle into a washing machine.

Keeping the bow pointed directly into the waves took all the strength she had. It fought her like a wild mustang, the rudder system straining against the intense force of the ocean.

Was she going to die out here? Alone? Fighting the ocean—just her against the incredible force surrounding her. Oblivious to her.

She'd never felt this alone, not even when a gunman had been spraying bullets nearby. At least then she would have died holding hands with her coworkers. Out here it was just her. At least she hadn't brought Ruby.

*Ruby.*

She didn't have time for the terror that wanted to swamp her. *Fight. Stay alive.* With her entire being, she focused on the enormous waves coming at her little boat as if they wanted to eat it alive. *Bang, slam, thunk.* How the hell wasn't the boat shattering into a million splinters? How long could it last under this pounding?

Of all things, that familiar bit of theme song from Gilligan's Island flashed through her mind. "...A tale of a fateful trip..."

"No. Not a fateful trip," she said out loud. Panting, wet from the spray, arms aching, she wrestled with the wheel. "Ruby needs me," she shouted at the ocean. "You're not taking me! Not today!"

Her radio crackled. She could hardly hear it over the wild ocean roar.

"Calling the *Forget Me Not.* Is that you?"

She couldn't take her hands off the wheel but managed to turn up the volume with her elbow. "Yes!" she yelled.

But of course no one could hear her unless she pressed the "talk" button and that would require one-handing the wheel. Stupid fucking design.

"*Jack Hammer* here. Can you hear me?"

The *Jack Hammer*! Lucas was out here somewhere. Where was he? She tore her eyes away from the oncoming waves long enough to scan outside her boat. She couldn't see anything through the flying spray and churning foam.

"If you can hear me, Megan, I got my binoculars on you." She clung to Lucas' calm voice like an anchor. "You're doing great. If you can steer two degrees to port you'll reach Ninlik Cove. I'm there right now and it's calm. You're about ten minutes out. Can you do it? Just watch the rocks to your starboard as you round the point."

*Ninlik Cove.* Yes. She knew it. A sheltered little jewel of an inlet in Lost Souls Wilderness where Varied Thrushes like to nest. A steep wooded bluff guarded it from the bay. But she couldn't see anything beyond the next wave. Water in the sky, foam in the water—everything upside down.

*Two degrees to port,* he'd said. She swung the helm slightly to her left, even though the force of the water against the rudder made it feel heavier than concrete. The shift in direction meant that she took the waves on the starboard quarter of her bow. As each one hit, the *Forget Me Not* rolled from side to side with a sickening dip.

*Ten minutes,* Lucas had said. She'd lost all sense of time and couldn't see a clock anywhere, so that didn't help much.

"That's it, you're on the right track," came Lucas' voice over the radio. Calm, commanding, and thoroughly reassuring.

"Don't leave me," she muttered, glad he couldn't actually hear her. Her hands were shaking so hard from exhaustion she worried they'd fall off the wheel. "Keep talking to me."

As if he knew what she needed, he spoke again. "You're over halfway there. Can you go another degree to port? You're a little off-course right now. That's right. You got it. I know you must be tired, but you're almost there."

Tired didn't begin to describe it, but the energy in his voice seemed to transfer right into her arms. She gripped the wheel tight and ignored the pain that screamed through her hands. *Almost there. Almost there. Another wave. Almost there.*

And then she crested a wave and saw something new—the bluff bringing dark green and solid brown into her world of watery gray. She almost cried at the sight of its blunt shape.

A big part of her learning curve here in Misty Bay had been studying the charts so she knew where the reefs and rocks and sandbars lurked. Luckily, the tide was high enough so most of the reefs were still several feet under. But there was that big rock at the mouth of the cove, the one Lucas had mentioned. It was tricky because it extended outward a fair distance, still close to the surface even at mid-tide.

"Give that thing a wide berth," said Lucas. "You don't want any sudden surges throwing you off course." At this point it felt like his voice was *inside her head*. It was unbelievably reassuring. She shifted her course another degree southwest, noticing at the same time that the force of the waves was diminishing. Maybe the sheltering effect of the bluff was already at work.

"That's perfect," said Lucas. "I'm coming down from the bluff now so I won't be able to guide you. Just come into the cove and idle. I'll take it from there."

She glanced up at the bluff, now larger and more detailed. She could make out individual spruce trees in the dark mass of the forest. Try as she might, she couldn't see Lucas. He was probably already deep in the woods on his way to her.

As soon as she rounded the big rock, holding her breath the entire time, the wind cut dramatically, from a blow dryer roar to an unsettled whisper. Even here in Ninlik Cove, restless ripples marred the usually glassy surface. But these waves were like baby kittens compared to the monstrous lions beyond the bluff.

The sheer relief made her light-headed. She had to peel her fingers off the wheel in order to throttle down the engine. When it reached an idle, the *Forget Me Not* settled into stillness with something like a sigh. Her poor boat.

She patted the dashboard with one numb hand. "We survived, my friend. You did so well. Thank you, thank you."

# CHAPTER TWENTY-ONE

"You did well yourself." Lucas' voice made her startle. She turned to find him pulling himself over the side in a power move that made his arm muscles bulge. He hadn't even waited for her to open the gate. He'd boarded her boat like a pirate and she didn't mind a bit.

In fact, she could kiss him right now, and it took all her willpower not to.

She slumped onto one of the padded benches in the wheelhouse as if her marionette strings had been cut. All the willpower she'd used to keep her boat from capsizing drained out of her. "I'm so tired," she mumbled.

"I bet you are. It's hard work, fighting the entire ocean." He must have gone through it too—his thermal shirt clung to his chest and his hair was thick with salt. While she recovered on the bench, he climbed onto the bow and dropped her anchor. Then he shut down her engine. Finally, complete quiet reigned in her little realm.

She let out a sigh. "I think I'm going to crawl into my bunk and sleep for a while."

"I suggest you come onto my boat. You may have sustained some damage you don't know about yet. I've checked the *Jack Hammer* thoroughly and she's in good shape. You can take a nap over there."

"Really? You don't mind?" For some reason, that simple kindness brought tears to her eyes. Probably a sign of just how exhausted she was.

"Of course. I'll keep an eye on the *Forget Me Not*. If you like I can give it a thorough inspection."

"Maybe later. I think she needs a break."

Lucas smiled at the affectionate tone in her voice. "I sense a new appreciation for your craft."

"Definitely. I thought there was a good chance I might die." Her voice cracked, and she cleared her throat to mask the sound. He caught it anyway—obviously—but didn't react. Bless him.

"You did great, really well. That storm came out of nowhere. They were calling for it to stay north, but it didn't."

"You got caught too?"

"I saw the wind shift. I've seen it before, so I knew what could happen. I took my clients back in and dropped them off, but then I saw you were still out." As he spoke, he opened the gate and dropped the ladder into place. He tugged his Zodiac up close.

"You came after me?"

"I came after you. I'm on the volunteer rescue crew so it's what I signed up for."

Ah. That made sense. He was doing his job. Being a hero.

She got to her feet and limped toward the ladder. Her entire body ached, as if she'd just gone ten rounds with a boxing instructor. "Well, I'm very grateful. I don't know what would have happened if you hadn't guided me here."

"I had a plan B. If it looked like you weren't making any headway, I would have come out and gotten you off the boat."

He held out his hand to help her onto the ladder. As she took it, she realized that hers were still shaking terribly. She couldn't make her hand close, so he shifted his grip to her wrist.

"And a plan C. The Coast Guard would have sent help. And then there was always Plan A minus—that the storm would die down quickly."

She smiled weakly. "I was rooting for that one every second I was out there. Didn't seem to work."

With his hand clasped around her wrist, she stepped down the ladder and into the Zodiac, which he'd tied to the *Forget Me Not*'s railing.

"Anything else you need from onboard?" he asked.

"My phone. That's it."

"No service in the cove. But we have contact by radio. Nothing from your magic cooler?"

She laughed as she settled onto the stiff rubber of the Zodiac. "No, I didn't expect to be out for long. No tours, no leftovers, no cupcakes."

He followed her down the ladder and into the dinghy. Before he picked up the oars, he handed her the radio. "Do you want to call anyone about Ruby? I'm not sure how long we'll have to wait out here."

She took her bottom lip between her teeth. Right now, with everyone in the harbor turned against her, the only person she trusted was Zoe. "How can I reach the pizza shop?"

"The harbormaster's waiting for your call. He can get a message to her."

"But he probably despises me after I basically trashed everyone in Lost Harbor."

He gave her an offended frown as he rowed them toward the *Jack Hammer*. She tried not to watch the way his muscles flexed with each stroke, but it was hopeless. With every move he made, he got sexier. She wanted to throw herself into his arms, snuggle against his hard chest, feel his warmth soak into her.

The impulse was so strong that she had to blink herself back to reality—Lucas at the oars, frowning at her as he explained Lost Harbor.

"What does that have to do with anything? You're a boater in trouble. That's all that matters. I told you we look out for each other here. Even my father would drop everything to rescue someone he was feuding with. Old Crow got stuck on a sandbar once and my dad swam two hundred yards from his boat to give him a hand."

A tear came to Megan's eye, then another one. It had nothing to do with any sentimentality over Jack Holt or fishermen looking out for each other. All the emotions from the last hour or so crashed over her.

"Go ahead and cry," Lucas told her, almost brusquely.

"But—"

"It's an emotional release. It's okay. Very common. Doesn't mean you aren't a badass survivor girl."

And with that, she burst into tears.

---

LUCAS HAD to remind himself over and over that Megan was in a very vulnerable condition at the moment. With a fierceness that shocked him, he wanted to take her into his arms and hold her so tight that the lost look on her face went away forever.

Seeing the *Forget Me Not* nearly swamped by twenty-foot waves, over and over, had scared the living shit out of him. Watching her through his binoculars while she made her painstaking way toward Ninlik Cove had nearly killed him.

Now she was here, knee to knee with him in his Zodiac, tears streaming down her face, and it was just something she had to go through. And he had to let her even though his heart was getting ripped right out of his body.

He focused on the things he could do for her. Like row this damn dinghy toward his boat. He hopped onboard, then reached for Megan and swing her over the side. She clung to him weakly, but he knew it was fatigue rather than lack of strength.

Megan Miller had plenty of strength and a big dose of courage too. The way she'd handled her boat through the sudden storm—she'd impressed the hell out of him.

Why had he ever thought she was too flighty and naive to handle life in Alaska? He'd dismissed her without getting to truly know her.

Once onboard, he guided her with a hand in the small of her back to the captain's berth. The *Jack Hammer* had originally been built with two berths up front but his father had combined them into one king-size sleeping spot that took up the entire bow. A skylight allowed light into the space and required regular caulking.

Lucas checked to make sure his last caulking job had held up. Everything seemed dry enough. A polyblend comforter covered the poly fiber foam mattress. Lucas had spent a pretty penny on it because it resisted mold. The scent of musty textiles always made him gag because it reminded him of the worst times with his father on this very boat.

"Go ahead." He gently urged Megan toward the bed. "It's all yours. Rest all you want. I'll get a message to Zoe for you."

"Tell her Ruby's at the library until four."

"I will. Don't worry about a thing. We got you. Sleep now. I'll be out there." He waved at the small galley and bench seats that made up the tiny living quarters of the boat. "Shout if you need anything."

"Do you have a towel?" she asked in a quivery voice. "I don't want to get your pillow wet."

God, she was adorable right now. Worried about his goddamn pillow when she'd just gone through a terrifying ordeal.

He plucked one from a small tote where he kept dry clothes. She tried to dry her hair but her arms were too weak to lift above her head. He took the towel from her and gently squeezed the ocean water from her hair. He lightly rubbed it across her scalp until he heard her sigh.

Megan sighing in his arms. It might be the most erotic sound he'd ever heard.

He balled up the towel and took a step back. Being this close to her was dangerous.

"Sleep now." His voice sounded like the scrape of a keel on a gravel sandbar. "You're safe. I'll wake you up if you're needed."

"I have to take my wet clothes off."

"Oh. Of course." He handed her the towel and turned his back to her. He took a fresh t-shirt from his tote and handed it to her without looking back. "You can use this if you want."

"Thanks."

Undressing in the cramped quarters of the *Jack Hammer* was no easy feat, and he heard plenty of banging and muttering until finally the familiar thud of the mattress told him she was now in his bed.

Megan Miller was in his bed.

"Is it my imagination or is this the most comfortable..." She trailed off and the next sound he heard was a snore.

Smiling to himself, he went into the galley and turned on the tea kettle. He needed a hot drink, and she probably would too when she woke up. He called the harbormaster on the radio and asked him to call Zoe.

"I can patch her in, hang on."

A few moments later, Zoe was on the line. "Everyone okay out there? It's blowing a gale here, the boardwalk's practically shut down."

"We're fine. Megan's asleep right now, but she wanted me to ask you to pick up Ruby at the library at four."

"No problem. Tell her I'll keep Ruby as long as she needs me to. I'll feed her pizza and we'll watch movies and have a good old slumber party. The twins can always entertain her. You guys stay where you are until it's safe to come back."

"Will do. Thanks, Zoe."

"Hey, thank *you*. Megan's good for this place, if only you idiots would get your heads out of your asses."

She might have a point there. He rolled his eyes and spoke next to Bob, the harbormaster. "What's the weather service saying?"

"Could go for a while. The advisory won't be lifted until morning. Use your best judgment. How's her boat?"

"Seems okay." He glanced over at the *Forget Me Not* bobbing peacefully a few hundred feet away. "Hasn't foundered yet."

"The Coasties are dealing with a tanker that ran aground— empty, thank God—so they're leaving this one to us."

"Is everyone else back in port?"

"Yup. Safe and sound. It's pretty rough in the harbor too. You're probably in the best place in the bay."

He glanced around the serene cove, with its soaring spruce trees reflected in the deep green water. "I'm not going anywhere for now, that's for sure."

"Funny thing," the harbormaster added just before he hung up. "They're saying this storm is related to climate change."

"Ha." Lucas snorted. "I guess that is pretty funny. Megan will probably laugh her ass off when she wakes up. Right after she writes 'I Told You So' in boat fumes."

His tea kettle whistled, so he clicked off the radio and went back to the galley. He jumped at the sight of Megan framed by the hatch that led to the captain's berth. She leaned against the fiberglass frame, blinking sleepily, enveloped in the clean t-shirt he'd given her. Her hair was a tangled mess, her face blotchy from her tears, the flesh around her blue-gray eyes swollen—but still, he found her beautiful.

The shirt read, "I Got Hammered on the *Jack Hammer*" and it covered her only to mid-thigh. The sight of her bare legs emerging beneath his shirt made him harden. *Trouble.*

"You couldn't sleep?"

"Not really, I was too worried about Ruby. Did you reach Zoe?"

"I did." He poured boiling water over a tea bag in an insulated mug. "Zoe says she and the twins will spoil her rotten until you get back. Want some tea or do you want to try again with the nap?" He offered her the mug.

She wrapped her hands around it gratefully and took a sip. "I think there's too much adrenaline in my veins to sleep much. Also, I—"

"What?"

"I—" She paused, then put down the mug next to the little sink. And threw herself into his arms.

# CHAPTER TWENTY-TWO

He caught her against his chest. Under the soft t-shirt, her bare breasts pressed against him.

"I just wanted to say 'thank you,'" she sobbed. "You saved my life. I know you'll pretend like you didn't and that you were just doing your job or something. But I was so scared and alone, and then your voice came on the radio and I knew I'd be okay."

He wrapped his arms around her. This wasn't sexual, then, even though every bone in his body reacted as if it was. This was gratitude. Emotional release. "You're all right. You're safe. It's okay." He stroked soothing circles across her back, feeling the delicate knobs of her spine under his palm. He kept his lower half tilted away from her. He didn't need her to know how turned-on she got him.

"I know I'm safe. You don't understand." She drew back, and now he saw something different in her eyes. Heat. "I'm alive."

"Yes." A drumbeat of anticipation came to life in the back of his mind. Something was happening here. He wasn't sure exactly what, but he could hope. "I can see that."

"Can you feel it?" She picked up his hand and placed it over her heart. He felt its rapid thudding beat. He also felt the curve of her breast. He fought to keep his voice neutral.

"I feel it, yes." He swallowed hard, his mouth suddenly bone dry.

"I'm alive and I want—I want—oh for Pete's sake." She grabbed the hem of the t-shirt and ripped it over her head. She tossed it into a corner—onto his best titanium halibut rod, but he didn't complain. There was only one rod that mattered right now.

And it was harder than ever as he took in her naked body. Naked. Body. As he ate up every curve and patch of silky skin, he knew he'd been imagining exactly this for quite a while now. "You sure about this? You might just be looking for a way to release tension right now."

"Who the fuck cares?"

Shit. He'd never heard Megan swear before. He found it—hot.

"I'm a grown fucking woman and right now, I want you. I want to fuck you in that incredibly comfortable bed back there and I don't want to think about anything else."

Electric energy vibrated through every word. Her eyes were wild flashes of blue light. Then she froze. "Unless you don't want to." Her suddenly tentative tone made him snort.

"You can put that out of your mind. I want to." He bent his head so his lips hovered over hers. "I think I've wanted to for a while," he murmured. He set his hands on her hips, her skin soft and pliant under his palms. The feel of her flesh sent the last of his misgivings flying off with the storm wind.

The first touch of her lips made the world shift around him. She tasted of salt and chamomile from the tea he'd given her. Beyond that, something else—something wild and rich and entirely new. She opened her mouth eagerly, urging his kiss deeper and sending her tongue to twine with his. The way she moved, her urgency, her heat—the message ricocheted through his system.

She didn't want hesitation or barriers. She wanted everything all at once.

Her leg slid up his side and curled around him. He pressed his erection into her nakedness. He was wearing a spare pair of fleece workout pants since everything else had gotten drenched. The fabric offered exactly zero way to hide his fierce arousal.

"I know this seems crazy." She pulled away long enough to murmur that statement, then descended on him again with a flurry of kisses on his chin, mouth, cheeks, stubble. "I know I might kick myself later. Can we just do this and not think about it ever again? Kind of a 'people do unpredictable things during a crisis' thing?"

"Yeah, but if you say 'what happens in Ninlik Cove stays in—"

She cut him off with a kiss so deep it left them both gasping.

"It's not like that. I just—I need this right now. I need you. I don't care where it is. And I don't know how I'll feel later, but this, here, right now, this is all that matters."

She pressed a hand against the front of his fleece pants. Holy God Almighty, the fever that shot through him at her touch. He groaned out loud, a sound she seemed to find sexy because it brought her grinding against him again.

With his hands on her ass, he added his own pressure to the rotation of her hips. He wanted her to feel his hardness right where it counted. Right there...the sweet spot in the valley between her legs, the hard little nub that grew as he increased the pressure.

She gave a screaming gasp as he worked her clit against his cock. "Yeah, honey, yeah," he muttered incoherently, barely aware of what he was saying. "God, you feel good."

He hoisted her up so her legs wrapped around his hips.

Ducking under the low frame of the hatch, he carried her to the bed. The comforter was still rumpled from her nap. She slid out of his arms and kneeled on the bed. With her skin flushed pink and her hair a wild tangle, he was seeing a new side of Megan Miller. A sensual, playful side.

Suddenly, all their verbal battles felt like foreplay.

She beckoned for him to come closer. He stepped to the edge of the bed. She ran her hands under his shirt. Eager, almost greedy, her palms slid across his skin and over his stomach muscles. Heat shot straight to his cock.

She noticed the swell of his erection—how could she not? Gliding her hands down his front, she traced the outline of hard flesh under fleece. First she used the pressure of her palms, then the harder scrape of fingernails.

"My God," he groaned softly. "What you're doing to me."

"I'm just hoping you'll ditch some of these clothes." She shot him a sassy wink that didn't do a thing to decrease his arousal. He obliged by ripping off his t-shirt.

She sighed as she feasted her eyes on his chest. "Do you know I sometimes ogle you from Zoe's while you're cleaning fish?"

"Do you know I've been imagining you naked ever since I saw you in that bikini top?"

With both his hands, he gently stroked the upper curve of her breasts, circling around the upswell of flesh. The texture of her skin was so smooth under his fingertips. Even though he hadn't touched her nipples, he watched them rise. Their light rosy pink turned to a dusky raspberry red. His mouth watered as he brushed his thumbs lightly across their tips.

She sucked in a breath and arched back to press her breasts farther into his hands.

Ah, she wanted more. So did he.

While he thumbed her nipples again, a little more forcefully, she slid her hands under the waistband of his pants. Heat pounded through his veins. *Touch it. Hold it. Now. Please. Fuck.*

He cupped her breasts in his hands, loving the springy weight of her flesh against his palms. In a weird way, they had just as much personality as Megan herself did. They weren't shy, those breasts. They stood up and spoke their mind—*kiss me. Now.*

Obeying, he bent to kiss her nipples, which met his tongue with eager responsiveness. As he licked and nipped, the dainty nubs turned to crystal hardness.

Almost as if she needed to stay even with him, she wrapped one hand around his cock. Her thumb flicked across his tip, drawing moisture to the surface.

Part of him had to laugh—this was how they did things, he and Megan. Always going up against each other, making those sparks fly.

He fought to keep his focus on the delicious flesh in his mouth rather than on the delicious things she was doing to his cock. That was the only way he could keep a grip on the fierce lust raging through him.

He wanted to be deep inside her, filling her to the brim, exploding into a million pieces. But he also wanted to draw this out and make sure she got what she wanted out of this experience.

If he was reading her right, she wanted oblivion.

*Coming up.*

She writhed under the deep suckling he was administering to her nipples. If she kept her hands on his dick much longer, this would be over before it really began. Time to take control.

He drew her hands away from his erection and pinned them with one hand. Urging her back onto the bed, with her arms overhead, he curled her fingers around the raised rim of the shelf above the bed. Its purpose was to keep items from sliding off the shelf during rough weather. Right now, it had a better job to do. Keep her from making him come too soon.

Her breath came faster as she held onto the shelf. "What are you doing?" she breathed.

"Reminding you that you're alive," he told her. He kneeled at the end of the bed and stared at her nude body. Round hips, a light sprinkle of downy hair between her legs, shapely thighs, a silvery horizontal scar on her stomach. Skin the color of sweet butter, nipples now scarlet, wet from his sucking.

Gently he placed his hands on her upper thighs and pushed them apart to reveal the shadowed realm of her most secret self. Her lower lips were already pouting and swollen, flashing a hint of wetness.

"Stay right where you are," he ordered. Ship captains knew how to boss people around, and this was his boat, after all. "Or I'll have to lash you to the mast and have my way with you."

Her breathing came more rapidly. "I don't know, that sounds like it might be kind of fun."

He should have known she'd have an adventurous spirit. How else would she have landed here at the ends of the earth?

"I'll have to get a proper mast installed then," he joked. "Who cares if it gets in the way of fishing?"

While she was still giggling, he surprised her with a long stroke of his tongue across her seam. Soft and wet, the sweet slippery flesh gave way under his licking, parting to reveal her clit. Rising stubbornly, as if to notify him of its presence, it snagged against his tongue.

*There you are.* He circled it lightly, listening for her reaction —a long and hungry moan. Just what he wanted to hear. Taking his time, setting a luxurious and sensual pace, he lavished attention on that excitable little bundle of nerves. He used his tongue, his entire mouth, his thumbs, even the scrape of stubble on his jaw, until every inch of her body was trembling with tension.

She was babbling something, or maybe just hissing at him. Definitely something about needing to come, and that she was going to make him pay for this, and oh God how good it felt.

He dug his hands into the flesh of her thighs and felt her muscles bunch in response. Her whole body went taut and her back arched. Something fell off the shelf. He couldn't remember what he'd left up there. But he did remember something else. He had no condoms onboard. Why would he have condoms on the *Jack Hammer*? Usually the boat was filled with his crew and clients. When he was meeting up with a woman, the last place he wanted to bring them was his father's fishing boat.

He buried his disappointment. This was about Megan and her near-death experience. This was about the sweet juicy flesh melting under his mouth, the tremors racking her body.

Time vanished as he feasted on her. The gentle sway of the boat, the whisper of waves against the hull, the howl of the storm hammering the bluff, it all wove together into a timeless lullaby.

And then a new sound pierced the air. A cry of joy. A fierce, primal, wild orgasmic yell. Megan came hard, a convulsive detonation that had her grabbing his shoulders and even his hair. He stayed with her, keeping his mouth clamped to her sex, milking every last spasm from her explosive orgasm.

"Oh my God," she gasped as she finally twisted out of his grip. "Stop, please, I can't take any more."

With a hidden grin, he eased his mouth away from her. The taste of her—wild satisfied woman—lingered on his tongue.

She collapsed her legs to one side and arched her neck back to look at the shelf. "Did something fall?"

"Yeah. Nothing big, just an old wrist brace I used to wear at night."

"I was terrified you were going to stop."

"Never," he vowed. He sat up on his heels. He still wore his fleece pants with a giant tentpole trying to pierce the fabric. "So, how do you feel? Alive or dead?"

He grinned at her. Even though he was still fully aroused, it almost felt as if he'd experienced a release himself. As if her climax had penetrated right through her skin to him. Like a secondhand orgasm.

It was a new feeling for him.

"Very very alive. Slightly unconscious." She raised herself on her elbows and tilted her head at his lower half. "You still have your clothes on."

"Got a problem. No condoms."

Her lips parted. "Oh. I can't believe I didn't even think about that. Where did my brain go?"

"That's what you wanted, right? To stop thinking for a while?"

"I suppose so." She met his eyes. Hers still had traces of bloodshot wildness, now softened by sensual satisfaction. "That was selfish of me. Sorry."

"Sorry?"

"I wasn't thinking clearly, about condoms and things. And now you're all—" she gestured at his crotch. "Like that. And we can't do anything about it. Well, except—"

She ran her hands up his thighs, then tugged down his pants. His erection burst out as if it was spring-loaded. He drew in a sharp breath.

"We don't always have to be even," he said softly. "You don't owe me anything."

She laughed, her face as open as a sunflower. Shifting onto her knees and heels, she dropped the lightest of kisses on the tip of his cock. "I can see how you might think that way. I'm not competing with you anymore. Or fighting. You saved my life."

He shook that off with a frown. "You'd better not be trying to thank me with a blow job."

"This isn't about thank you's. It's about..." She put a little more force into the next kiss. "It's about being alive, remember?"

"Oh, it's alive, all right." He gritted his teeth while his penis jumped under her soft lips. She slid her mouth over the tight knob and its hot, bursting skin. Enclosed in that wet embrace, his shaft swelled even harder. His hips pumped, his thighs strained. He filled his hands with her softness—shoulders, neck, back, anything he could reach. Gathering up her hair, he pulled it aside so he could watch her mouth sliding up and down on his cock. The sight—lips open wide around him, her neck exposed and bent—worked like an erotic fireball.

"I'm going to come," he gritted. "Watch yourself."

And then he closed his eyes as he shattered into a thousand shards of pleasure. His climax sent him soaring through dark space, stars streaming in hyper speed all around him. *Seeing stars* —that phrase made sense for the first time. Not just seeing stars, but flying with them high overhead in a space where nothing existed but pure joy and pleasure.

# CHAPTER TWENTY-THREE

After that mind-melting experience, they went back into the galley and warmed up their tea. Megan resolutely refused to think about the consequences of what they'd just done. She'd gotten naked with him. Seduced him. Not much of a seduction routine, really. Getting naked and begging a man for sex didn't qualify as seduction, did it?

Her seductress days, such as they were, seemed like ancient history. Ever since Ruby had arrived, there had been very few men in her life—a fellow grad student, her dentist. She'd enjoyed herself but the experiences had barely registered. In both cases she'd ended the relationship shortly afterwards.

This situation was completely different. For one thing, she and Lucas weren't in a relationship of any sort. Maybe that was why it had felt so good, so freeing. She didn't have to worry about how Lucas was going to fit into her life with Ruby. After they got back to Lost Harbor, they'd both forget about this.

"Have you had a lot of girlfriends?" she asked as she sat cross-legged on the bench in the galley, nursing her mug of tea. "I know of at least one."

"Who?"

"The police officer. Officer Badger."

He whipped his head around from his position over the tiny stove. Still bare chested, he was stirring sugar into his mug. His hair, still stiff with salt, stood up in all directions. The long muscles of his torso made her mouth water.

"How'd you know that?"

"Honestly, it was just a lucky guess." She smirked at him. "Something I picked up on when she came to check on me."

"Well, you're right. It was a long time ago, but yes, we did date in high school. She dumped me."

"Aw. Sorry. What did you do wrong?"

"Thanks for automatically assuming it was my fault."

"Am I wrong?"

"Not wrong." With a wink, he left the stove and sat on the bench opposite her. He stretched out his legs, filling the entire space between the two benches. "I screwed up."

"What'd you do?"

"Brought her home without warning my parents that she was black. They didn't know her because her family had just moved here. Her dad was in the Coast Guard. I didn't generally tell my parents shit about my personal life. But my mom really wanted to meet the girl I was texting with all the time, so I invited her over."

"So what happened?"

"My father was a rude asshole, like always. Said something about her being bussed from Africa or some shit. My mom tried to shut him up but then she started talking about recipes for collard greens and it was all just terrible. I drove Maya home and she was furious at me. Said I'd blindsided her. She even wondered if I'd done it on purpose to get back at my dad for something. Surprising him like that, I mean. I fought a lot with my father so it wasn't totally out of left field for her to ask that. But I got all insulted and offended. She broke things off and I didn't fight it. That's that." He gave an uncomfortable shrug, as if the memory still bothered him.

"She said nice things about you. Are you friends now?"

"Sure, we're fine now. I've apologized to her. She accepted my apology. I never called out my dad, though. Not about that. It's one of my regrets."

He dunked his tea bag in and out of his mug. A seagull landed on the deck with a harsh caw. He jerked his head toward it. "Look at that. The birds are up and about."

"Does that mean the storm's almost over? What time is it?" This time of year, it could be hard to tell. The daylight lasted past midnight.

He checked his phone, which sat on the counter. "Almost five. Do you want to check in with Ruby?"

"Yeah, I should."

He handed her the radio and watched quietly as she contacted the harbormaster. A message from Zoe awaited her; Ruby was fine and helping her out at the pizza shop.

She handed the radio back to him and he spoke for a few moments with Bob about the storm.

"He says we should give it another hour or so before we head back in," he told her.

Wistfully, she thought how nice it would be if the storm picked up again and they could spend the entire night in his bed. Back in Lost Harbor, she'd be facing a storm of another kind.

"What's the matter?" He clicked the radio back into its cradle.

"Oh, nothing. Just not really looking forward to all the fireworks when I get back. Think they'll drum me out of town?"

"No," he said firmly and immediately. "If they let Yanni stay after he advocated for declaring independence from the Earth, they'll let you stay for speaking up about climate change."

"Independence from Earth?"

"Yes, he said we should join the planet Jupiter. I think they straightened out his medication shortly after that." He rested his mug on the bare muscles of his abdomen. She forced herself not to visually devour him, but it wasn't easy.

"This place really is full of characters, isn't it?"

"Where do you think the name 'Lost Souls' comes from?"

"Actually, that's a good question. I've heard so many different things. What's the story you heard growing up?"

He swallowed his tea and tossed the plastic mug in the sink. "I heard a few different things. Some Russian missionaries came here around the turn of the century and tried to convert the villagers. It was a mix of natives and trappers and fishermen at that point, and none of them wanted anything to do with orthodox religion. They left in disgust and announced that we were nothing but a bunch of lost souls."

She screwed up her face. "That sounds like a made-up story."

"Could be. Some people end up here like birds lost in a storm." He rubbed his knee lightly against the side of her thigh. The touch sent fire along her skin. "Maybe that's where the name comes from."

"A bird reference! You just made my day."

He grinned at her, white teeth flashing through his scruff. "So how do you feel about this place after your first big storm?"

She looked out the back of the boat, over the big twin engines, across the rippled surface of the cove to the wild chop that still churned outside the shelter of the bluff. "I survived, didn't I? I could have been lost at sea."

"Maybe. I told you about plan B and C, though. We would have been okay."

"I'm just saying, the ocean let me live, so why would I leave now?"

Glancing back at him, she caught him staring at her with a look of surprise on his face.

"What's wrong?"

"I don't remember telling you that part."

"What part?" He looked spooked, as if he'd seen a ghost. What had she said to cause such a reaction?

"That phrase—'the ocean let me live'—that's exactly what I kept thinking after the current pushed me up. You know, after my father tossed me overboard. But I didn't mention that, did I?"

"I don't think so. But maybe you did." She couldn't remember word for word what he'd related to her. "Or maybe it's just a funny coincidence."

"Right. Of course." He shook himself and his normal unshakeable expression reappeared. "Here's the thing, Megan Miller, as you've probably heard. Strange things happen around Lost Souls Wilderness. Things that can't necessarily be explained by logic or rationality or common sense. Or science," he added pointedly.

"That's what they say, but I think it's just a marketing angle. I haven't seen anything that strange."

"It's just a matter of time," he said ominously. "Fair warning. It will start with an odd coincidence and you won't think anything of it. Then it will escalate to a mystery you can't explain. Why did that current rise to the surface just when I needed it to?"

Goose bumps were rising on her arms. "I'm sure there's a perfectly good scientific explanation."

"Maybe. Why did Carmen leave town right after you arrived?"

"Probably because she knew a sucker when she saw one."

"Let me ask you this. How did you even find out about the *Forget Me Not?*"

This conversation was giving her chills, and not the good, panty-melting kind.

"Stop it. You're trying to scare me away so you can get the office to yourself."

He laughed, then his tone shifted from ghost-story ominous to merely curious. "Seriously, how did you first hear about Lost Harbor?"

"It's kind of a funny story," she admitted. A tote of food stored under the bench caught her eye. "Mind if I grab a cracker?"

He pulled out the tote and tossed her the package of rice crackers. "Crackers in exchange for a funny story. Shoot."

"Well, I was with Ruby and we had just come from visiting Dev at his office in Palo Alto. It's in one of those giant high-rises with fifty floors, and he works on the fiftieth, so it's a long elevator ride down. Two executive types were talking about their vacation plans, and one said he was going to Alaska. My ears perked up because I've always been fascinated by Alaska. He said he was going with his wife, and that he'd booked a fishing charter but she had no interest in that so she was doing a bird-watching cruise at the same time. And Ruby piped up with, 'my mom is a bird scientist.'"

"Has Ruby ever been shy at any point in her life?"

"Not yet, but she's only eight. The teenage years could change everything." As always when she thought about Ruby being a teenager, she muttered a little prayer under her breath.

"Okay, so Ruby started talking to the corporate dudes."

"Yup. She kept pestering them for details. By the time we got to the ground floor, we knew they were going to Lost Harbor, that the nature cruise was on something called the *Forget Me Not*, and that those two gentlemen were not especially patient with genius-level eight-year-olds."

Lucas gave a crooked smile. "Let me guess. She went straight to a map of Alaska and found Lost Harbor."

"And looked up airplane tickets. *And* googled the *Forget Me*

*Not.* We found out that the owner was looking for a tour guide and the rest is pretty much history. Her heart was set on coming up here. And I—" She stopped herself. She wasn't ready to share more about her state of mind at that time.

He waited for her to finish.

"Agreed," she said lamely.

A flash of disappointment crossed his face. "So looking back, do you think it was just random chance that put you in that elevator with those guys?"

"Of course." No way was she buying into this crap. "Random chance and Ruby's refusal to let anything go. That's why we're here. Not some weird woo-woo Lost Souls magic."

He laughed and rubbed his hands down his fleece pants. "I'm sure you're right. I'm just a humble fisherman, what do I know? Hey, do you want to take a quick trip up the bluff since we're stuck here for a while longer? It's either that or get naked again." His wicked grin sent a pleasant thrill through her system.

But if she got into that bed with him again, she wouldn't ever want to go back. She had to draw a firm line before it was too late for her heart.

"The bluff. I want to see what the storm looks like when I'm not in the middle of it."

# CHAPTER TWENTY-FOUR

Once they'd thrown on their rain clothes, he rowed them to the shore. They carried the Zodiac above the high tide line and beached it face down do it didn't fill up with rain. He led her to a winding path that switchbacked up a steep incline. The fresh mossy scent of rain-soaked woodlands went to her head like fine wine. The twisted trunks of ancient spruce soared overhead. How long had these trees been standing guard here on this quiet spot of coastline?

The wind had felled some of the giants and transformed them into fallen logs thick with emerald moss and gray lichens. Giant ferns, ornate as lace, grew as tall as Ruby.

The canopy was thick enough to stop much of the rain, but nonetheless a steady *drip-drip* sounded all around them. A raven perched on a high branch and watched them curiously. A gray jay—the locals called them "camp robbers"—swooped overhead, then flapped away with a disappointed *caw-caw* when he saw they had no food.

"This whole area is protected, but you probably know that." Lucas spoke in a hushed voice. With his long legs, he took the incline easily, barely losing a breath. For her it was more of a struggle, especially because she still wore her rubber boots—not the most comfortable for walking longer distances. "Lost Souls Wilderness State Park. I used to come out here in the spring and help with trail maintenance. I ran into a bear once, right up ahead."

"Good to know." She glanced around nervously.

"Oh they're all upriver now hunting salmon. Very doubtful we'll see a bear today, especially with this storm. They take shelter just like everyone else."

"I've only seen bears from afar," she admitted. "Even through binoculars it felt a little too close."

"Rule of thumb, talk loudly and make a lot of noise. Sound like you're a crowd. When I was a kid we used to bang pot lids and yell crazy shit."

"Should we do that now? I know all the words to every one of Abba's greatest hits."

Quickly, he put a stop to that. "I was up here before when I was looking for you and I didn't see any bear sign. No need to torture the wildlife with Abba."

"*Dancing queen*," she murmured under her breath. "*Young and sweet...*"

"Actually they say bears are drawn to the sound of Abba. Just saying."

Oh, that smile, aimed over his shoulder at her as he strode up the switchback... it really did something to her insides. Her pulse picked up a notch and her breath fluttered.

Then again, that could have been because of the ridiculously steep slope they were climbing. If she laughed, it would be even harder to keep up with Lucas. He was so fit, so made for striding up mountains and braving storms to rescue someone he didn't even like.

Well, hopefully that part wasn't true anymore. He wasn't

acting as if he hated her. He'd not only rescued her, he'd been nothing but sweet to her since then. Not to mention the time they'd spent naked.

Her opinion of him was definitely taking some rollercoaster twists and turns, so maybe the same was true for him.

Lucas came to a stop as they rounded the last curve in the path and came out on a promontory that jutted into the ocean. She'd seen this point from the water—it was shaped almost like the prow of a ship. The view from up here was even more spectacular than she'd imagined. It literally snatched her breath away —or maybe that was the wind, still howling across the bay.

As soon as she stepped out of the shelter of the forest, rain slashed against her cheeks and the entire side of her body. Lucas shifted his body so he took the brunt of it, but even so she had to brace herself against the buffeting of the wind. Down below, so much foam swirled across the ocean's surface that she saw more white than gray. One after another, waves flung themselves against the base of the cliffs, then hissed back to sea so the next one could take its place.

"It's calmed down a bit." Lucas squinted against the cold rain pelting his face.

"You mean, it was worse when I was out there?"

"Oh yeah. The *Forget Me Not* was rocking and rolling like a rodeo bull. The scary part was when it disappeared between waves. Scared the crap out of me. Nothing I could do from here, obviously."

She watched the wild waves with fascination. Even from here, several hundred feet up, she could hear the din of ocean and rock and wind. "You did plenty from up here. You have no idea how comforting it was to hear your voice. Until then I was all alone. Even the voice of my nemesis was better than that."

She hugged herself, wrapping her arms around her body to fend off the chill. Lucas added his arm for another layer of protection. Sheltered from the storm by the powerful arms of a handsome fisherman—things could be worse.

"Your nemesis?" His laughter vibrated through her. "Didn't know I had that status."

"I'm sorry to say that you're slipping on that front." She leaned against him; he was just too warm to resist. "All that life-saving and body-heat sharing, you know."

"You didn't even mention the orgasm-inducing."

"Right. I forgot about that."

"*Forgot?*" He looked so offended that she had to laugh.

"I guess you'll just have to remind me. Show, don't tell." She smiled mischievously up at him, nearly forgetting that it was supposed to be a one-time event. They'd helped each other feel alive and shared the sheer joy of survival with the only nearby human being—that was it.

Or was she fooling herself?

His solid body held her close, so warm and vital, and for the life of her she couldn't think of a good reason why they couldn't go to bed together again.

*Ruby?* She didn't have to know for now.

*Lost Harbor gossip?* People always gossiped.

*Her vulnerable heart?* She was a grown woman and could handle the fallout.

Or was she fooling herself about that?

She watched the churning surf and remembered how it felt to be battling the storm with her boat as her only ally.

"You know, I think the *Forget Me Not* and I really bonded out there. The old girl was there for me."

"She sure was. She's a good tub."

"It's funny—I was more interested in the 'nature tours' than the actual boat. I wanted to do something scientific that didn't involve school. I never thought I'd fall in love with my boat."

*Fall in love* —interesting choice of words, fortunately snatched away by a sudden gust.

"Think we should head back down?" She braced herself against another howling blast of wind.

"Yeah, and we should check in with Bob because it looks to me like it's picking up again. We might want to shelter in the cove overnight." Still shielding her with his body, he walked the two of them back into the forest. As soon as they stepped into the shelter of the tall trees she could breathe freely again.

"Overnight? Is that safe?" She pushed her hood back from her face as they made their way among the towering spruce.

"We'd have to stick together," he said solemnly. "Bears, you know."

"Bears are a threat on a boat?"

"It's Lost Souls Wilderness, you never know. Strange—"

"—things happen around here." She finished the phrase with him.

In the storm-dark woods, with no one around for miles and the wind still keening in the treetops, she actually believed it, and shivered.

"If you're trying to invite me to a slumber party on your boat, you don't have to scare me into it. You could just say so."

"You're invited to a slumber party on my boat," he said promptly.

"Will there be ghost stories? Because I'm spooked enough just walking through these woods."

"I'm not surprised. They say these woods are haunted by the ghosts of all the hikers who—"

She swatted his arm to make him stop. He laughed and hugged his arm around her again. "Sorry. I'll stop now. I'm an idiot."

"No, it's funny. I'm just easily spooked. Is it getting darker? I feel like it's getting darker." She shuddered as a raven cawed and flapped to a higher branch as they passed.

"Ravens are well known to be harbingers of doom," he intoned, back to his ghost story voice.

But now he'd gone too far. As an ornithologist, no way was she going to stand by while he slandered one of her favorite species.

"Okay, now you're way off base because ravens are highly intelligent birds who have demonstrated logic and empathy and playfulness. Did you know they make toys out of sticks and—" She cut herself off. "Oh. Wow. You did that on purpose, didn't you?"

"Looks like your bird nerd side is a lot more powerful than your easily spooked side." He waved at the raven perched in the branches overhead. "Hi, guy. We'll take a pass on the harbinging of doom. Is that a word? Harbinging?"

"I have no clue, but I accept and appreciate your efforts to distract me. I'm actually impressed that you found the one thing that would get my undivided attention."

"Oh, there are plenty of things like that. Birds are just one."

"You think you know me that well? What other things?"

"I know you well enough." His deep-set eyes gleamed down at her. "We could talk about how climate change is making storms more intense. That would definitely get you talking. We could discuss whether Ruby is actually named after a Rubik's Cube."

"She isn't. That's absurd. Well, Dev might have been thinking that but he's completely wrong." She laughed, and realized that he'd managed to un-spook her with just a few words.

"Then there's your obsession with pistachio ice cream. Is it the color or the flavor? Because either way, I'm not getting it."

"I wouldn't call it an obsession, more of a long-standing love affair between a consenting adult and an iconic dessert." Her mouth watered as she pictured the double-scoop cone she was going to treat herself to as soon as she reached the harbor.

When her mouth was watering, she couldn't be scared. Amazing how that worked.

"We could also talk about your hopeless crush on me," he added, almost casually.

"*What?*" She swung around, filled with indignation, to find him laughing down at her. "Where'd you get that ridiculous idea? Oh. I see. You did it again. When I'm mad at you I can't be spooked."

"I have your number, Bird Nerd."

"You really do. I have to hand it to you. Which makes me wonder." She tapped a finger against her chin. "To know that much about me, maybe the shoe is on the other foot. Maybe you're the one with the crush on me."

"I guess we'll never know." He gave her a cryptic smile as he helped her over a log that blocked the path.

With her hand gripped, her foot sliding across the mossy log, she thought how very strange *that* would be. All this time, a crush? On both sides?

Talk about strange things happening in Lost Souls ... she shivered and picked up the pace.

## CHAPTER TWENTY-FIVE

The unpredictable Misty Bay weather played more tricks on them. By the time they made it back to the cove, the wind had petered out to nothing more than a steady breeze. The rain, so fierce just an hour earlier, had decreased from a torrent to a slow drizzle.

The wind had shifted, said Bob over the radio, and was now knocking down the waves. He gave them the go-ahead to leave the cove and wished them a safe trip.

Probably for the best, Lucas knew. One hot encounter was one thing; repeating it would lead to complications. He had enough of those in his life and didn't need any more.

They headed back around nine in the evening. The receding clouds crowded dark and sullen on the horizon to the west, with the low sun breaking through in jagged bursts of copper.

So dramatic, like a toddler stomping away after a tantrum.

The bay was still pretty choppy, so Lucas insisted on sticking close to the *Forget Me Not* as they convoyed across the strait. He stayed behind Megan so he could keep a close eye on her boat. Checking for leaks and all.

Yeah right. He also kept checking on her slim form braced at the helm, so bright with her yellow slicker and spray-sparkled hair.

Megan Miller was so much more than he'd realized. He knew she was smart and idealistic and determined. He knew she was attractive, obviously. But he hadn't predicted that she'd be so much fun to be with. In a situation like this, with her guard down, every moment with her made him either laugh, smile, or experience a hard-on. Sometimes all three at once.

He usually loved being alone on his boat, with no customers to chat up. But now it felt lonely. He missed her vivid, sexy presence. Every time he looked in the direction of his bed, he missed her even more.

When they reached the midpoint of the bay, cell service picked up again. At least the storm hadn't knocked that out. He called Megan and watched her answer, then prop the phone between her neck and her shoulder.

"We're not in the harbor yet. How about some last-minute boat sexting?"

She looked over her shoulder and wagged a finger at him. "Boat sexting? I'm pretty sure they didn't cover that in my boating safety class."

"I'll teach you myself. Private lesson."

"With an offer like that..."

He lowered his voice to a hot growl. "I'll start off easy. What are you wearing, you sexy woman? Under that industrial plastic rain slicker, that is?"

"Well, since you ask, everything on my body is extremely... wet." She spoke the word "wet" in a breathy whisper.

Figured she'd be good at boat sexting.

"The wetter the better." His mouth had gone dry so he couldn't think of a good enough response.

"In that case, I'm very, very good. Good and wet."

"I think you're very, very bad. And I'm not just talking about the way you're steering a little too close to Mussel Shoal."

She adjusted course immediately. Good, now he could focus on the fun stuff again.

"So about this wetness...tell me more."

"Why tell when I can show?" And then she surprised the hell out of him by turning all the way around so she faced him. She put her phone down and with her back to the wheel, she opened her jacket and yanked up her shirt to flash him.

Great. Now he'd be pulling into the harbor with a massive hard-on and honestly, it served him right, trying to play games with her on the water.

He'd much rather play games with her on dry land. In a bed.

"You win," he growled. "I'm hanging up now. See you in the harbor."

Laughing her ass off, she tossed aside her phone and put both hands back on the wheel.

Since he couldn't stop thinking about her naked breasts and damp skin under her rain gear, the rest of the trip was not comfortable. Not one bit.

But at least she didn't hit Mussel Shoal, so things could have been worse.

He slid into his berth just past the *Forget Me Not*. Several fishermen jogged down the ramp as soon as they docked.

It was a tradition in Lost Harbor—as soon as anyone returned from a run-in with a storm, the entire harbor community gathered in support.

Megan reacted with alarm when she first saw the guys swarming the tie-up float to help out. But when Old Crow handed her a thermos of hot chocolate, she brightened right up.

"You don't mind a little extra something in your drink, do you?" he asked.

"I could use it," she assured him after taking a long swallow.

Then another one. Uh oh...she probably had no idea how strong these guys poured their drinks. "That was the most terrifying experience of my life. Well, except for childbirth, of course. Nothing really compares to that."

If there was one topic fishermen didn't generally discuss, it was childbirth. With impressive speed, they changed the subject and asked both Lucas and Megan what they needed boat-wise.

For the next half hour or so, the other fishermen helped rinse the salt off the decks, coil ropes and stow buckets. When Lucas saw Megan sway with exhaustion—and probably a little too much rum in her hot chocolate—he gestured for her to grab her things and follow him.

"We'll finish up in the morning, guys. Thank you."

"Thank you soooo much," Megan gushed, her face pink and glowing. Yup, that hot chocolate must have quite a kick. "You guys are the *best*. I'm so happy you're not mad at me about the things I said in the show."

"Yeah, you pretty much trashed us," said Ralphie, Lucas' deckhand. "You made us sound stupid."

Megan's face fell. "I didn't mean to. I'm sorry."

Lucas glared at his deckhand. Megan didn't need this shit right now. "Did you ever think that maybe we are stupid?"

"That's not what you said on the show."

Megan stopped Lucas from answering and put a hand over her heart. "Don't get mad at Lucas. I'm the one who insulted you even though it definitely wasn't my intention and I never thought that part would make it on the air because it's so boring. I never meant to imply that you were stupid, just more like, in denial and—"

"Okay, I think we've done enough here." Lucas took the thermos from her limp hand and gave it back to Old Crow. "It's been a long day and we're a little loopy here."

"Still listening for that part about not being stupid," grumbled Old Crow.

"Not stupid," said Megan, "just uninform—"

"We're going," Lucas said firmly. He clapped a hand over Megan's mouth and practically dragged her down the ramp. "It's been a long day. Getting caught in the storm really takes it out of you, right, Megan?"

Megan scowled behind his hand, her wide eyes shooting daggers at him.

He hauled her up the ramp to the sound of the fishermen grumbling. They knew perfectly well what she was getting at. They probably even knew that she was making a valid point. But getting them to accept it—that was another matter.

Right now, whatever she said was guaranteed to rub them wrong.

Hopefully she'd understand tomorrow—if she remembered. After that big scare, no food beyond a few crackers, an orgasm and a rain-soaked hike, it hadn't taken much alcohol at all to knock her on her ass.

"You're driving with me," he ordered as she tried to veer off toward her own truck in the nearly empty parking lot.

"You're being very bossy." She elbowed him in the ribs. "But that's okay because I don't want to drive. My arms hurt. Especially my wrists. And hands."

They reached his truck, a burgundy crew cab with a bumper sticker that read, "Hammer Time." His brother had found it and slapped it on the truck without permission. She tugged away from him and leaned against the side of the truck. Her eyes half closed as she tilted her head toward the sky, which was finally showing hints of darkening.

He lifted her left hand in his and gently rubbed his thumb across her wrist. "It's hard work, what you did out there. You're taking tomorrow off, right?"

"Can't. I have two tours tomorrow. I never have that many tours."

"Reschedule them. It can take a few days for the aftereffects of a storm to die down."

She rolled her head back and forth against the truck. "I'm not rescheduling. Storms bring rare birds, you know. They get blown away from their usual habitat. It's a great opportunity. Hey, you should come with me." Her face lit up with delight. "You'll get to see some amazing wildlife and you won't even have to kill it."

"Then what's the point?" he said dryly.

She sighed. "You're hopeless. It's a good thing you're so attractive. That makes up for a lot."

"Good to know. Get in." He opened the door for her.

"Where are you taking me?"

"Home." Where did she think he was taking her? What happened to the one-time only-in-Ninlik Cove thing?

She blinked at him innocently. "Ruby's staying with Zoe. I'm available. And I'm quite buzzed. It's like a perfect storm, so to speak."

"Haven't you had enough storms for one day?"

"I think I could manage one more." She hooked a finger through his belt loop and tugged him closer.

He laughed and opened the door of his truck for her. "I'll think about it. Now would you get in already?"

"Bossy."

---

BACK AT HIS PLACE, Megan spent some time drunkenly admiring the pioneer-days construction and profusion of woven and quilted things. "Your mother did all that? She must not have had TV or Internet."

"She told me once it was more about the socializing than anything else. She and her friends called it 'stitch and bitch.'"

"That's funny. Or maybe it's not. Sounds inappropriate." She reeled over to the big stone-cut hearth that dominated the main room. "This is amazing. Can I sleep in that fireplace, like Cinderella?"

"Nope. You're coming with me." He swooped her into his arms and carried her into his bedroom. She yelped in surprise and clutched at his shoulders—as if there was any chance he would drop her. He marched past his bed and into the bathroom beyond.

"Oh my God, is that a shower?" She peered over his shoulder. "I thought I wanted to sleep, but that's only because I forgot that showers existed. It's been a long day."

"That's for damn sure." He plopped her onto the floor with the tiles he'd laid himself as an early construction project. He could still point out every flaw—because his father had pointed them out first. "Can you handle this part yourself or do you need me for anything in there?"

"I'm fine. I'll be right out. You're an angel. At first I thought of Lucifer but I'm rethinking that. You're just an angel from heaven. I'm sure people tell you that all the time." She was already unzipping her fleece jacket. The damp swell of her t-shirt over her breasts made him clench his teeth.

"Oh yeah. It gets tiring, really." He left her then, determined not to lose control over a simple thing like a shower. Despite her teasing "perfect storm" come-on, he knew what she really needed. A shower and some sleep.

Why did this woman bring out his protective side so strongly? He didn't want to think about it too much; he had a feeling he wouldn't like the answer.

# CHAPTER TWENTY-SIX

Megan woke up the next morning in a state of floating bliss so unfamiliar that she wondered for a moment if she'd died in the storm.

She was so warm, first of all. Surrounded by heavenly warmth, snuggled in the most luxurious comfort. Maybe clouds in the upper atmosphere felt like this, the big fluffy white cumulus clouds.

She'd always wondered what it would be like to dive into one of those clouds.

But why was it so warm? Clouds were generally about sixty-five degrees Fahrenheit, unless they were ice clouds, in which case...

As her scientific side kicked in, she opened her eyes and realized something else. Someone was in the bed with her.

That person was naked. Or at least the upper part of him was. His shoulders could have been chiseled from some especially durable rock. His head was turned away from her, but the curve of his jaw showed some heavy-duty dark stubble.

Lucas Holt. Sleeping like a hero after coming to her rescue.

His dark hair curled against the tendons of his neck, which were extra prominent because of the way his head lay on the pillow. She wanted to stroke that strong line all the way to his shoulder. Maybe she could lick it.

Her mouth watered. This man got her juices flowing in a way no one had in a very long time. At least since Dev, and maybe before that too. She'd stopped desiring Dev long before they'd ended their relationship. She'd gotten so tired of his manipulative ways.

For a moment, she dwelled on her ex and the constant worry that he might be up to something. She wanted to trust him. He was trustworthy in so many ways—financially, for instance. But Dev always had a hidden agenda or two. Sometimes more. That made him an excellent chess player, but not the best partner in a relationship.

Lucas, on the other hand, was blunt to a fault. If he had a problem with something, he had no trouble speaking up about it. She knew where she stood with him. Even if he was unhappy about something she'd done or said, she'd much rather know about it. Dev never came out and *told* her when he was upset with her. They could never resolve anything without the professional help of Eliza Burke. Outside of mediation, he deflected and distracted and moved on. Quarreling with him was like wrestling an eel.

Maybe that was why she and Lucas argued so much. Because she *could*.

If someone had a problem with Lucas—like her, for instance —he didn't pretend to listen but really just scheme about how to change her mind. No. He listened. He might disagree. Okay, so he often disagreed. But then he *said* so. Right out in the open. It was freaking intoxicating.

She licked the hard curve of flesh on the outer part of his shoulder. Clean skin. No salt. He must have showered after her.

She remembered the shower. The sheer stunning joy of warm water sluicing over her skin. She remembered stumbling out in nothing but a towel. Silky oversized pajamas had lain on the bed.

She'd called for Lucas, but gotten no answer. Then she'd spotted the note—"Checking on my mom. You can borrow the PJs if you want. Mis-order from Amazon. Brand new unless you count Fidget sleeping ON them one night. Be back soon."

She'd tried to stay awake, but didn't last long once she'd put on those amazing jammies and crawled into this ridiculously comfy bed—seriously, how did Lucas have so many comfortable beds? He was such a rugged dude. Did hard-edged fishermen always live in luxury like this?

It made sense after working his body so hard during the day.

She slid her tongue along the bulge of his triceps. She didn't normally thirst after muscles. Brains were her catnip. That was what had drawn her to Dev, who had been studying statistics before he decided to use his skills in the business world.

But Lucas was smart too. Not in a "savant" kind of way, but in a real-world, observe-and-act kind of way. Not just on the water, but in every situation.

Like the Harbor Commission meeting, where they'd spoken for the third and most annoying time.

The hot issue at the meeting had been whether or not to allow a disabled oil tanker to berth in the harbor while a crew of welders worked on repairs. Even though all the oil had been removed from the tanker, Megan had been part of a group opposing the idea. They didn't want to provide a safe haven for anything having to do with the oil industry.

On the other side of the argument, the company was willing to pay full rate for every day its tanker stayed in the port. That money could do so much for Lost Harbor—fund new ramps, a pavilion that had been talked about for years, new public restrooms.

For days, the community had argued and taken sides; two fishermen on opposing sides had even come to blows at the Olde Salt one night. Everyone remembered the *Exxon Valdez*, and not everyone was ready to trust an oil company.

Then had come the big meeting. Because interest was so intense, it had to be moved to the auditorium at the local high school. Even so, the crowd spilled into the hallways.

Advocates on both sides had taken turns coming to the microphone and presenting testimony. Megan had given a dire speech about the potential risks of diesel seeping into the harbor during the repairs. Sea otters would be harmed, the bird populations would be affected, fish could be tainted. Children would no longer be able to wade in the harbor water.

She'd had the audience in the palm of her hand. As she finished painting her post-apocalyptic vision of an oil spill in Lost Harbor, she just knew she'd swayed everyone to her side.

And then a tall man had casually strolled to the microphone. She recognized the man from the slip next to hers, the one who'd been so rude just a couple days earlier. A low rumble had swept through the crowd; the sound that means people are sitting up and taking notice.

"Lucas Holt here. As you all know, my dad lost everything thanks to the *Exxon Valdez*. That's why he started fishing for tourists instead of King Crab."

*Oh good*, she'd thought. Anyone who'd been a Valdez victim would hate this plan. Lucas Holt—so attractive with his dark hair, black jeans, black sweater, strong build, casual posture, deep baritone, confident manner, at ease in the spotlight—was going to back her up.

Then he kept going.

"Unlike for some people, it's personal to me." She'd looked up sharply. Was that a dig at her?

"The way I see it is, the oil companies owe us. If they're

willing to hand over large sums of cash in exchange for parking their empty tanker here, I say what are we fucking waiting for? Excuse me, kids."

That was a joke because salty language was part of harbor life.

"I vote we say yes and charge them for every single little thing we can think of. Use of our water? There's a fee for that. Occupancy? Charge them extra for every person onboard past the first five. Require them to hire local. We've got world-class welders here in Lost Harbor, let's put them to work. Require their food vendors to be local. Charge them for the fricking air they're using. Let's make these bastards pay."

By the time he was done, the entire crowd was on its feet. The final vote was a crushing defeat for the anti-tanker forces.

Megan had been so furious that she'd dodged through the crowd to snag Lucas before he could slip out the auditorium side door.

"Is that all that matters to you? Money?"

"Sorry, who are you again?" Propping the door open, he'd lifted an arrogant eyebrow at her.

"Megan Miller. We met before. My boat is in the slip next to yours. As a boat operator I'm horrified at the thought of a big oily tanker seeping chemicals into our harbor."

"Well, as a boat operator myself, sorry, but your side lost." The brusqueness of his answer sent steel through her spine.

"This isn't a game. It's not about winning or losing."

"Isn't that what losers always say?"

She set her jaw. Never in her life had she met such an instantly irritating man. "Call me a loser if you want, but if the ecology of the harbor is adversely affected, we're all going to pay for it."

He studied her for a moment with those dark eyes, as if

seeing her for the first time. "Adversely affected...What are you, a scientist?"

"Yes. Ornithologist, to be exact. That's a branch of zoology specializing in birds, but it's all connected." He seemed to be listening, so she jumped at the chance to change his mind. "Sea birds feed on the fish, so if anything hurts the fish the effects ripple throughout the environment, and—"

He cut her off with a wave of his hand. "The tanker is empty. What are you all ranting about?"

She planted her hands on her fists. "Why do you call a coherent, reasonable argument 'ranting'? That tanker is like the Pig Pen of ships. You don't know what kind of toxic substances it's giving off."

"Pig Pen, huh? That's your coherent argument?"

"That's my attempt to create a picture that you might understand."

A muscle ticked in his jaw. "I appreciate your effort to speak on my level."

"That's not what I meant—" But of course it was what she meant, and her face flushed as she stumbled to repair the faux pas. "It's my science background talking."

"I have no problem with science."

"Then what's your problem?"

He leaned closer to her and she caught a whiff of soap and clean skin. "Right now my problem is that I'm trying to get to my truck because I left my dog inside the cab and he's probably torn the seats apart by now."

He turned and strode away down the hallway past trophy cases and homemade school banners.

That was the third time he'd gotten the last word.

But the first time she'd noticed what a killer ass he had.

# CHAPTER TWENTY-SEVEN

It was honestly very hard to believe she was now in bed with the very same man who had been such a thorn in her side. He'd turned onto his side, facing away from her. She glided her hand down the long muscles of his back. In a few places her fingertips slid across a raised patch. Looking more closely, she saw scars marring the smooth bronze of his skin. Maybe three in total—like slash marks. From a fight? A beating?

Had the man who'd thrown Lucas into the harbor taken a whip to him too?

"I snuck out one too many times to see my girlfriend," came Lucas' rumbling voice.

"So it was your father."

"He was a hands-on kind of parent," he said dryly, "who didn't know his own strength when he was drunk. They would have healed better if I'd gone to the hospital, but Mom wasn't having it. She put antibiotics on me and called it good."

"Jeez." She shivered. "I just can't imagine doing anything like that with Ruby."

"Ruby's a good kid. I was a troublemaking asshole. Haven't you figured that out about me yet?"

He rolled onto his back and gently tugged her on top of him. Fire swept through her at the contact of skin through silk.

"Actually, there's something I've been thinking about that relates to that."

"To me being an asshole?"

"Yes. That tanker last year. We were on opposite sides, remember?"

"Hard to forget, after you yelled at me in the hallway."

"Please stop calling any opposition 'yelling,'" she said with all the dignity she could manage while resting her folded forearms on his bare chest.

"You're right. Point taken. You didn't 'yell' at me, you enlightened me."

She lifted her eyes to the ceiling and muttered, "lord give me patience." Then addressed Lucas again. "I tried to make you see another perspective. I didn't think it worked. I thought you totally blew me off. But then I noticed someone taking samples from the water near the tanker. I asked him what he was doing and he said that Lost Harbor had requested EPA monitoring while the tanker was in port."

"Hm," he grunted. He snuck one hand under her pajama top and skimmed it across her waist. "Imagine that. Who the hell would request monitoring?"

"Was it you?"

"Me? I'm nobody. I'm not on the city council, I'm not part of the Harbor Commission. Why would it be me?"

His innocent look didn't fool her. "You intervened. They respect you. You won the argument for the tanker and so they deferred to you about the testing."

"Do you have any evidence for this?"

"No, but it makes sense and I don't hear you actually denying it. You *did* hear me that day." She drilled him with a stare worthy of a prosecutor. "Did you or did you not actually listen to me?"

His teeth flashed in a grin. Above his thick layer of stubble, his skin looked fresh and clean. Was he more handsome with or without the scruff? She couldn't decide. "I always listened to you. I don't always completely agree, but I do listen. You're so educated. Persuasive. Extremely adorable."

"Are you mocking me now?"

Both of his hands were under her top now, and he spread them apart so his warm palms covered her back. "I am not mocking you. I'm lusting after you. There's a big difference."

The little fingers of both his hands pressed against the upper curve of her ass. She arched in pleasure. "I mean, that's fine. I can live with that." She sounded so breathless. "But I want you to respect my viewpoint as a scientist."

"Everyone should." He slid his thumbs alongside her spine. Her skin heated and pleasure sparkled between her legs. She wasn't sure if his words or his touch was more arousing. "You have valuable knowledge. We should fucking listen to it."

"Oh my God," she groaned. "This is like porn. Are you saying all this just to turn me on?"

"Is it working? But no," he added quickly. "I'm being real. It's what I think. What I always thought."

"Then why—" She cut herself off with a sharp inhale as he slid his hands upwards along her rib cage, to the sensitive sides of her breasts.

"Why do we fight?" He shrugged his big shoulders. "I still don't always agree with your proposals. I know this place. I know the history, the personalities. I know how hard it is to make a living from the sea."

"So you see things I don't. Fair enough."

A slow smile tugged at his lips. He skimmed his thumbs toward her nipples, which rose in anticipation of his touch.

Maddeningly enough, he didn't quite reach them. "But that's not the only reason we fight."

"It's not?" Distracted, she wriggled in his arms. Her entire being was focused on the next move of those taunting, teasing thumbs. "Why then?"

"Well, it's starting to seem like it's been a year's worth of fore-play, no?"

Finally, *finally*, he brushed against her nipples. Her entire body reacted to the jolt of pleasure.

"That's a lot of foreplay," she managed.

"Oh yeah. Worth every second." At that point he took command of her nipples, playing with them until she wanted to scream from the wild sensations tumbling through her.

"But I didn't...did you think..." She wasn't even sure what she was trying to ask. Something about—had he known it was all leading up to this? Because she sure hadn't. "I thought you didn't like me."

"Shhh. Hold that position, right there."

She paused, her back arched like a bow. He unbuttoned her pajama top and gently slid it across her breasts. With the tips already sensitized, this new silky friction was almost too much for her. Her hips pulsed against his groin, where his arousal was swelling against the fabric of his boxer briefs.

There was entirely too much clothing involved here.

Except that the things he was doing with that silk top were sinful. Sliding it across her skin, tweaking her nipples into tighter and tighter peaks. Teasing her with it until even her scalp tingled. When she was practically bursting out of her skin, he finally tossed the top aside.

"Naked Megan. Nice to see you again," he murmured. "I was afraid I wouldn't get another chance to worship your body, with all that one-time-only talk of yours."

"I meant it at the time. Times change."

"Then I guess you're mine until moonrise." He brushed his lips across hers.

"Moonrise? When's that?"

"That's the thing. This time of year we barely see the moon. Too much light. In other words, you're not going anywhere yet, lady."

She sighed happily. "Not arguing, especially when you do that thing with your mouth..." She thrust her breast closer to his lips. With a grin, he took the tip of her breast into his mouth. Ah, there it was, the incredible pleasure he'd generated on the boat with nothing but his lips on her nipples.

Good God, that feeling ought to be regulated like some kind of mind-altering substance. Heat shot straight to her lower belly and her entire body tingled.

"This thing?" he murmured against her breasts.

"Yes, that. Other things, too."

With his mouth still working its magic, he slid his hands under her pajama pants. No underwear, because it had been soaked by the storm. He spread his hands across the globes of her ass and moved her against his penis.

Long and hard, it nestled into the notch between her legs, with the silk of her jammies and his boxers between them. Like a lethal weapon waiting to be unleashed. Her breath hitched at the memory of his erection swelling between her lips. She wanted that hard shaft to pierce her. She wanted him stoking the fire inside her, she wanted to feel every inch of him straining toward her core.

"What...um...what's your condom situation here?" She gasped as he shifted her in just the right way to stimulate her clit.

"Abundant. But I'm not ready for that yet. First I want to make you come like this, dry humping like a couple of teenagers. Then I want to spread you open and fuck you senseless."

His hot words made her squirm almost as much as the

pressure of his hardness against her sex. She gave over all control to him and let him manipulate her body as if she were a toy. He slid her up and down, faster and faster, with more and more pressure. Finding those perfect angles and then working them until her body quivered under his firm grasp.

"Oh my God, oh my God," she whimpered as light spangled her vision. "I'm going to come, ohmigod don't-stop please don't stop right there harder ..." And then she stopped all words because a wave of pleasure curled over her head and capsized her senses. She pressed herself against him and let the pulsating orgasm go as long as it wanted. Like riding a rogue wave onto a perfect beach.

With a long sigh, she relaxed back into a sitting position with a sigh and pushed her hair behind her shoulders. It had fallen across his chest as she rode out her climax. "Wow," she whispered, still catching her breath. "Wowee woweee."

"You said it." Lucas' chest rose and fell with his ragged breaths. Between her thighs, she felt the hard press of his cock. Lifting the waistband of his underwear, she slid her fingertips across the bulging head she'd exposed. It felt hot to the touch, and so eager.

He groaned and lifted her off his body, then stripped off his underwear. She curled on her side and watched him with shameless admiration as he stretched toward the nightstand next to his bed.

"This whole supremely fit bod thing you've got going on just really works for me," she said lightly. "Who knew I was so shallow?"

"I can relate. I know you're wicked smart and have degrees and all, but you're also sexy as hell." He snagged a condom from the drawer and rolled back over.

From her lounging position, she shrugged one shoulder.

"Glad you think so, but I don't know why you would since you've only seen me in rubber boots and rain gear."

"And that bikini."

"My second best bikini," she corrected.

"So when do I get to see you in the best one?" With a glint of a smile, he tore open the foil packet. She stuck out her hand to take charge of the condom. He let her take it and fell back on the bed, arms spread wide.

"Letting your bossy side out to play?"

"I don't think of it as bossy. I think of it as right." Still holding the condom, she allowed herself a moment to slide her tongue the length of his erection. Yesterday on the boat, the conditions had been a little cramped. Here, they had space and plenty of light and the bed wasn't rocking back and forth on the waves.

But he tasted just as good as before—his hardness filled her with hot excitement. She swirled her tongue up and down and around, feasting on firm flesh and subtle ridges and soft veins. From the hazy corner of her eyes, she saw his thigh muscles flex as if he was working hard to keep himself in check.

"Ahhh, Megan," he groaned, loud and long. "That feels so damn good."

She smiled around the shaft filling her mouth. "Good. Ready for this?" She waved the condom at him and went back to her sensual licking. She lapped up a drop of salty moisture from the smooth head of his cock.

"Too ready." The strain in his voice made it drop an entire octave. "Might not last long. Why I made you come first. Knew it would be like this."

Smart man, just as she'd known. With her lips still tingling, she drew away and set the condom at the tip of his penis. She rolled it down, sheathing him safely behind an almost see-through layer of latex.

She wondered, in a quick flash, if he wanted children. Maybe he didn't. Maybe that was why he possessed "abundant" condoms.

Just as quickly, she shoved the question away. This thing between them wasn't about the future. It was about the present.

She was just about to lift herself back into the same position from earlier— stretched over his body—when he flipped her onto her back.

Heat rushed through her at the intensity written all over his face—jaw tense, eyes burning.

*I'm going to fuck you senseless*—those had been his words; they were scorched into her memory.

While she lay on the bed, still trying to catch her breath, he stood up. Completely nude now, his entire physique revealed, he swept her breath away faster than yesterday's windstorm. Not only was every muscle powerfully defined, but he had that sexy pattern of hair arrowing down to his crotch. A nest of black hair curled at the base of his jutting erection. His cock was still slick from her saliva. That wetted flesh caught the morning light with an almost terrible beauty.

"Jesus, Lucas. You belong in a porn magazine or something."

He gave a tense grin as he leaned over the bed and took hold of her ankles. "If the whole charter thing doesn't work out..."

He dragged her to the edge of the bed, pulled off her pajama bottoms and pushed her legs apart. Her climax still lingered in the form of a pleasant buzz, but apparently that wasn't enough for him. He knelt between her thighs and put his magic tongue to work. It didn't take long for the smoldering embers of arousal to spark back to life. Within moments, she was twisting and moaning under the fierce strokes of his tongue.

"Please, Lucas. Please. I want you inside me. Please."

"You know I always listen to you," he murmured. Hot gravel roughened his voice. His muscles bunched as he braced himself over her. He found her entrance with his blunt tip and in a long, slow, sensuous move inched inside her. Her inner channel opened for him with slick ease. She must be so juicy inside, so aroused and ready for him.

When he'd fully seated himself inside her, balls deep, the feeling was one of deep satisfaction. As if something had clicked into place, key in lock, hand in glove, boat in slip.

That image—boat in slip—wouldn't leave her as he rocked his hips against hers. They were together on this bed, her and Lucas, as if they were still out at sea. Tied together like a knot around a cleat. Alone on the waves as they rocked against each other.

*Find that rhythm.* Feel that newness. Hold each other. Whisper to each other. Raw words of want and need. Open begging, even.

How did they fit together? How didn't they? What felt good? What felt awkward? They were like two explorers in a strange new land. In this new place, they were equals. Both completely open and vulnerable, both laying themselves bare for the other.

"God, I want you, Megan," he muttered. "Ever since you came after me like a pit bull at that meeting. I wanted you then. How's that for nuts?"

She heard him, as if faintly in the distance, but his words didn't really sink in. That was because he was flexing deep inside her and he'd found a spot that rang a bell of pleasure that resonated throughout her body.

"Lucasssss," she moaned. "Oh sweet Jesus, that feels good."

"Yeah? How about this?" Hands on her ankles, he pushed her legs up, knees bent, opening her even more deeply.

She cried out, neck arching, hands scrabbling against the bed covers.

"Too much?" he asked quickly, ready to withdraw.

"No! Not too much," she panted. She tilted her hips to draw him in again, to locate that magic spot he'd discovered.

And there it was—another slow surge filled her to the brim with joy.

"Lucas," she whispered, disoriented by how deep he was taking her. What kind of ride was this? It was transporting her somewhere she'd never gone. Every thrust sent her further into that new land, where everything was more intense. More colorful. More rich. More joyful. She lost herself...and found something else.

Each thrust blended into the next, like fireworks going off in a cascade of spectacle. Bursts of sensation racked her body. Explosions of light filled her vision. Sound too—shouts from Lucas, moans from her own lips, the banging of the bed, the sticky slap of flesh on flesh. Everything went high-definition, as if they'd stepped for one wild moment into another dimension.

The orgasm ripped through her before she even knew she was close. She opened her mouth to release a wordless cry of release. As if he'd been waiting for that signal, Lucas went tight and rigid, a low groan riding his hot breath. They pulsed together in a timeless, endless, throbbing climax.

It was...it was...the word finally came to her as the spasms slowed. It was almost otherworldly.

# CHAPTER TWENTY-EIGHT

Sex—not just any sex, but mind-altering, universe-expanding sex —broke some kind of dam between her and Lucas. All of a sudden they couldn't stop talking to each other. They talked on the phone during free moments on the water. When they couldn't talk, they texted.

They talked while Ruby was in her art class or immersed in her math books or playing cards with Hunter. They talked while Lucas was cleaning out his father's accumulated piles of tools and cars and junk.

Lucas told her about his father—the rough and the good.

"Sure, he nearly drowned me—"

"Just a minor detail—"

"I think maybe he meant well. He wanted to teach me, and he taught me a lot. He always stood up for the underdog. He would get into fights over shit people would say about the Natives. He used to live in the bush and always said it was the happiest time of his life. Mom didn't like that much."

"She's pretty tough herself."

"Oh yeah. Tough as beef jerky. Refuses to leave the homestead even though she could make a fortune if she sold it."

"Hang on. Got a phone call." She hung up without saying goodbye. This had become their habit. Every conversation was really just a continuation of the one before, so there was no need for hello or goodbye.

She dealt quickly with the call—a booking for a tour the next day. She was in her tiny back-office space designing new brochures that might attract more business. The new version featured a banner that read, "As seen on *Trekking*." Maybe that would do the trick.

"I'm back," she told Lucas. "Got a customer, yay!"

"Good job. Hey, I just found a 1940s era set of binoculars in my dad's stash of crap. Are you interested? Vintage bird-watching?"

"Sure. Why not? They're probably not much older than my boat. Oh, speaking of your dad, I keep forgetting to tell you that I talked to Boris."

"Yeah?"

The cautious hope in his voice tugged at her heart. Lucas might act the tough guy, but she knew how much the weirdness of his father's death bothered him.

"I think he saw more than he let on that night. But he's afraid to talk about it."

"What did he say, exactly?"

"It's not so much what he said." She screwed up her face, trying to piece together her memory of the conversation. "It's the *way* he talks about it. It's the way traumatized people talk about things they'd rather forget." Refusing to meet her eyes, deflecting, scratching at invisible bug bites—he'd been jumping out of his skin when she'd mentioned Jack Holt.

She couldn't exactly criticize him for that, since she rarely talked about that trauma that she'd experienced. She still hadn't even told Lucas about it.

Not even on the 4th of July, when she'd spent the entire day and night inside her cabin to avoid the sound of firecrackers.

Why hadn't she? She didn't know exactly. But this thing with Lucas was so new and fun and fascinating. She didn't want to weigh it down with something from her past. She was moving on. That was why she'd come to Alaska—to start fresh.

"Sounds like you've seen that before?" The question in his voice offered the perfect opportunity to share her story.

But not like this. Not over the phone. And not yet.

She returned her focus to the brochure, moving a photo of a Tufted Puffin closer to the top of the page and shifting the background photo of Lost Harbor. She'd come to this rugged faraway harbor to escape, not dig up the past.

*Moving on. Moving on.*

"Well, Boris has lots of other issues too. But I think I'm making progress with him."

"Anything I can do to help?"

"Be nice to him. Earn his trust. He's scared of you."

"I'm always nice to him." The irritated edge in Lucas' voice kind of proved her point.

"Be *nicer*. Bring him muffins from the bakery. Nothing with nuts, though. He's scared of nuts."

"I'm a little scared of nuts too," he muttered.

"Very funny. He's not a nut. He's a lost soul like the rest of us. Oh—gifts for his chicken go a long way."

"What gift can you get for a fucking chicken?" His outrage made her laugh.

"I told you already. Mealworms always go over well. Once I brought him an old coconut husk."

"Okay, okay. I'll study up on it. Maybe the feed store has some ideas."

"Perfect!" She sat back to admire the design she'd created. "My new brochure rocks."

"Yeah? Can I have a look?"

"Let me take a screenshot." She aimed her phone at the screen just as Lucas' real world voice sounded behind her.

"Love it." A kiss landed on her head. He twirled her around to face him and braced his hands on the arms of her chair. Instantly her heart went into a wild pitter-patter of excitement. "But you know what it's missing?"

"Lucas..." She peered behind him into the *Jack Hammer* side of the office, where his receptionist and a customer were studying the big chart of Lost Souls Wilderness mounted on the wall. "You're living on the edge here."

"We're all living on the edge here. Might as well enjoy it." He claimed her mouth in a lingering, luscious kiss that raised goose bumps on her skin. Then he spun the chair back around so they were both looking at her computer screen. "I like it, but it could use a photo of the gorgeous tour guide. You should get rid of that bird and replace it with the stunning Megan Miller."

"You're ridiculous."

"Just calling it like I see it."

"What are you doing here? I thought you had a Harbor Commission meeting today." This was a bit of a sore point. The head of the Harbor Commission had asked her to stop attending the meetings because she kept creating too much controversy. To keep the peace, she'd said yes. But she didn't like it.

"I skipped it. Been busy with something else."

A text message flashed on her screen.

*From: ExCel Studios*

*Hi Megan, just checking in to see if you have any more questions about our offer.*

Leaning over her shoulder, Lucas frowned at the screen. "Offer? What offer?"

"Are you spying on me?" she teased.

She felt his body go tense behind her.

"I'm hardly spying. It popped up right in front of me."

"I was teasing, relax. It's just some crazy movie studio offer. They saw my boat on the *Trekking* show and they want to buy it."

"*Buy* it? For what?"

She laughed at his astonishment. "Thanks for the vote of confidence that the *Forget Me Not* is worth anything. But, in fact, you are correct. It is worth something to them, but only because they want to blow it up."

He frowned down at her, just as confused as she had been at first.

"They're filming an action movie about an alien invasion in Alaska," she explained. "My boat would be collateral damage between warring planets or something. They said they want a boat with a humble and nostalgic kind of look. It's more poignant that way."

"So they want to buy your boat and blow it up?"

"Yup. I thought the *Trekking* show might be my big break, but this isn't exactly what I had in mind. On the plus side, it's a big chunk of cash. On the minus side, that would be the end of Forget Me Not Nature Tours."

Lucas was studying her face, probably trying to gauge his reaction to hers. "What did you tell them?"

"That I'd think about it." She tugged her lower lip between her teeth. Maybe it was childish, but the thought of her boat getting blown up—on purpose—made her want to cry. "I'm barely making a living right now, so I have to consider it. What do you think?"

He cupped her face in his hand and brushed his thumb across the curve of her cheek. His touch was always so perfectly attuned to the moment. Gentle when she needed comfort, rough when they were going wild in bed.

"Are things really so bad?" he asked cautiously.

"Well..." She hated to admit it, but... "Yes. They're pretty bad. I'm a very optimistic person but even I am having doubts. And I have to think of Ruby first. She loves it here, she loves the harbor, but if I can't make a living I can't justify staying here."

His expression went shuttered. In all their conversations, they never talked about a future together. She knew that he missed his life in Colorado and that he intended to go back as soon as he wrapped things up related to his father.

And he knew that her life here was just as tenuous. If the lack of customers didn't drive her away, the hostile fishermen might.

"The Harbor Commission might throw a party if I left," she said with a weak laugh.

"I don't know about that." He straightened up and held out his hand to her. "There's something you should see."

"Did they finally rescue that baby otter?"

He laughed. "You sound like Ruby. That's the first thing she asks me whenever she sees me."

"I know. She's obsessed. I can't blame her, that little guy is awfully cute." She took his hand, but then dropped it quickly as they walked through the door to his side of the office. She wasn't ready for the tsunami of gossip that would explode if people know about her and Lucas.

Carla clapped her hands together when she saw them. "Oh good! Finally. Hang on. Stay right where you are, Megan. Don't move."

Megan stopped where she was and shot a confused glance at Lucas. With a smug look, he folded his arms—no help there. Carla made a quick phone call, and a few seconds later people began filtering into the office. Yanni the fisherman, Ralphie the deckhand, Zoe, Trixie from the ice cream shop, the lady who sold sweaters, the Inupiat man who sold furs and carved narwhal tooth earrings.

"What's going on? Is it someone's birthday?" she asked Zoe, whose wild dark curls were piled on her head and tied with a bright orange scarf.

"I'm sure it's *someone's* birthday."

"Ha ha."

Zoe just laughed at her confusion. "Patience, child. Patience."

When the office was packed full of "harbor rats," Zoe raised her hand for attention. "Since I have the loudest voice, I got the lucky job of speaking for the group."

"What group? What's going on?" Megan asked.

"Remember that part about patience?" She pulled a manila folder from behind her back and held it in front of her. "After the *Trekking* show, a discussion was held. It was loud. It was unpleasant. But the end result is that Lost Harbor has realized that you, Megan Miller, with your constant and admittedly irritating ecological pestering, are making some good points. And that we need to step up and show a little more support."

Megan's mouth literally fell open. There was so much to process here, beginning with the fact that discussions had taken place *about her*—behind her back.

Zoe continued as she tapped the folder. "Contained herein is our collective effort to help Forget Me Not Nature Tours. These are coupons from each of our businesses. Every one of your customers is welcome to select two coupons. They're all pretty valuable, but I'd say my seventy-five percent off the pizza of your choice comes out on top."

The sweater lady waved her hand. "Two-for-one hats ain't bad. Most of your customers come in pairs, I've noticed. Everyone needs extra hats."

Megan opened her mouth to say what an amazing deal that

was, but got preempted by Tremaine, who ran the best fish and chips restaurant on the boardwalk. "Everyone just gonna ignore my free fish burger offer to anyone who sees an eagle on one of Megan's tours?"

"Everyone sees eagles," Megan said faintly. "They're about as common as crows here."

Tremaine offered her a high-five. "God bless America."

"You guys...this is...really incredible." She felt like crying. She'd tried so hard, for months now, to find her place in Lost Harbor. But she kept messing it up. And now...either dust had blown into her eyes or she was about to sob like a baby. "You didn't have to—"

"Hey. Yes, we did." Zoe's voice rose above the others. "You've been out here fighting the good fight for the rest of us. We've been slacking and letting you take the heat. It's our harbor too. We need you here. These coupons aren't much, but it's a helping hand. People love coupons."

"Oh, I know my clients will go crazy for these." She clutched the folder to her heart. "This is so amazing, I can barely believe it. A week ago I thought you all might kick me out of the harbor."

"Some people wanted to." Yanni piped up from the back of the crowd. "Lucas told them to eat shit."

Laugher rippled through the group. She glanced up at Lucas. His dark face wore its usual stern, all-business expression. "Lost Harbor doesn't kick people out for being annoying."

She let out a spurt of laughter—better than crying. "Thanks for that, Lucas."

He shot her a wink.

"And thank you all for this incredible gesture. It means a great deal to me. I know I can be a little too pushy and that I don't always have the bigger picture when it comes to Lost Harbor history and so forth. I'm working on that."

"You picked the right teacher," a fisherman said—she couldn't make out who.

Her face flamed. Did he mean Lucas? She became aware of how close Lucas was standing to her. Were people starting to catch on or was it an innocent comment? *Change the subject.*

"I'd like to offer something to you as well. You're all welcome on a *Forget Me Not Nature Tour* any time you like, for free. If you aren't interested in birds, I always have cupcakes. Actually, hang on." She skipped to her side of the office and set down the manila folder next to her computer. Another message had flashed on the screen while she was away.

The producers had just added twenty thousand dollars to their offer—and a deadline. She had a week to decide.

Swallowing down the lump in her throat, she grabbed the batch of cupcakes she'd made that morning. Ruby had decorated them with rose petals.

Ruby—if only Ruby was here to see this amazing show of support.

But Ruby was playing with Hunter, as she often was lately. Megan often caught them whispering together as if they were hatching a plot.

Whatever it was, Megan hadn't had a chance to pry it out of her yet. She'd been so distracted by a certain tall, broad-shouldered fisherman.

*And who could blame her?* she thought as she reentered the office with her stash of cupcakes.

Lucas was so mouthwatering, even in his current outfit of paint-flecked Carhartts and a t-shirt with a stylized print of a bear. With his thick pelt of dark hair and his powerful build, he could be a bear himself, especially if "bear" meant gruff on the outside, mushy on the inside.

She handed out cupcakes and smiles to all the "harbor rats." But she couldn't stop thinking about that comment—"you picked the right teacher." How much of this sudden support did she owe to Lucas? He was so respected and influential in this little community. If he spoke up on her behalf, people would listen.

That made her a teensy bit uncomfortable.

Since it was the middle of summer and everyone had work to do, the crowd dispersed quickly after that. Even Carla disappeared for her break.

She and Lucas were left alone in the *Jack Hammer* office. Hauling in a deep breath, she faced him.

"Don't take this the wrong way."

"Uh oh."

"This is all really sweet. But I don't want you thinking you have to ride to my rescue just because we're sleeping together."

# CHAPTER TWENTY-NINE

"*Excuse me?*" Lucas could barely believe what had just come out of Megan's mouth. "What are you talking about?"

She lifted her chin. "People follow your lead. Was all of this thanks to you?" She gestured at the folder of coupons.

"No. It wasn't even my idea. It was Zoe's."

"Oh." She bit her lower lip. "But you supported it."

"Sure, why not? It's a great idea. What's wrong with that?"

"Nothing. I just want to make sure that nothing changes because of our personal relationship."

He had no idea what she was going on about. Didn't sex always change things? "I thought you didn't want a relationship. That's what you said in Ninlik Cove."

A quick expression of confusion crossed her face. "You don't think we're having a relationship?"

He felt quicksand under his feet. "Hey, don't put words in my mouth. We have something, obviously. Sex, when we can. Lots of phone calls. What would you call it?"

She tugged at her lower lip. "I'm not sure. I have to be careful because of Ruby. I don't want to confuse her."

"Good. Neither do I." He rubbed at the back of his neck. "But now *I'm* confused. What exactly are you looking for here?"

"Respect. That's all. I want respect. I don't need a rescuer."

Should he point out that he had, literally, rescued her? Or would that piss her off? "Okay. Noted. Where is all this coming from? Why are you so..."

"Annoying?" she supplied.

"I didn't say that."

"Irritating?"

"That's kind of the same thing, and I didn't say that either."

A quick flash of a smile, which she bit her lip to hide. "All right. Bring out the dictionary, there's got to be something in there that fits."

"Infuriating?" he suggested.

"Good one. Wow, am I really infuriating?"

"Sometimes, yes." He put his hands on her shoulders and steered her into the far corner of the office, away from potential prying eyes. The privacy itself, the fact that he had her alone, made his cock twitch. With Ruby around, their opportunities for sex were few and far between. "But it's a turn-on, so there's that."

"I doubt that."

To prove it, he put her hand on his crotch. The swell was hard to miss. "Can't argue with this."

"Okay, but we can't get distracted." Her voice had turned breathy. "I really don't want you riding to my rescue like a knight in shining...boat paint. I'd rather have you be my nemesis than my savior."

The fragrance of her hair was driving him crazy, but he kept his focus on her words. "I'll try to keep that in mind."

"I mean, I'm grateful that you rescued me from that storm."

"I can't promise not to do that again."

"Of course not. That's different. I'm talking about the business, my place here, that sort of thing." She put her hands on his chest to give herself some space, and he took a step back. Obviously she had something important to say and it wasn't her fault he got a hard-on every time he was alone with her. "I want to do this on my own. Dev always undermined me. He made me feel less than capable. Like a scattered student who didn't understand the real world."

Her mention of her ex made him remember that he still had the man's business card in his pocket. It had the weight of a guilty conscience. Irritated, he said, "I'm not your ex."

"See, that's the thing. When I first met you, I thought you were just as arrogant as Dev. I thought you'd be the last person I would ever want to get involved with. I was completely wrong about that, obviously."

She ran her hand down his chest, lingering on his stomach muscles, no longer pushing him away. He liked this direction much better. "Go on."

"You're very different from Dev. But I've worked really hard to stand on my own two feet. I get antsy when it seems like that's being threatened. So, I'm sorry. The coupons are a great idea and I really appreciate the support."

He blinked at her in confusion for a moment. "Wait." He captured her wrist. "So this is an apology?"

"Yes. What did you think it was?"

"I thought we were fighting."

"Oh. Well, I suppose we were fighting at first, but then I realized I was freaking out over nothing so now I'm apologizing. And explaining."

Amusement filled him, along with something like fierce affection. He shaped her waist with her hand. "You really like to talk things through, don't you?"

She laughed out loud. "You should see me in mediation. I'm a beast."

Under the strokes of his hand, he felt her tension give way to surrender. Her morning-blue eyes, shadowed by dimness of the corner, smiled into his.

"I really am sorry. The whole thing was so sweet. All of it. Including your part, whatever it was."

"Any chance we can stop talking now?" He cupped her ass and pulled her lower half toward him.

"But this is a big deal. We just survived our first fight."

"We've been fighting since we met."

"Our first fight as a…you know. Two people who are sexually involved."

He burst out laughing. "You really have a way with words. Say it, babe. Our first fight in a…"

"Couple-ish sort of partnership otherwise known as a relationship?" The smile curving her lips sent a shot of heat to his groin.

"Okay, that's it. No more talking." He crowded her up against the wall and with one hand, pinned her arms over her head. "I locked the door. No one can see us. I want you bad and I want you now. You good with that?"

She nodded breathlessly. With his free hand he fondled her breasts. Rough and hungry, showing her how much he wanted her, he plumped up her flesh and squeezed her nipples together. Her sharp breath and pumping hips told him she liked this, that she ate up the edginess.

He pumped up the volume and kneed her legs apart. "Face the wall so I can take you from behind," he growled. He loosened his grip so she could follow that command. She turned and rested her flushed cheek against the cool wall.

He moved his hands to her hips but she left hers where they were, over her head, palms spread open. Her chest heaved with her excited breaths.

Reaching around her front, he tweaked her nipples into diamond-hard peaks. That pebbled flesh rolling under his fingertips made him wild. He dropped one shaking hand to the front of her work pants and undid the snap and the zipper. As soon as he plunged his hand inside he felt the steam heat already building.

"So wet for me," he whispered in her ear. He tugged her earlobe with his teeth, like a lion claiming its prey. "I love how you get so hot for me."

She gave a wordless squeak and pushed against his hand. "You want to come already, you wild thing? Want me to pinch that clit for you? Make it all plump and juicy?" Moisture sprang under his fingers with every word he spoke. Her creamy essence slid onto his hand. Ah God, it was sweet to feel her so willing and responsive under his touch.

"Pinch it," she murmured. "Touch me."

He found the hot little bundle of nerves, pinned it between his thumb and finger and rubbed—gently at first, testing how much she could take. When she moaned and thrust her ass toward him, he increased the pace. Keeping his thumb firmly planted on her pleasure center, he used his other hand to pull down her pants and expose the creamy flesh of her hips and rear. He skimmed lightly across that sweet skin, each curve enticing him further.

He needed to be inside.

"Stay right there," he whispered hoarsely. "Gotta put a condom on."

Even though she gave a moan of protest, she let him go. She slumped against the wall, panting, her exposed flesh pale in the shadows. He dug in his pocket for a condom. Ever since the storm, he'd taken to carrying one with him at all times. His chances with Megan were as rare as a summer storm, and he wasn't going to miss another one.

Lightning fast, he unrolled the condom onto his straining shaft.

"What's taking so long?" she complained, peeking over

her arm.

"I just set a speed record for condoms, what are you talking about?"

He came back to her and picked up right where he'd left off—she let out a cry as he touched her hyper-sensitized clit again. "Sorry. Too rough?"

"Sort of. Not rough exactly, just—you surprised me." He pulled his hand away and licked his own thumb, then tried again. This time she moaned in pleasure as he slid through her folds to the sweet spot. He found a rhythm she seemed to like and stroked her until shudders racked her body and her hands clenched into fists against the wall.

"I'm coming inside you now," he growled into her ear. "I want to watch you come apart. I want to hear you shout."

"Is...it..."

"No one can see or hear you. It's just us. You and me and this hot little clit of yours." He increased the speed of his strokes and watched her body jolt against the wall. "Step back a bit. Toward me. But keep your hands on the wall."

He needed the right angle and for that, her ass had to be right in his lap. She did as he instructed, with a little help from him. "Perfect. God, you're fucking sexy. I want to take you so hard..."

With one hand still deep in her folds, massaging and stroking, he used his other hand to guide himself to her entrance. The slick channel gave way for him. Her body seemed to pull him in, deeper and deeper, as if some magnetic force was at work. Lion-like, he hunched over her, using the strength of his thighs to read-just to the perfect angle.

And there it was. The exact place he wanted to be, so deep inside he wanted to never leave. The world reduced itself to nothing but intense sensations ... long, slow thrusts...deep moans...slippery flesh...

She came just before he did, tipping over the edge into a

series of convulsions that rippled through the flesh enclosing him so tightly. The fierce grip of those spasms felt like a fist, like a command, and even though he wanted more—so much more—he wanted this pleasure to last for hours, days—he gave into the demands of her body and plunged off the cliff. A waterfall of pleasure caught him as he fell. Round and round he floated, dizzy and wildly blissed out.

His orgasm seemed to touch off another round of tight contractions inside her. He kept the momentum going and filled her with his cock. Her clit pulsed against his fingers—so delicate yet so fierce.

When the tension drained from her body and she relaxed boneless in his arms, he gently pulled out of her. He tugged up her jeans and removed his condom. She rolled over so her back rested against the wall and finished fastening her pants.

"Be right back," he told her. The tiny bathroom was in the *Jack Hammer* side of the office.

"Wait." She clutched at him, peering around his body. "Carla just came back."

"Shit." He tried to fasten his jeans but with a handful of condom he couldn't manage it.

"Stand still," she ordered him in a whisper. She zipped up his jeans and fastened the top button.

"Bra." He jerked his head toward her top as Carla's voice came toward them.

"Yoohoo! Anyone around? I brought extra fries from Crabbie's."

He blocked Megan's body as she quickly tucked her breasts safely back into her bra and pulled down her top. The neckline was stretched too loose and there was drool on her shoulder. Had he drooled on her? Or was that from when he'd fastened his teeth on her collarbone?

Note for the future: no sex in a goddamn shared office.

Scratch that. Sex anywhere and anytime they could manage it. He wouldn't take this back for anything.

He grabbed her jacket off the back of the chair. "Put this on. You look disheveled."

"What about your hair?" she hissed as she pulled on her fleece jacket. "Hi, Carla! Oh, are those fries? I'm starving."

Carla waltzed into the *Forget Me Not* section of the office with her Styrofoam container. "So weird, the front door was locked. Good thing I had my key with me. Megan, aren't you hot in that jacket?"

"Oh you know me. California girl. I'm always cold."

Carla narrowed her eyes at her for one suspicious moment, then turned her gaze on Lucas. "You two aren't getting into a fight back here, are you? You really can't be trusted alone, can you?"

"No, we definitely can't," Lucas said soberly. Megan disguised her smile with a cough. "I should get going. Think about what I said, Megan. I think you'll come to see that I'm right."

"Oh really?" Her wide eyes sparkled at him. "I think you're going to have to do much better than that."

"Is that a challenge? I accept."

Grinning, he went to grab a French fry from Carla's container, only to remember just in time that he still held a condom gripped in his fist. He switched hands, but not quite smoothly enough.

"What's in your hand?" the receptionist asked curiously.

"He hurt it," Megan blurted at the same that he said, "none of your business."

"Men," Carla said as he strode out the door. "Why is it so hard to admit they get hurt? They think they're Superman. Band-Aids are next to the sink!" she called after him.

In the bathroom, he disposed of the condom, washed his

hands, then met his own eyes in the mirror. And started laughing so hard his balls hurt.

## CHAPTER THIRTY

Over the next weeks, Megan lived for those stolen moments of pleasure in the arms of Lucas Holt. It wasn't always about sex—often it was just a kiss in the alley that ran behind the boardwalk businesses, or a quick chat while hosing off their boats.

The rest of life continued in the background, almost like a dream. When Ruby wasn't with Megan on the *Forget Me Not*, she usually stayed with Hunter and his mother, Grace, at the Wild North office. Megan and Grace settled into an easy handoff routine. Megan would text Grace when she reached the breakwater and Ruby would head down to meet the *Forget Me Not* at the float. That bit of independence thrilled Ruby to no end.

Word spread about the lost baby otter who had imprinted on the marker buoy. All the tourists wanted to take videos of him as the *Forget Me Not* cruised past at the required safe distance.

Megan made yet another version of her brochure, adding "Choice of 20+ coupons," and left them everywhere around town, from the airport to the Chamber of Commerce. Between the coupons and the otter, she finally saw an uptick in bookings.

While she wasn't yet operating in the black, she could at least *imagine* it happening soon. So she emailed the movie producers and told them the *Forget Me Not* wasn't for sale. But the shoot had been postponed due to a cast change, so they told her they'd check in with her again in a few weeks. Apparently people rarely said no to movie money.

She and Lucas made a tiny bit of progress with Boris. Lucas went online to research gifts for chickens and came up with something amazing—a custom-made basket for Boris' bike. It had a built-in water bowl and a plastic dome for when it rained and a self-serve feeding contraption that responded to a chicken's pecking.

Boris was bowled over by the gift. He told everyone in the harbor about it, and began following Lucas around with an expression of awe, as if he was a god on earth.

Megan didn't entirely disagree with that—for her own reasons.

One day Lucas invited her to the homestead so she could pick through his father's stash. She met his mother and the yak and the cows. Jane Holt watched with interest as she picked up one item after another—a propane cookstove that would be useful for longer cruises, a Hudson Bay blanket that needed a serious cleaning.

She couldn't believe the sheer amount of stuff Jack Holt had left behind.

"You can't call it stuff," Lucas informed her.

"That's right. These are 'resources,'" Jane Holt agreed. "If we get cut off from the rest of the world, all this could come in handy."

"Is that likely?"

"It's possible. Strange things happen..."

"...near Lost Souls," they all finished. Even tough Jane, in her corduroys and steel-toed boots, laughed.

"There's still so much here," Megan marveled. "How much have you gotten rid of?"

"Being generous, between one and two percent," he admitted. "It's a process."

No wonder it was taking a while for Lucas to wrap things up at the homestead.

Which was fine with her. She didn't want anything to change. Right now, everything was perfect just the way it was.

An unusual warm spell held Lost Harbor in its grip. Long days of nothing but sunshine made the big storm seem like a distant memory. The grocery store ran out of kiddie pools and fans, and paddle board rentals skyrocketed. Megan loved the heat. The Alaska summer usually skidded by like a runaway skateboarder, but the endless bluebird skies made it seem as if this one would last forever.

The one fly in the cream of this perfect stretch of summer days was that Ruby refused to share what was on her mind. Whenever Megan tried to ask, Ruby would shake her head and run off to play with the latest crazy puzzle Dev had sent her.

"If something's bothering you, I want you to tell me," she lectured her daughter one evening after a busy day on the water. "If it's in the middle of the night, or I'm busy with the boat, it doesn't matter. You're the most important thing, you understand?"

"Yeeeeessss, Mom. I know." Wasn't her eight-year-old too young for that irritated tone of voice? Shouldn't she wait until middle school?

And she skipped off to splash in the Ariel-themed kiddie pool Megan had set up on the deck.

Megan settled into the Adirondack chair with a glass of white wine and watched her daughter.

It was past ten o'clock but with so much light it could have been six or seven. She really should get Ruby to bed, but her daughter was having so much fun Megan didn't have the heart to end it.

She debated texting Lucas but knew that he was busy with an extra-large charter group—an extended family that had flown up from Louisiana to fulfill their grandfather's lifelong dream of fishing in Alaska. The *Jack Hammer* crew had planned some extra events for them—a bonfire on the beach, a clambake, a sunset singalong at midnight.

Her phone buzzed with a text. Her instant excitement plummeted when she saw it wasn't Lucas, but Dev.

*Test results came back. Ruby is testing at college level in math.*

Her heart sank even further. Dev was really pushing this "our kid is a genius" line and she didn't like it at all.

*We already knew she was good at math.*

*Now we know how good. You can't deny it. You can't hold her back anymore.*

*She's 8. How am I holding her back?*

Ruby stomped across the pool, sloshing water over the sides onto the deck. Good thing it was weatherproof. Megan snapped a quick photo and sent it to Dev. *She's good at playing too. How cute is this?*

*Is that safe? What if she slips?*

Megan laughed out loud, causing Ruby to look over in surprise. "Sorry, sweetie, just a joke your dad told."

She texted back, *You're nuts. It's a kiddie pool. Didn't you ever play in a kiddie pool?*

Rigidly overprotective with a dose of judgmental Dev was her least favorite version of her ex. Didn't he want Ruby to have fun and explore new things? Why did everything have to be about her IQ or her math talents?

*Ruby told me about the storm. What if you'd died? You need to be smarter.*

*That was a freak storm and my boat held up fine.*

She left out the fact that she also could have died in that admissions office shooting on a normal day at work. She didn't want to talk about that.

*I'm serious. You need to model wiser behavior for Ruby. You're too impulsive. Why were you even out on the water during a storm?*

Stricken, she remembered her brief debate that morning about whether it was safe to go out. Was Dev right?

*Don't worry, Ruby takes after you when it comes to caution. She's never impulsive.*

She wished she could throw her damn phone in the kiddie pool, but Dev would find some way to hold that against her in the next mediation session.

That little text exchange totally ruined her glass of wine. Why was Dev in such a mood? She wondered if something had gone wrong at work. He often lashed out at her when that happened. She hadn't really picked up on the pattern until lately, once she'd seen a different way of operating.

When something went wrong in Lucas' life, he just dealt with it. He didn't yell at innocent bystanders or point fingers at other people. If it was their fault, like with his crew, he corrected them and moved on. Like the time Ralphie had forgotten to pack the full complement of life jackets. Lucas had come back to port, picked up the jackets, dropped off Ralphie, and set him on the task of cleaning barnacles off the wooden skiff.

The next day, everything went back to normal. That made sense. Appropriate consequences, no drama.

Lucas would make an amazing father.

The thought flashed through her mind the way cheesecake did when she had a craving. Like a fantasy she knew she should ignore. Lucas never talked about having children, and she had a good sense of why. He'd been scarred by his father. He didn't want to pass that pain to the next generation. He'd said as much when he'd spoken of his brother, who'd recently gotten married in Reno.

"They want a big family, and I'm rooting them on. I'll be the uncle who takes the kids fishing and doesn't rat them out when they sneak into bars."

"Cool Uncle Lucas?"

"That's me. My contribution to the next generation. Cool Uncle Luke."

He would be a cool uncle, but he'd be an even better father—if only he could see it that way.

Not that it was her job to point that out. She had Ruby, and their little family was perfect. So what if she sometimes mourned the fact that Ruby was an only child and at this rate always would be. You couldn't get everything in life. At this point, all she wanted was a place where she and Ruby could be happy and safe. And a job that allowed her to spend time with Ruby and put her scientific background to work. And a place where she could make a difference...okay, maybe she did have big dreams.

Add Lucas to all that...her heart nearly burst from the dazzling joy of that possibility.

Oh no. *Oh no*. Was she in love with Lucas?

# CHAPTER THIRTY-ONE

The next day, she and Ruby drove down to the boardwalk early enough to snag the last sugar donuts before the bakery sold out of them. They walked down the ramp to the *Forget Me Not*. Its soft blue trim—the color of forget-me-nots—sparkled in the morning sunshine. They ate their donuts and watched the seabirds floating past on their own hunt for breakfast.

"Can I go play with Hunter?" Ruby asked after she'd devoured her last donut.

Megan brushed sugar off her daughter's cheek. "At the kayak office?"

"Sometimes at the kayak office, sometimes at the beach," Ruby said in her meticulously accurate way. "Maybe a little more at the beach."

"Let me see if that's okay with his mom." She texted Hunter's mother and got a quick "yes" of response. "Okay. That's fine. You know the rules. Grace is in charge. Don't cross the boardwalk alone. Don't talk to strangers or tourists. No going in the water *at all*. Not even just your feet."

"I won't go into the water." Ruby put on her backpack and climbed over the side rails to hop onto the float. She waved goodbye and ran up the float toward the ramp. Megan frowned a little—something about Ruby's promise felt off, but she couldn't quite put her finger on it.

Her passengers began filing down the ramp shortly after that. Captain Kid appeared, yawning widely from an all-night bonfire party. This was one of her biggest groups so far, and she launched enthusiastically into her spiel about the incredible abundance of wildlife in Misty Bay and Lost Souls Wilderness in general.

"Please take this list of the many species we're likely to spot on this trip." She handed out photocopies to all. "Anyone who fills it out completely gets an extra cupcake."

The tour went wonderfully—they saw a raft of Pigeon Guillemots riding the waves, a family of sea otters floating on its back while nibbling on a mussel, even a small pod of Dall porpoise. The tide was just right so she could take them into her Ninlik cove—definitely one of her favorite new spots—and show them the spiny starfish clinging to the exposed rocks.

Since the tide was coming in, they tied up to an overhanging tree branch and ate their lunches in the cove. Bobbing up and down on the gentle incoming waves, they alternated between searching for bald eagles and snacking on turkey sandwiches.

A text came in from Lucas. *Albatross spotted out past Little Peak. Looks like he's hanging around for a while.*

"Okay, everyone, who's up for extending this tour? Word has it there's an albatross awaiting us. Did you know some can fly for six hours without flapping their wings? Are you up for an adventure?"

It was unanimous, so she gave the signal to Ben to untie the boat and head out toward the mouth of the bay, where Little Peak guarded the entrance to a long inlet.

The hunt for the albatross took an hour, but everyone agreed it was absolutely worth the extra time. By the time they headed back to the harbor, the group was buzzing with satisfaction, slathered in sunscreen, and fighting off sleep. Megan had to give them credit for hanging in there for the adventure.

As Ben steered them around the breakwater, she texted Grace, Hunter's mother. *Just getting back now. Can you tell Ruby to head to the slip?*

Grace texted back. *Crazy day here, sorry. I dropped my phone in the water. Just got it dried out. Ruby left a little while ago to meet you.*

A little while ago? That wasn't the routine at all.

*How long ago?*

*Maybe half an hour? She should be there waiting for you. She's so responsible.*

Grace was right. Ruby would be sitting on her backpack at the float, waiting for the *Forget Me Not* to dock.

Except she wasn't.

Megan's heart thumped as she scanned up and down the float and the ramps that led to the boardwalk. Ruby knew the other floats and ramps were off-limits. She wasn't allowed to walk up and down the aisles because anyone could be berthed there. She took that rule seriously, as she took all the rules.

As the passengers filed off the *Forget Me Not*, Megan called Grace, but she got no answer. Maybe her phone was still screwy from being dropped in the water.

Next she called Zoe. "Have you seen Ruby?"

"Not today." Her harried voice could barely be heard over the background noise of hungry pizza fans. "Is she missing?"

"No. Yes. I don't know yet. Maybe just a miscommunication." But what could the miscommunication be? She'd come back into port later than usual, but not so much later that Ruby wouldn't know what to do.

"Ben, can you get the boat squared away? I need to run up to the office."

She darted away before he could even answer. *Please be in the office. Please be in the office.*

But only Carla and Lucas were in the office. Lucas looked up from the paperwork he was filling out and immediately dropped it and strode toward her. "What's wrong?"

"Have you seen Ruby today?"

He shook his head, then glanced at Carla who did the same.

"She wasn't at the ramp when I got back and she's not with Grace and Hunter."

Panic clawed at her throat. The walls seemed to close in around her, and she spun around and dashed outside. If Ruby wasn't here, she had to go somewhere else, look somewhere else. She didn't even know where—just not here.

Lucas followed her out the door and took her by the shoulders. "Talk to me, Megan. Where would she go? Have you checked the ice cream shop?"

She grabbed his wrists in gratitude. "No, I didn't. She loves that place. Come on." And she took off in that direction.

But Trixie hadn't seen Ruby all day. Neither had anyone at her other favorite haunts.

"Where was the last place she was seen?" Lucas asked her. She could tell he was trying to keep her calm. It wasn't working.

"Wild North Kayaks."

"Come on then."

But the kayak office had a "be right back" sign hanging on the doorknob.

The world around her seemed to tilt in all directions. The edges of her vision blurred. She couldn't breathe. *Where was Ruby?*

"I'm sure there's an explanation." Lucas kept a reassuring

hand on her shoulder. The weight of his hand anchored her; otherwise she might go floating off in a cloud of terror.

"Ruby never does this. Never. She's always where she's supposed to be when she's supposed to be there."

"Is there a chance she found a ride home?"

"Without someone telling me? Absolutely not. Oh!" She clapped a hand over her mouth. "The hospital. Maybe she got sick or something. Where's my phone?" She patted herself all over, but couldn't remember where she'd left her phone.

Lucas pulled his cell out and dialed the emergency room at the small hospital that served all of the Misty Bay peninsula. When someone answered, he passed his phone to Megan.

"My eight-year-old is missing, I'm just checking to see if maybe she came in for an emergency and I wasn't notified—"

"No kids here today at all."

"Okay." Numb, she handed the phone back to Lucas, who ended the call for her.

Where? Where was Ruby?

And then—disaster. From the harbor came the sound of an engine backfiring.

She jerked at the sudden *pop*.

She couldn't catch her breath. Her lungs heaved, trying desperately to draw in air. It didn't work, and dancing spots of light filled her vision.

"Take it easy, Megan. We'll find her." Lucas voice seemed to come from a great distance. His words held no meaning; they were nothing but air. She spun away from him, then staggered, so light-headed she nearly fell.

"Hey!" Lucas caught her in his arms and lifted her up. He carried her to a patch of grass behind the kayak office and set her on the ground, shielded from view by a rack of kayaks. "Slow breaths, sweetheart. Nice and slow. Put your head between your knees."

His voice vanished as terrible images flashed through her brain—Ruby, lifeless on the ground. Ruby on the floor. Blood pouring from her. A man with a gas mask looming over her. Then she wasn't in Lost Harbor anymore, she was in that quiet admissions office where a fly was buzzing against a windowpane and Chun was texting *beep-beep* and everything was ordinary-boring-mundane until an alien figure appeared in the doorway.

The noise—relentless rattle of gun...angry shout...crash of her chair as she hit the floor...crawl to the cabinets...go, go...where was Chun? On his back, seeping dark fluid...no, no, it can't be... something overhead, flying past on a mission to make her dead. It wanted her dead. *He* wanted her dead. And she would be unless...

Zoe kneeled in front of her. She smelled like flour and tomato sauce. "It's okay," she was saying, over and over again. She took Megan's hands in hers. "Are you with me? Are you conscious?"

"Ruby." She uttered her daughter's name through a dry mouth. What the hell had just happened? Panic attack. Just like the ones she'd experienced after the shooting, except this was much worse because it had interrupted the search for Ruby and she had no idea how much time had passed.

"Everyone's out looking. We'll find her. Are you okay? Here, have some water." Zoe unscrewed the top of a stainless steel water bottle and eased it into her hand.

Megan took a sip. The coolness against her dry throat made her feel instantly more awake. "Where's Lucas?"

"He's looking with the others."

"How long have you...have I..." She still couldn't quite catch her breath.

"Only a few minutes. Lucas called me so he could go search the other floats."

"Help me up. I'm not doing any good here."

Zoe helped her to her feet. She took another swallow of water and gave the bottle back to Zoe. Her friend still wore the flour-covered apron she made pizzas in. "You left work."

"Of course I left work. Don't worry about that—even though the twins are in charge." She smiled with a touch of wryness. "This is Ruby we're talking about. I'd shut down the shop if I needed to."

Megan swallowed hard as another wave of dizziness passed over her. *Ruby. Where are you, my heart?* She closed her eyes, as if she could somehow communicate with her daughter psychically. *Where are you, where are you?*

Nothing. Of course not. That was what language was for. She was being ridiculous and desperate.

She opened her eyes and found herself staring at the rack of kayaks. Several were missing. Which was normal, at the peak of summer. But what if...

"Oh my God," she whispered. "She took a kayak."

"What? Why?" Zoe looked from her to the kayaks. "Why would she do that?"

"No, I'm not sure, but she said, '"I promise I won't go into the water.' I thought it was strange. Maybe she meant she was going into a kayak. Where's my phone?"

Once again, no matter how much she patted her body, she couldn't find her phone. Zoe handed over hers, and she called Lucas.

"Lucas, where are you right now?"

"Ramp Three. I'm checking all the boats."

Beckoning for Zoe to follow, she set off at a run toward Ramp Three. "I think she might have taken a kayak."

"Why would she do that?"

"I don't know. But we need to look for her on the water."

"I'll meet you at the *Jack Hammer*. I'll drive, you look. Bring your binoculars."

"See you there."

Still at a half-run, she handed Zoe's phone back to her. "I'm on it, Zoe. You go back to work."

"Are you sure?" Zoe jogged to keep up with her, both of them dodging tourists strolling down the boardwalk.

"Yes. I'm good. I know we'll find her. She's good with kayaks and they're very seaworthy. I don't think she'd go far—" A thought occurred to her. "Oh my God. I think I know where she went." But Zoe had fallen behind, so she just waved at her and increased the speed at which she was racing toward the docks and skipping past pedestrians.

The paralysis that had gripped her before was gone. Now she was energized and ready to tear the world apart to find Ruby.

Lucas had already cast off the *Jack Hammer* and was idling next to the float. She leaped onboard as if she were a champion hurdler. He caught her against his chest. "You okay?"

The concern in his eyes nearly made her lose it again.

"I think she went to help the baby otter."

"At the buoy?" He hurried to the helm and eased the boat out of the slip. Megan grabbed her binoculars and aimed them at the far point of the breakwater. There were too many boats in the way to see anything beyond closeups of masts and the occasional startling swoop of a seagull.

"Yes. She sometimes gets these intense connections with animals. Like Fidget. That's one reason we don't have a pet, because she goes overboard with her attachments. We had a hamster when she was five, and when he died she cried every night for two months."

"So she feels that way about that otter?"

"She's talked about him a lot. Actually, *her*. She's convinced it's a baby girl. Maybe she wanted to help her. It's Ruby, you never know what she'll come up with."

They glided through the still water of the harbor.

Something vibrated in the lowest pocket of her cargo pants.

So that's where her phone was! She dug it out and saw it was a call from Dev.

Crap. She had to tell him what was going on, but he was going to flip out. Of all moments for him to call.

She'd barely said "Hello" when he interrupted. "Did you find her? Tell me you found her."

For a moment she was too confused to respond. "Not yet, but I think I know where she went. Remember that otter she's—"

"I'm coming. I'm on my way to the airport."

"Really? No, that's not—just give us a few minutes here, Dev. We'll find her. She's been obsessed with that otter, I think she went—wait, how do you even know she's missing?"

"Lucas called me."

She swung her gaze over to Lucas, who was intently scanning every boat they passed as he steered through the harbor.

"But—how did he—"

"I gave him my number. I asked him to call me if you had a panic attack or if Ruby's safety was at risk—or all of the above, in this case."

The steady rumble of the engine hummed in her ears. Lucas knew about her panic attacks? He'd been acting as—what, some kind of guard dog on Dev's behalf?

"That's unacceptable," she managed.

"Honey, it's not your fault that you were in a shooting. But the reality is that it happened and it affected you and you were never especially tough to begin with. I'm only concerned about Ruby, you—"

"Dev—" She cut him off. "I can't get into this now. I have to find Ruby."

"Don't hang up—"

She hung up on him.

The stench of baitfish filled her nose as they passed a trawler. In stark contrast to her state of mind a few minutes ago, everything around her was crystal clear. The purr of the engine, the caws of the gulls, the seaweed floating past, the breath of air against her cheeks.

Most of all, the harsh, inevitable truth. She and Lucas were over. She could never trust him again.

# CHAPTER THIRTY-TWO

As soon as Megan was off the phone, Lucas called to her, "What was Ruby wearing when you saw her last? What color?"

"Red jacket," she said shortly. He tried to catch her eye, make sure she was herself again, but she ignored him and lifted the binoculars to her face.

"What else, in case she ditched her jacket?"

"Just look for a kayak." Her stiff tone, her glacial cold shoulder...something was up. She was probably just worried about Ruby. He shrugged it off and returned his focus to scrutinizing every boat they passed.

"There's the buoy," she said when they reached the tip of the breakwater. "I don't see the baby otter. How close can you get?"

He steered toward the warning markers the Coast Guard had installed to keep boats from bothering the otter. The big green can buoy stood guard at the end of the breakwater, about fifty yards out.

Sure enough, the little otter, with its soulful eyes and curious twitching whiskers had vanished. There was no sign of a kayak either, or a little girl.

Megan let out a hiss of disappointment. "Damn it. I was so sure she'd be here."

He shot her a cautious look as he throttled down to a near-idle. Was she going to have another meltdown like the one earlier?

But one glance told him that wasn't going to happen. Her expression was steely, her jaw set in determination. Her feet were braced apart on the rolling deck. If a pirate had boarded just then, she'd be ready. "What next?"

"Well, we're out on the water, might as well keep searching. Maybe she got caught in a current." She put the binoculars back to her face. "Oh!"

She flung her arm up to point past the green can buoy. "I see something. Go that way."

He translated "that way" into south-southwest about fifteen points, and aimed the bow of the *Jack Hammer* in that direction. As he brought the boat around the green can, he caught sight of what she was referring to. A spot of red rising and falling with the waves.

"Kayak?" he asked her.

"Could be. Maybe she got caught by the tide."

"Yup, happens all the time." Hope flooded through him, and he realized in that moment just how worried he'd been about Ruby's disappearance. By God—this was what being a parent must feel like—sheer terror that something might happen to your child. How did people like Megan—parents—do it?

The closer they got, the more the dot of red resolved into a definite kayak shape. And then a head appeared. Dark hair.

"It's her!" Megan finally cried. "It's Ruby. She's waving at me. Ruby!" She jumped up and down on the deck and waved back like a maniac. Tears ran down her face. She still didn't look his way.

Lucas throttled down so they didn't rock the little kayak with their wake. At a slow chug, they glided across the water toward her. The girl waved both hands at them and he realized the problem. She'd lost her paddle.

When they got close enough, he backed the engine to bring them to a standstill.

"Come take the helm," he called to Megan.

"Why?" *Still*, she didn't meet his eyes.

"I'll get her onboard. I've done this many times before. Just keep us steady."

Reluctantly, she came toward him and took his place at the wheel. "Be careful," she told him, as if he were a stranger. "She's probably exhausted."

"Don't you worry. I got this."

He lowered a ladder off the side and climbed down. Every time the boat rocked to that side, icy water lapped at his legs. One glance at Ruby's face told him Megan was right, she was completely wiped out. *Don't let her fall into the water.*

"Okay, honey, I'm going to reach out my hand and all you have to do is grab it and hold on. Got it?"

She nodded. Such a smart girl and yet for some reason she'd taken a kayak out alone. She ought to know better than that.

When he had a tight grip on her wrist, he pulled the kayak right up close to the side of the *Jack Hammer*. Reaching down, he unfastened the spray skirt that anchored her to the kayak. When she was free from that, he put both hands under her armpits and hauled her out of the cockpit. She wrapped her arms around his neck. Her thin body was shuddering with cold.

"That's it. Hold on tight, we're going up the ladder."

"But the kayak..."

"I'll get it next. You first."

Getting her up the ladder was a little awkward, but Megan helped from above. She gave a sob of joy when Ruby tumbled into her arms.

"I was so worried, Rubes. Are you okay? You're freezing."

Ruby nodded, teeth chattering.

Megan lifted her off the deck, her arms wrapped tightly around her bundle of shivering child.

"You need a blanket. Lucas, can she use your bed? Come on, sweetie, we need to get you warmed up. What were you thinking? No, don't answer that, we'll talk about all that later."

The two of them disappeared in the direction of the bunk. As he fished the kayak out of the ocean, he heard the low murmur of Megan's voice as she tucked Ruby into his bed. So cozy together. Such a tight little family of two.

He stowed the kayak on the deck, where it dripped onto the floorboards, and went back to the wheelhouse. His phone buzzed. Dev had texted him.

*Did you find Ruby? Megan won't answer.*

A chill shot through him as he put it all together. Megan knew he'd called Dev. That was why she wouldn't meet his eyes or talk to him normally.

Maybe their other arguments and quarrels had been like foreplay. This—felt very different.

---

MEGAN BARELY HELD it together as they cruised back to the harbor. She couldn't bring herself to look Lucas in the face. She was too furious with him. Embarrassed, too. That was her personal business Dev had spilled. Lucas probably thought she was just as irresponsible as Dev did.

But she didn't want to talk about any of that in front of Ruby. All that mattered right now was getting her daughter home.

Ruby finally told them what she'd done as Megan and Lucas carried the kayak back to its rack. "The baby otter just needed some help to get to her mother."

"But her mother's probably dead," Megan said as gently as she could. Her heart was still pounding from the adrenaline of the scare.

"No, she isn't. She was injured and scared of all the boats so she couldn't come close."

"How do you know all this, baby?" Megan adjusted her grip on the kayak. Lucas paused to give her time. Thoughtful—but he *couldn't be trusted. Never again.*

"Because I saw her. Hunter helped me take the kayak down to the ocean. He promised not to tell anyone so don't blame him."

Oh, she was definitely going to have a talk with Hunter, if his parents hadn't already. Grace had sent her a flurry of horrified and apologetic texts once word had spread.

"I paddled out to the baby otter. She was scared of me at first, but I just played with her until she wasn't anymore. I brought her some mussels from the rocks and opened them up for her. Then I told her to follow me. And she did! She kind of flip-flopped over to the water and jumped in. I paddled away from all the boats because that's what was scaring her so much. She stayed right behind me."

Ruby's pride shone in her wide smile. Megan didn't have the heart to scold her about all the things she shouldn't have done.

"And then another otter came swimming over. An adult otter with a scab across her face, like she'd been hurt. I know it was her mother, because right away the baby went paddling over to her. The mama sniffed at her and kind of nuzzled her face. It was so cute. And then they both swam away. They were happy to be back together."

They reached the top of the ramp. Megan put down her end of the kayak to take a breath. Lucas did the same and they rested for a brief moment while she tried to take in this story.

"You broke the rules, Ruby. There are going to be consequences. You went out on the water *alone.*" She shuddered as she pictured what could have happened.

"I'm sorry, Mommy. I'm sorry! I just had to help her." When Ruby was dug in like this, it could be hard to get through to her.

"But...where did you get the idea that she needed your help?"

"I don't know."

Megan felt her patience snap. "Ruby. *Where?* What made you break so many rules and put yourself in danger?"

"I don't know! Every time we passed that buoy I thought about her and what if her mom was hurt and couldn't get to her and..."

Ruby choked on a sob and every ounce of Megan's anger vanished into the ether.

She crouched down and wrapped her arms around her sobbing daughter. "It's okay, sweetie. Everything's okay. I'm here. I'm okay. Your little baby otter is okay. I love you so much, honey. I'm right here. Not going anywhere."

With Ruby's trembling body pressed against her, she dug deep for every reassuring word she could find. *You're safe. You're loved. I'm here. I'm okay.*

But inside, a dark hole had opened up in her soul. This was her fault.

Of course Ruby feared for her mother after the shooting. The terrible incident had shattered *her* sense of safety too. That was why she'd gone off to help the otter. Because from her perspective, what could be more disastrous than being ripped away from your mother?

Worst of all—Megan herself had made it worse. She'd never talked about the shooting with Ruby, aside from the basic details that were common knowledge. Ruby hadn't asked about it, and she hadn't wanted to talk about it. She'd come here to Alaska to start new. To escape. To fill her life with new sights and experiences and never have to think about the shooting again.

But some things couldn't be escaped. She shouldn't have tried.

---

ONCE RUBY WAS SETTLED into her car under a pile of blankets, she turned to Lucas. The evening sun turned his face a warm gold and picked out the evergreen flecks in his eyes. He'd never looked more handsome. And she knew that she *did* love him.

But it was over now.

"You're angry that I called Dev," he said in a low voice.

"You were spying on me for him."

"No. He wanted me to, but I told him to fuck off."

Empty words. He'd called Dev, hadn't he? She couldn't fall for his excuses. "You called him."

"Yeah. I still had his card in my pocket and when I saw you like that—I remembered what he said about your panic attacks. I didn't know what to do. I didn't know how long it would last. I didn't know anything. You've never *told* me anything."

She wanted to scream and cry and yell at the heavens. But she couldn't get her jaw to unhinge.

"You've never talked to me about the shooting."

"It's...it's over," she managed.

"I've rescued enough victims to know it doesn't work like that," he said gently. "It's not over."

"Not that. This." She waved a hand between them and choked out the words. "This is over. I can't trust you. Dev's going to...he thinks I'm..." The words tumbled out of her now. "You should have told me before you called him! You should have told me he wanted you to be his spy! This is...it's over. I should never have come here. It was a big mistake." Her voice cracked at the end, but she refused to give into any more emotion. She had to get through this, then she'd break down.

Lucas' face turned stony. He held her gaze for a long moment, as if measuring her sincerity. Then he gave a curt nod, turned on his heel and strode away.

Over.

# CHAPTER THIRTY-THREE

"Sorry, the *Forget Me Not* is on hiatus and no, I don't know when it will be operating again. You can write down your name and number if you want."

Lucas shoved a pad of paper across the counter to the Japanese couple with field glasses dangling from their necks.

Since when had he become Megan Miller's receptionist? Easy question. Since she'd whisked Ruby back to San Francisco with barely a word to anyone in Lost Harbor.

Megan hadn't disappeared completely. Zoe was watering her plants. Ben was checking on the *Forget Me Not* between fishing trips. Carla was answering her calls—when she felt like it.

Lucas? Not a word since that scene in the parking lot.

"Are you birders?" he asked the couple, indicating their binoculars.

They nodded eagerly. "From Japan. We always want to see puffins. We have many friends who also want to come here."

He suppressed a sigh. An endless flow of Japanese birders would be a godsend for Megan—if only she hadn't skipped town.

If she lost this opportunity, what did it matter to him? This was her business, not his.

"I can take you on a fishing trip. We often see puffins."

"Is expensive?"

"I'll give you a special birder's rate. Same as the *Forget Me Not*."

They eagerly accepted his offer and he passed them the paperwork to fill out.

He couldn't let Megan's clientele slip away, could he?

"Stealing Megan's customers?" Ralphie lounged against the wall, nursing a soda. They'd only stopped in for a second to pick up a new shipment of life jackets that had been delivered to the office.

Stealing her customers? Megan would probably see it that way too. Let the feuding continue. "They came to me, what am I supposed to do?"

"When the fish are running..."

"Exactly." They each grabbed a box of life jackets and headed toward Ramp Two. He avoided the sight of the *Forget Me Not* bobbing sadly in the slip next to his. He and Megan were like...ships in the night. And the day, and that back corner of the office, and the *Jack Hammer*, and...

He shook off those distracting memories as they neared the *Jack Hammer*. Someone was waiting there. Boris. Without his bicycle, for once. The man shrank into his hoodie when he saw the two of them.

"Ralphie, go grab us some coffee, would you? I'll take it from here."

When Ralphie was gone, Lucas stepped cautiously toward his visitor. "Hi Boris, are you looking for me?"

"Yeah. Where's Megan?"

Oh. That was what he wanted. Well, Lucas could relate.

"She's taking care of some things in California. Do you miss her? I do."

That frank admission pulled Boris' gaze to his face. "Yeah."

"She's nice, isn't she?"

"Yeah." He fiddled with the strings of his "Get Wrecked at the Olde Salt Saloon" sweatshirt.

"Where's Anushka? She okay?"

Miraculously, he'd stumbled onto the right words. The fear cleared from Boris' face. "She's home. I came to talk to you. About Mean Jack."

Mean Jack...Lucas' father. Well, he couldn't really disagree with that nickname. "Do you mean about that night? What happened?"

"Yeah. What I saw. It was stupid."

"Stupid?"

"Ayup. Stupid. He was..." Boris walked with his hitching stride to the stern of the *Jack Hammer* and gestured to a spot on the gunwales. "Right there. He had a suitcase. He was laughing a lot. Like this." He mimicked Jack Holt's cackling laugh with eerie accuracy.

A nearby seagull took flight, flapping across the harbor with a startled caw. Maybe the seagulls remembered Jack Holt and how he'd toss beer cans at them when he was drunk.

"What was in the suitcase? Was he going somewhere?"

"Nah. He wasn't going nowhere. It was a dumb prank. It was full of lead weights, like for fishing lines. But they were painted like eyeballs."

"What? Jesus." Lucas scrubbed a hand through his hair. Jack Holt had always loved a mean prank and he could absolutely imagine him in his shop with a pile of lead balls and some paint.

"He was muttering stuff. He didn't know I was there."

"Where were you?"

"Up there." He pointed to a bench on the boardwalk. Next to

it an industrial telescope anchored to a concrete block was aimed toward the glaciers on the other side of the bay. "On the bench. But I could hear. I hear everything."

"What was he muttering? Can you remember?"

"He was talking about Old Crow. How he was going to scare the smile off him. Old Crow smiles a lot. Maybe Jack didn't like that."

"Jack and Old Crow had a forty-year feud, you know that."

"That's what they say." Boris jittered back and forth on his feet. This was the longest conversation they'd ever had. Megan said he could only handle short talks.

"Thanks for telling me, Boris."

"Ain't done yet."

Okay then. Apparently the guy had more gas in his tank. "Go on. I'm listening."

"He was back here at the stern pulling the dinghy around. It was tied up behind. I couldn't see how it happened, but I think he was trying to get the suitcase into the dinghy."

"Oh god." Lucas cringed as he imagined the scene. "Drunk, right?"

"I think. I wasn't so close to know for sure."

"Well, it's a safe bet. So he was trying to get the suitcase loaded with lead weights into the dinghy—Lord only knows how he got it onboard in the first place."

"Maybe a deckhand?"

"Yup, that's probably it. Good thinking, Boris. For a strong young kid it wouldn't be hard. For my dad..."

"It was too heavy. I think his hand got stuck in the handle and it pulled him overboard."

"Probably hit his head on the railing. Or inhaled water because he was too drunk to think right." Anything could have happened at that point. Once you were immersed in Alaska ocean water, the clock was ticking. Had he fought to the surface? Had a current come to save him? Or the opposite—maybe a swift current had claimed him in a final watery embrace.

Boris twisted his hands together. "I didn't go down because Anushka was sick—too far—so I called from the phone—"

Lucas stopped him with a hand in the air. "Forget it."

Once his father had gone overboard, his chances were slim. Maybe someone close by could have saved him. But not Boris from the boardwalk.

"My dad died the way he lived. Being an ass and pulling a stupid drunken prank on his longtime feuding buddy. You couldn't come up with a better end for him."

Boris shoved his hands deep in his pockets. "You're not mad?"

"That's why you never said anything, because you thought I'd be mad? No, Boris. I'm not mad. I'm—" He shook his head and rubbed the back of his neck. He wasn't sure exactly what he was. Many emotions were coursing through him, but "mad" wasn't one of them. "I'm glad you told me. Thank you. I owe you one."

"One what?"

"It's a figure of speech. You need anything, ever, you come to me and I'll help you out. That's what I mean."

Boris sniffed and swiped a hand across his nose. "Okay."

Lucas took a chance and squeezed him gently on the upper arm. He sensed the man's fear and dropped his hand immediately. "Friends?"

"Okay. Will you get Megan home soon?"

Now that was an odd question. Why would Boris think he could get Megan back? Megan didn't trust him. Probably hated him even more than she had at the start. And did Megan even consider Lost Harbor her home?

"She might not want to come back," he told the man.

"Why not?"

"Well..." He paused. Boris had shared his story. Maybe he

should do the same. "I screwed up. She's very angry with me and she has a good reason."

Boris nodded wisely. "Get her a basket. She'll like that."

Fighting not to laugh, Lucas nodded seriously. "Good tip. Thanks."

# CHAPTER THIRTY-FOUR

"I'm your last stop before court," warned Eliza Burke. "I know you both know that. You've done so well up to now. I'm sure we can work this out."

"She endangered my child," Dev said stubbornly.

*My* child? Megan gritted her teeth to stop herself from losing her cool. Dev always knew how to say things that got under her skin, but she couldn't fall for that trick. "Ruby is perfectly fine. She had an unauthorized adventure, but we found her before any harm came to her. She understands that she screwed up. This is a normal part of childhood. A normal part of a *normal* childhood."

"And that's exactly where we differ." That British colonial accent of Dev's was driving her nuts. It always made him sound more rational than he actually was. "Ruby is not normal. We need to stop treating her as if she is. She needs more advanced educational opportunities. She needs special tutors, foreign travel, all the things I and only I can provide."

"You're complaining about a kayak but you want her to have foreign travel?"

"It's entirely different. I'm talking about raising her level of sophistication. I'm talking about not allowing her so much free rein that she decides an otter is her sister."

"It was just an expression," Megan told the mediator, who was looking at her askance. "Ruby felt an emotional connection to the otter."

"And that sounds 'normal' to you?" Dev smirked.

Megan wanted to wipe Dev's smug smile right off his face, but forced herself to behave like an adult. "It sounds like Ruby to me. Not everything is always logical, you know. Not even with high-IQ kids."

He lifted his eyes to the ceiling and let out a long-suffering sigh. "You see what I'm dealing with here, Eliza. She doesn't even believe in logic."

Trying to get the mediator on his side—Megan recognized that trick.

But this wasn't Eliza's first time navigating Megan and Dev's relationship. "Where is Ruby now?"

"With me," Dev said.

"It's a previously scheduled visit," added Megan quickly. "I *always* abide by the agreements we make. I brought her down a little early so we could make time for this session."

"So this is..." Eliza checked her notes. "The agreed-upon three weeks of the summer she spends with you, Dev?"

"Yes. I enrolled her in a programming camp. She loves it." Dev wasn't lying about that. Every time Megan talked to Ruby, she sounded happy.

But she didn't know there was a chance they'd never go back to Lost Harbor.

"Good. So the issue before us is how to divide the time starting this fall."

"I found an excellent school tailor-made for prodigies like Ruby," Dev said. "It's here in the Bay Area, where she's already comfortable and where she won't wander off into dangerous situations. I believe she should attend this school, and that I'm the proper parent to oversee her education. I should have custody."

Megan's jaw ached from clenching and the heels of her hands throbbed from her fingernails digging into her flesh.

"And Megan? What's your preference?"

Dev started to speak again, but Eliza raised her hand for quiet. "Megan?"

Megan relaxed her jaw so she could speak. All the arguments she'd practiced ran through her mind. *Ruby deserves a real childhood. The focus shouldn't be only on her education. She loves Lost Harbor. The ocean and the wildlife, the freedom, the beauty, it all feeds a part of her that might get buried under formulas and math studies. I'm the proper parent to raise* all *of her, not just her brain.*

But then something else came back to her—the terror of realizing Ruby was missing. And worse—the horrible paralysis that had seized her. The images that had flooded her mind in that moment. How fucking useless she'd been when Ruby had needed her most.

"I— Can I—" Try as she might, nothing else would come out of her mouth. The silence in the room ticked away, second by agonizing second.

Eliza looked at her watch. "Oh goodness, I'm sorry, we've run out of time. We'll pick this up at our next meeting. Megan, I want to hear your ideas for the next school year."

Megan nodded. Message received: *get your act together or lose Ruby.*

"Saved by the fifty-minute hour," Dev said snidely as they left the mediator's office. It was located on an upper floor of a high-rise near the Transamerica building. Dev stayed back to pay the receptionist, while Megan hurried toward the elevator. She couldn't bear to endure an entire elevator ride next to Dev's smug gloating.

She stepped into the elevator and the doors slid shut. As the car glided toward the ground, a memory came back to her—the moment she and Ruby had first heard of Lost Harbor. That elevator had been full of men in prosaic business suits, but the mention of Lost Harbor had hovered in the air like a magical beckoning siren.

"There's no place quite like Lost Harbor. It's not just the fishing or the scenery. One old geezer told us about some local legends about the wilderness there. Talking animals, lost tribes, that sort of thing. I normally don't buy that crap, and don't get me wrong, I didn't have any conversations with the wildlife. But once you've seen Lost Harbor, you start to wonder. It's more than a fishing port, I can tell you that."

Had Ruby encountered a local legend? Had some of that Lost Harbor magic fairy dust landed on her daughter?

Maybe, maybe not...it didn't really matter. One thing Megan knew for sure. Ruby had been obsessed with the otter as a stand-in for Megan herself. Her daughter was worried about her. Megan got that message loud and clear, right down to her soul. That was why she was here in the Bay Area.

And yet she still hadn't done what she came to do.

The elevator doors whispered open. *Time's up.*

---

THE CENTRAL COAST University admissions office hadn't changed much from when Megan worked there, if you didn't count the memorial plaque mounted on the wall between the windows that looked out over the quad. The atmosphere was still half sleepy, half industrious, as if everyone was one nap away from springing into action.

That was the other thing—she didn't recognize any of the new staff members. Everyone she'd worked with had either transferred to another department or quit working for the university.

"Can I help you?" asked the wiry young Asian man behind the reception desk. A nameplate said his name was Lee Jin.

She swallowed hard. "I was working here last year, when... well, I was just wondering if I could..."

"Wait. Are you Megan Miller?"

"Yes."

The young man leaped to his feet. "You saved my friend's life. Chun. He was wounded in the shooting. I recognize you."

"I know Chun, of course. But I didn't save—"

"You did! He told me. He said you dragged him behind those cabinets—" he waved in the direction of the bank of storage cabinets. Even in her peripheral vision, they loomed large—a reminder of the nightmare she'd tried to forget.

"That was nothing." She waved her hand in dismissal. "Really, I didn't save him. He shouldn't be telling people that."

Lee's lively dark eyes wouldn't let her go. "He said he would have kept getting shot by that monster. He was lying there with no way to move. You saved him."

Well, she supposed that part was true. He couldn't move by himself, and the gunman might have shot him again. Or he might not have. It was hard to say.

The kid reached for her hand with both of his and shook it vigorously. "I am very grateful. So is Chun. If he knew you were here—"

"Please, I just want to kind of, see where it happened, maybe..." Now she wasn't sure anymore what she wanted, exactly. Confront the memories instead of running from them? Would coming here help? Or would it make things worse?

"Come on." Lee Jin beckoned her into the area past the reception desk. "We have metal detectors now and other safety features, but Chun still didn't want to work here anymore. He referred me to the job and I absolutely love it."

He kept talking as he led the way toward the filing cabinets.

Which was completely unnecessary—she didn't need a guide. But his company eased the raging butterflies in her stomach, so she didn't ask him to leave.

But as she got close to where she'd been when the figure in the gas mask appeared, a funny thing happened. The kid's voice morphed into...Lucas'.

Lucas, who she'd never told about the shooting. Lucas, who had known about it all along.

*"So this is where it went down,"* she heard Lucas say with that *dry humor of his. "Can't imagine a more mundane setting. What was he mad about? Did you misfile his college essay?"*

*"He'd gotten expelled. You shouldn't joke about this."*

*"I'm not joking. I'm not even really here. Why are you mad at me?"*

*"I'm not mad at you."*

*"You sound mad."*

*"How do you know? You're not even really here."*

*"Which means you're arguing with an invisible friend."*

*"If you're my friend, why'd you call Dev on me?"*

*"So that's what you're really mad about. Now we're getting somewhere."*

*"We're not getting anywhere. You're not here. I'm arguing with air."*

*"And winning. You're stronger than you think, Megan. I've always seen your strength. Why would I bother feuding with a weakling? Wouldn't be worth the bother."*

*"Is that a compliment?"*

*"Take it or leave it."*

"Chun said this is where you dragged him," Lee Jin was saying. "When you saved his—"

"I didn't save...oh forget it. Fine, maybe I did help him a little. I'm so glad he's okay." A sudden burst of emotion overwhelmed her for a moment. "He's okay, right?"

"He is. He'll be graduating in the fall. A bit behind schedule but his family isn't too upset about that. He has a good excuse."

She laughed at that. "That he does." Her glance lingered on the floor where she and the others had crouched. The possibility of an incoming bullet had given each moment a terrible weight.

But they'd survived. And she'd helped Chun. And then *forgotten* that she'd helped Chun. How strange that she'd focused on how powerless she'd felt. That was what she'd remembered, not the way she'd taken action.

Why? Why had that part stood out?

*"If you ask me, it's because you're afraid."*

*"Oh, so you're back again? More wise words from the ghost?"*

*"Yeah, more wise words from your invisible friend Lucas, the one you should try listening to."*

*"Okay, what am I so afraid of then?"*

*"Yourself."*

*"That makes no sense."*

*"Sure it does. You're afraid to claim your own power."*

*"You can say that to me after all the times I went against you in the town council?"*

*"Perfect example right there. It takes a strong person to stand up to all that mockery. You have the strength. You just don't admit that you do."*

*"I can stand up to all that because it's not about me. It's not for me. It's for the ecology of Lost Harbor and the wildlife and all that."*

*"So you can stand up for everything else but not for yourself? You're going to let Dev tell you that you're a weakling? What about Ruby? Aren't you going to stand up for her? Don't you think she needs you?"*

"Stop it!"

"Sorry?" Lee Jin blinked at her. "You don't want to hear about Chun's new job?"

"No. Sorry. I—" She passed a hand across her forehead. Was she feverish? Hallucinating? "It's hard to be here, that's all. Maybe you could give me a moment?"

"Sure, sure. Of course." He backed away from her; she couldn't blame him for his suddenly wary expression. She was acting like a lunatic.

In the quiet space behind the filing cabinets, with only the dust motes for company, she sank onto the floor on the spot where she'd hidden from the gunman.

*That sound.* Bullets into metal, just overhead. That sound never left her, not really.

Those bullets had ricocheted through her life. They'd sent her fleeing to Alaska. They'd ripped apart her already shaky self-confidence. They'd left her with trauma that Dev was now exploiting. So the ricochets continued. If she didn't stop them now, they'd keep going. They'd leave her with nothing.

But how could she stop a bullet that was no longer flying? How could she stop a ghost bullet?

*"Talk to a ghost friend?"*

*"Jesus. I've heard enough from you, Lucas. Leave me alone."*

*"You really want that?"*

*"No. I really don't. I need you, Lucas. I think I love you. You bastard. I wish I didn't, but I do."*

*"Then get up. Find your strength and get up."*

The sound of a fly buzzing against the window brought her back to reality. Beads of sweat studded her forehead and her face felt flushed. Wow. Trauma did strange things to the human brain. Hallucinating the voice of Lucas Holt, former and maybe once-again nemesis? It didn't get much stranger than that.

It also didn't get much better than that. Even in her imagination, his voice made her happy.

"Are you sure you're okay?" Chun's friend asked her as she left the office. "You look a little flushed."

"Might have a touch of fever. Or it might be fairy dust." She sneezed.

"Excuse me?"

"The dust. It's building up back there."

"Oh, I thought you said—"

"No. Definitely not. That would be ridiculous." With Lee Jin still staring at her oddly, she left that place and knew she had no need to ever go back.

# CHAPTER THIRTY-FIVE

"Well, you can make it official, Officer Badger." Lucas lounged against the doorframe of Maya's office at the police station. "My dad wasn't murdered. He died of being an idiot."

"It already was official, but thanks," she said dryly. She leaned back in her chair and bounced a pen off the palm of one hand. "Did you learn something new?"

"I did. Boris saw the whole thing. Dad was trying to play a prank on Old Crow."

"So he died as he lived."

"That's about the size of it."

"And you're satisfied. You'll return to your regular programming and let us law officers do the job we're paid for."

He cocked his head. "You'd like that, huh?"

Maya clicked her pen in a way that sounded vaguely like a bullet pop. "I'd like that because that's how it's supposed to be around here. You going to keep causing me trouble, Lucas? Don't you have a life to get back to somewhere in Colorado?"

"Not going back to Colorado."

Her eyebrows drew together in a way he remembered all too

well. The time he'd been late to pick her up for a movie, and then the time she'd stormed away from the homestead after that disaster of a dinner. "Why not?"

"It's home." He shrugged. His real reasons were a lot more complicated and involved a big question mark in the form of Megan. "What can I say? There's just something about the place you grew up..."

"Bull crap. You couldn't get out of here fast enough. What are you going to do, take over the *Jack Hammer* and carry on your dad's legacy of ridiculous feuds?"

"I—no." He looked at his feet. "Can I ask you a question?"

"Will I deputize you? No."

"God no. Not that. Do you think...I mean, you knew my father. And you know me." This was a lot harder than he'd thought it would be.

"Spit it out, Holt. I got work to do."

"Do you think I'm like my father? Do you think I'd make a decent...partner?"

At first she looked startled, as if that was the last thing she'd expected him to say—which it probably was. "You had your decent side. And then you had your idiot side."

"Like when I brought you home and sandbagged you. So fucked up. It was the kind of thing my father would have done. So I guess I want to know..."

"If you're like your father?"

He winced. It sounded so inane. Why was he dumping this on Maya after so many years? "I'm sorry, I know you have bigger problems on your hands."

"Well, yeah. I am the only detective in Lost Harbor. All the crimes come to this desk."

He nodded, getting more embarrassed by the minute. "I'll get out of your hair." He turned to go.

"Lucas," she called to him softly.

He swung back, one hand gripping the doorjamb.

"Give yourself a break, why don't you? You were a good kid. Now you're a good man. Maya Badger has good taste in men, always has."

"Aren't you single right now?"

"Yes, and you just proved my point about my discriminating taste."

He smiled slightly. "I get your point."

"Don't be so hard on yourself, Lucas. By the way, on the downlow, I heard a position's opening up that you might want to look at."

"What position?"

"Head of the Harbor Commission."

His eyebrows lifted. In Lost Harbor, that role rivaled that of mayor for importance. The harbor powered the local economy, brought tourists, served as the heart of the community.

"Then again, I heard Megan Miller might run for it. She's got the science background and a lot of good ideas. She's more forward-thinking about certain things."

Maya kept going, but Lucas hadn't heard a word after "run." Hope rushed through him with the force of an ocean current lifting him up. "Megan's back?"

She burst out laughing. "No, but it's pretty obvious you want her to be. What the hell are you doing blocking my doorway when you should be going after her?"

He frowned at her. "That's not—"

"You come in here asking for my opinion, you're gonna get my opinion. How long have I known you? How *well* have I known you? You're pining after Megan. I don't even need my police superpowers to see it. Everyone knows it."

"Bullshit."

"Fine." She threw up her hands and kicked her chair back to

stand up. "Lie to yourself if you want, but stop taking up space in my damn office."

He stepped backwards, just in time to let Bob the harbor-master past. "Hi Bob."

"Hi Lucas. Any word on when Megan's getting back?"

He left to the sound of Maya's laughter.

On his way out the door, his phone pinged with a text.

*We put another bid on that boat.* The message came from an intern at the movie studio that was eyeing the *Forget Me Not*. When he'd first heard about the potential sale, he'd contacted the studio and offered the intern some under-the-table cash to notify him if there was any more action on that front. As a fellow harbor tenant, he liked to know what was going on with the other crafts.

*Is she going for it?* he texted back.

*Looks like. It's a very good offer.*

Damn. His gut tightened into a hard knot. If she was selling the *Forget Me Not*, that meant Megan wasn't coming back.

*Thanks for the heads up,* he messaged back.

*Want to know when it's a done deal?*

*No need.*

It wasn't really about the boat. It was about Megan, and how she was floating away like a boat that had slipped its mooring.

She hadn't returned any of his calls. Desperate, he'd even tried Dev. Dev hadn't answered either, and he hadn't left a message. He didn't trust that dude not to take his words and remix them to say something completely different. He was smooth, slippery, manipulative.

Such a bad match for someone as genuine and idealistic as Megan. Not to mention kind and sparkling and beautiful and brilliant and—

Holy Mary, Mother of God. Officer Badger was right. He *was* pining for her. This strange, unsettled feeling that had followed him around ever since she left—this hollow pit in his heart—this constant wondering about her, thinking about her, missing her—Jesus Christ, it was so obvious now. *He loved Megan Miller.*

With her forget-me-not eyes and her give-as-good-as-she-got and her devotion to her daughter and her struggle to believe in herself and her homemade cupcakes and her bird nerdiness and the fun and whimsy she put into everything she did...*He loved her.*

And he had to tell her. In person. Not only that, he had to win back her trust and beg her to give him another chance. In other words, some serious groveling was about to go down.

ON HIS WAY to the airport, he swung by the homestead to drop off Fidget. "Mom, I need you to watch the dog for a few days."

"Why?" In her mud boots and a long gray sweater, his mother stood at the fence of the enclosure feeding carrots to the Tibetan yak.

Jack Holt had always loved carrots. The yak seemed to as well.

Lucas squinted at the beast; there was a certain resemblance, come to think of it. Something about the shaggy hair.

"I'm going to a very important meeting. I'm going to see Megan," he admitted.

"What about your father's junk?"

"What about it? It's not going anywhere."

"Yes, exactly the problem. We've been thinking. Let's put a notice out on the radio and people can come get what they want. The rest we'll take to the Goodwill."

He thought about that for a long moment; it was like spotting a glimmer of sun peeking through storm clouds on the horizon. "I'm okay with that if you are."

"We are."

He cocked his head at his mother. By "we" did she mean...? He looked over at the yak, which was chewing placidly on a carrot top. No. She couldn't be referring to the yak. Could she?

His mother serenely passed another carrot through the fence. Was it his imagination, or did she get along with the yak better than she had with Dad?

He chased away the absurd thought. "I'll put Fidget in the house."

"Have a good trip."

He gave her a quick side-hug, winked at the yak—just in case —and jogged off toward his truck.

After letting Fidget inside—the old fellow trotted directly to his favorite rug for a nap—he cruised down to the guesthouse to grab his travel bag. As usual, he had to wend his way around rusting cars and piles of "resources" to get there.

A "come and get it" radio announcement. What a great idea. He didn't need this stuff anymore. It had served its purpose. It had kept him in Lost Harbor long enough for him to lose his heart to a confounding, compassionate woman by the name of Megan Miller.

Now he just had to convince her to come back.

# CHAPTER THIRTY-SIX

He finally tracked Megan down at a friend's house in Palo Alto. She emerged from under a cloud of jasmine vines just as he pulled up at the curb. He almost didn't recognize her in her pantsuit and low-heeled shoes. To add to her professional look, she wore a tooled leather over-the-shoulder bag and her lips moved as if she was rehearsing something.

Was she applying for a job? Had he missed his chance? Even though she looked so different, he ate up the sight of her. Yes, she still walked with that springy stride; yes she still hunched her shoulders just a tiny bit. Yes, she was still Megan, and she still graced his world. The feeling of relief nearly overwhelmed him.

He swung out of his rental car, causing her to jump about a foot as she caught sight of him.

"*Lucas?* What are you doing here?"

"I'm...here. To see you." Ugh, maybe he should be the one rehearsing.

"Well, this isn't a good time. At all. I'm already late for an appointment and I absolutely *cannot* be late." Looking distracted, she dug in her purse for her keys.

"I'll drive you," he offered. "Brand-new rental car. Very high-tech, I think it might have jet packs instead of air bags."

She barely smiled at his joke. "No, that's okay. I'm meeting with Dev. You don't want to get in the middle of that—any more than you already did."

He winced. "Please. That's one of the reasons I'm here, to talk about that."

"It's not important anymore."

"It's important to me." His firm tone finally got her attention. "Everything to do with you is important to me."

Her eyelashes fluttered. Was she finally softening? "Come on. I'll drive and you can yell at me about it."

"You're not the one I want to yell at. Not the only one, anyway. You're...okay, you're in the top two. I wouldn't be in this situation if it weren't for you." Despite her words, she was heading in the direction of his car.

That was all he asked.

He opened the door for her and she slid into the passenger seat. Quickly, before she could change her mind, he got behind the wheel. The cinnamon fragrance of her hair filled the car. He breathed deeply. "Where are we going?"

She rattled off an address, which he punched into the GPS that came with the car. In seconds, they were on the road to downtown San Francisco.

Good. He had at least half an hour to say his piece.

But judging by the way her nails were bitten down to the cuticles, she had other things on her mind.

"What situation are you in?" he asked her. "What's going on?"

"Dev wants custody. He claims I put Ruby at risk because of the kayak fiasco."

*Shit.* No wonder she blamed him. His grip tightened on the steering wheel. "That's complete crap. You didn't put her at risk.

She's fine. She had an adventure and she reunited an otter family and no harm done. Do you know how many times I fell down the stairs as a kid, or jumped off the roof trying to fly?"

"Yes, but you're 'normal.' Dev doesn't want Ruby to be 'normal.' He wants her to be exceptional."

"She is exceptional. But that doesn't mean she isn't a kid."

"Exactly." She fully turned her gaze on him for the first time. He felt her scan his face, as if she was looking for something. "I wish Dev saw it that way."

He should have tossed Dev overboard when he had the chance. *No.* He quickly buried that thought. Dev was Ruby's father, and she loved him. If he wanted to be part of Megan's life, he'd have to get used to Dev.

Holy shit. Was he really thinking this way? Long-term? Permanent? He shot a glance at Megan's hands, which were twisted in her lap, obsessively pushing at her cuticles. *Yes.* The answer was yes. He was thinking this way. His heart ached for her. He loved her.

But she was in the middle of a crisis; still not the right moment to drop that bombshell. He cleared his throat. "So what's this appointment about?"

"Mediation. I'm supposed to present my plan for the next year for Ruby."

"Which is?"

She hauled in a long breath. "I sold the *Forget Me Not*. I'm going to buy a house near a school that Dev found for Ruby. That way I can keep custody even if Dev wins the argument about school. That's my plan."

That sounded like total surrender to him. "I thought you wanted Ruby to put down roots in a community like Lost Harbor."

"I did. I do. But Dev—maybe he's right about Ruby's school. I don't want to cheat her out of the education she deserves. We can always visit Lost Harbor in the summer."

He fought to keep his breath even and steady. If this was Megan's decision, he had to respect that. "What does Ruby say about it?"

"She dreams about Lost Harbor every night," Megan said softly. "She wants to check on the baby otter. But kids are adaptable."

"But Ruby..." He clamped his jaw shut so he wouldn't say any more. Megan was trying to do her best for Ruby, and the hell if he would get in her way. If she wanted—or needed—to stay here, he'd have to accept that.

"Ruby what?"

"Nothing. Like you said, it's not my business." *Keep your mouth shut, jackass.*

"Oh, now it's not your business? After you called Dev in the first place? Didn't you kind of make it your business when you did that?"

His hands flexed on the steering wheel. "Megan. Try to see it from my point of view. Ruby was missing and you were having a panic attack."

"So you call someone who's over a thousand miles away? What was he supposed to do?"

He winced under the force of her anger. "He was supposed to tell me how to handle it. I've rescued people from drowning, from dehydration, from exposure—but I'd never seen someone have a panic attack like that. I called him for guidance."

"Why him?"

"He was the one who told me you were still struggling with PTSD issues. I figured he would know how to handle the situation."

The computerized GPS voice told him to get on the freeway,

so he did. If only the voice could tell him what to say to Megan to get her to stop hating him.

"But I was wrong. He was no help. All he said was that it wouldn't last long and to keep looking for Ruby. So I called Zoe to stay with you while I kept searching."

She dropped her head into her hands, as if the memory of that time was too difficult even to think about.

"I'm really sorry, Megan. Truly, I am. That's why I came down here, to apologize. I never intended to cause trouble for you. The custody issue wasn't even on my radar. I was just trying to help."

Her shoulders were shaking. Tentatively, he reached a hand out and touched her shoulder. When she didn't resist, he rested it between her shoulder blades and gently soothed. "Do you think you can forgive me?"

"I...you..." She took in a shuddering breath and looked over at him. "You did nothing wrong. Truth is, Dev had a right to know Ruby was missing. We're supposed to be completely open with each other about anything concerning Ruby. It's part of our co-parenting agreement."

"Okay." So was he off the hook? Why did she still look so distressed? "Then what—?"

It's me," she blurted. "I failed Ruby when she needed me. She was out there on that kayak drifting with the tide while I was freaking out."

"Honey. No." Steering one-handed, he brushed the hair away from her face. The curve of her cheek was damp with tears. "You didn't freak out for long, and it was very understandable."

"*No.* I mean, yes, but no. Dev's partly right. I wasn't dealing well with the trauma from the shooting. I was running away from it. I didn't even tell *you* about it, and you know how much I like to talk things through. I pretended everything was fine and it was a fresh start. But really I was just trying to escape." She tucked her hair behind her ears and sat up. "That's another part of my plan. Therapy."

He gently squeezed her shoulder. Should he tell her there was an excellent therapist in Lost Harbor? Someone who worked with trauma patients?

"You want to know something funny?" She took a small mirror from her bag and dabbed the tears off her face. "I went back to where the shooting happened and had a big argument. With you."

"Excuse me?"

"Yeah. It helped a lot." She clicked the mirror shut and turned to him with a shaky smile. "Arguing with you made me feel strong."

If only she could see herself the way he saw her. "You are strong."

Finally a real smile spread across her face. "I'm going to have to be. Dev is set on getting his way and I don't know how to stop him. But I can outlast him so that's what I'm going to do. I'm strong like a weed. I won't just go away. I'll always be there for Ruby, wherever she is."

The poignant little throb in her voice nearly ripped his heart out. In that moment, he would have opened a vein if it would help her. His love for her pulsed inside him with the force of a solar flare.

"Megan, I lo—" He snapped his mouth shut. Did she really want to hear that right now? It would be a total distraction. All that mattered was Ruby, not the fact that his heart was breaking into lonely pieces right now.

"What was that?" She glanced over at him and then waved at a building up ahead. "That's where we're going. That tall silver phallic building. Dev's probably already there charming the mediator."

"We'll be on time." He pressed down on the accelerator. It was the least he could do.

"What was it you were about to say?"

"Nothing, just—" Something tugged at his memory. Something she'd said about Dev and their agreement. "I was going to ask you about what you said earlier. That you and Dev are supposed to be open with each other?"

"Yes, it's part of our agreement. We don't hide anything related to Ruby from each other. Trust and communication are the building blocks for successful co-parenting."

"So in other words, when I called Dev about Ruby being missing, I was honoring that agreement even though I didn't know about it?"

"Well, yes. I guess that's true."

"Whereas he..." Like a bolt from the sky, a plan came to him. "What are the chances I could say something to this mediator?"

# CHAPTER THIRTY-SEVEN

Ever since Lucas had shown up in Palo Alto, everything had taken a surreal turn. Megan was so distracted with her worry about the session that she hadn't taken the time to figure out what he was actually doing there.

Had he really flown all the way from Alaska just to apologize? Drive her to mediation? That seemed over the top. Sweet, but not necessary. Touching. Amazing, even, especially because the sight of him, even the smell of him, made her feel better. As if she had an ally.

And now he had some kind of mysterious plan. "The only way Dev will let you in is if he thinks you're going to help him."

"Okay then. Done. That's our plan." He jerked to a stop in front of the high-rise. "Better run if you want to get there on time. I'm going to call Dev."

She looked at her watch and saw she had a total of three minutes to make it to the twenty-third floor. "Thanks for the ride. And the grovel. I enjoyed that."

"I didn't *grovel*." With a grin, she closed the door on his protest. She'd really missed sparring with Lucas. It felt good not be angry with him anymore. In fact, it felt amazing. As if the entire world had been washed clean and now sparkled with joy.

When she reached the mediator's office, she discovered that Dev had requested a fifteen-minute delay so that someone else could join them.

"Are you okay with that?" Eliza asked Megan. "It's a bit unusual, so if you have any objections I'll disallow it."

"No objections." She shrugged, trying to look defeated when she was actually the exact opposite. "This is about trust, right? Trust and communication. I have nothing to hide from Dev and I'm sure the same is true with him."

"Correct." If Dev found her statement suspicious, he didn't show it. He was always so smooth.

*That doesn't mean he's a better parent*, she reminded herself. *Don't fall into that trap anymore. You know better.*

When Lucas arrived, they all stood for hand-shaking and introductions.

"We're not technically under oath here," said Eliza once they sat down. "But we always behave as if we are. The goal is to sort issues out here in this room instead of putting Ruby in the middle."

"That makes sense to me. I promise to tell the whole truth and nothing else." A crisp white shirt set off Lucas' dark good looks. With his natural air of authority, he commanded the room without any visible effort.

"Well," Eliza laughed. "Consider yourself under oath then."

Lucas had charmed her without any visible effort. Take that, Dev.

"So what are you here to tell us, Mr. Holt?"

"Holt was the one who called me when Ruby went missing," said Dev, obviously trying to regain the spotlight. "He witnessed the entire debacle."

"That's right," Lucas said calmly. "I did. I run a charter in

Lost Harbor. I took Dev out when he was there last month. That's when he—"

"That's not relevant," Dev said quickly. "We're not here to talk about fishing."

"We're here to talk about anything relevant. Is it relevant, Mr. Holt?"

"I think so. It's the reason I called Dev."

Megan shot a glance at Dev, whose face was slowly turning a shade of brick red.

"Okay, go ahead then."

"On our fishing trip, he asked me to report back to him on anything I witnessed regarding Megan and Ruby, especially anything relating to her panic attacks. He offered to pay me to do this."

Lucas wouldn't meet her eyes as he spoke. He kept them fixed on Eliza, who was taking notes on her familiar legal pad. "He offered to pay you?"

"Yes. I think he knew that Megan and I were...adversaries at that time. He wanted to use that to his benefit."

"I see."

Megan's heart began to flutter madly. She knew that tone of voice from Eliza. It meant she was Not. Happy.

"Did you accept his offer?"

"No. I thought it was ridiculous and I told him so. But I did take his card. I still had it in my pocket when Ruby went missing."

Dev pointed an accusing finger at Lucas. "You called me because Megan had a panic attack and you didn't know what to do."

"Right. I was hoping you would be able to help. You didn't have much to say, though. You said it wouldn't be long and you were right. As soon as she came out of it, she figured out that a kayak was missing. That's how we found Ruby."

Dev's nostrils flared until he looked like a snorting bull. "The point is, Ruby nearly got lost at sea because Megan couldn't keep her shit together."

His harsh words hung in the quiet air. They kept ringing in Megan's ears, so accusing, so—right?

Lucas leaned forward, elbows on his knees, hands loosely clasped, his calm manner the opposite of Dev's. "I guess to a city boy it might seem that way. In Lost Harbor, we have more than our share of people lost at sea. Fishermen. Adventure-seekers. The occasional dare-devil. But we never lose anyone without a fight. Especially not a kid. Ruby had all of us behind her that day. All of Lost Harbor. She always will. Every child does."

Megan's throat closed up. As many clashes as she'd had with the harbor folks, they'd circled around her after the storm.

That was what she wanted for Ruby. That sense of being part of something a community that looked out for each other. Tears welled in her eyes but she blinked them back.

Important business going on here. She had to pay attention.

"Getting back to your first statement, that Dev tried to hire you to...what, spy on Megan?"

"More or less. The words he used were 'keep an eye on her' and 'be a bodyguard.' But he wanted me to report back to him, which does add up to spying."

Eliza turned to Dev. "What do you have to say about this?"

In that moment, Megan was quite happy that she wasn't Dev being pinned with Eliza's level gaze.

"It was for Ruby," Dev said with his usual smoothness. "You can't blame me for wanting to keep an eye on Ruby given Megan's condition."

"My *condition?*"

"PTSD is no joke. You weren't taking it seriously. I did."

"Bullshit." She leaped to her feet. "You just want to undercut me. You want me to doubt myself so I won't fight you. You think

I'm weaker than you, but I'm not. I'm stronger than you. Do you think I could have gone to Alaska and made a life and started running a boat if I wasn't tough? You don't really know me, Dev. And hiring spies behind my back is crossing a major line."

Her words that rang with the clarity of truth. And God did it feel good to stand up for herself like this. Lucas' eyes gleamed with something like pride.

Eliza caught her eye and gestured for her to sit back down. She did, wondering if losing her cool like that was going to cost her.

"Thank you, Megan. Dev, I get that you were worried. That's understandable. But you never brought it up *here*. You had the option of airing your concerns in this very room. That's why we're in this mediation process. We could have instituted some kind of aboveboard agreement. Instead you chose to go behind Megan's back."

Megan had to bite her lip to keep from shouting, "exactly!"

"It was for Ruby," he said sullenly.

"For Ruby's safety or so that you could gather material to gain custody of Ruby?"

Dev's jaw flexed and he looked everywhere except at Eliza. It was so rare to see him at a loss for words like that.

"We stick to the truth here, remember?" Eliza said gently.

"Fine. The second choice. That one. Ruby needs to be with me. She needs a real education. The teachers up there in the backwoods don't know how to handle someone like Ruby."

Eliza swung her head around to pin Megan with that laser-beam gaze. "Response, Megan?"

She drew in a long breath. Here was her opportunity, created for her by Lucas with an assist from Eliza.

Now she had to believe in herself...and grab it.

"I think Ruby needs a quality education, absolutely. But she's more than a math whiz. She also loves animals and art. She doesn't make many friends, but when she does she's incredibly loyal to them. Those attachments are important too. She needs people who love her for things other than her IQ. She needs a community. She needs...me. Despite all my many flaws—no need to list them, Dev—she needs me. Right now, she needs me to fight for her because our life in Lost Harbor is what's best for her. I truly believe that to the bottom of my soul."

Her passionate words echoed in the air even after she'd finished speaking.

Until Dev spoke up. "But that ridiculous boat is no way to make a living."

"I sold the *Forget Me Not*. I plan to use that money to hire a private tutor to come to Lost Harbor." Where had that idea come from? It had flashed into her brain at the perfect moment. "It's the best of both worlds. A quality education and a community she loves. Dev, you can even select the tutor. Maybe it's two tutors. Three, four. Whatever works."

"But the resources here—"

Eliza cut him off. "Dev, I hope you understand that you're on thin ice here. You violated the agreement we all worked out. I'd even call that an egregious violation. I wouldn't blame Megan if she pulled out of this process altogether. Megan, what do you have to say about that? Would you rather take this process to court instead of mediation? You'd have a compelling case."

Megan gave that a moment of serious thought. Did she want to become courtroom adversaries with Dev? Her child's father? The mediation sessions were tough, but they did help her and Dev understand each other. "No. I think we can work through this. Unless you're giving up on us?"

"No. Of course not, not after all the many, many sessions that got us here." Her touch of dry humor lightened the moment. "So, keeping our focus where it should be, which is the best interests of the child, I repeat. Dev, would the hiring of tutors satisfy you?"

Dev slouched back in his seat. A lock of his dark hair fell across his face—a sure sign that he was rattled. "Partially. I'd still like the option of enrolling her in a few advanced courses or short-term programs."

"Megan?"

Megan drew in a long breath. Was Dev actually giving up his battle for full custody? She stole a glance at Lucas, who wore an impassive expression. The decision is yours, he was silently saying.

"That should be fine," she finally said. "But Dev, you can't pull something like what you tried with Lucas. No spying. I would never do that to you and you shouldn't do it to me."

"Agreed," he managed through gritted teeth. "Should have known I picked the wrong guy," he added.

Lucas' head shot up and he fixed a fierce stare on Dev. "What's that supposed to mean."

"You still consider yourself under oath, don't you?"

"Yeah."

"Answer this, then. Are you in love with Megan?"

The entire room went silent. Megan froze in her chair. Goose bumps rose on her skin and her head felt light enough to float away.

"What does that have to do with anything?"

"It's pretty clear. If you're in love with her, you might lie for her."

"Where's the lie? Is anything I said a lie? You're just as much under oath as I am."

"So you're not going to answer the question?" Triumphant, Dev looked over at Eliza. "He can't be trusted. He's trying to weasel out of a legitimate question. He had an ulterior motive. We can't consider..."

Dev kept talking, but Megan tuned out. She felt as if she was on a rollercoaster that had just taken a sickening plunge. Amazingly, things had been going her way. But now Dev had found an opening and was gnawing at it like a pit bull. Was Eliza going to fall for his bullshit?

"Yes." Lucas' calm voice interrupted Dev's stream of complaints. "Since I'm under oath, I will say that yes, I am in love with Megan. That is the truth along with everything else I've said today."

Megan gripped the edge of the table. Where was this crazy roller coaster going next? "You're *what?*"

He glanced over at her, almost casually, as if he wasn't dropping a major bombshell on her. "In love with you. Why else would I follow you all the way down to California, of all places? You know how I feel about California. Too many people."

*California?* What did California have to do with anything? None of this was making sense.

"You...you said you wanted to apologize. Grovel. And you didn't even grovel completely because you should have told me Dev wanted to pay you to be his spy!"

"You're right. I should have. I forgot because I think you got mad at me about something else right after that."

"That's very likely," she admitted.

That amused glint in his eye brought it all back—the sparkling energy that fueled their quarrels, the feistiness he inspired in her.

"You heard him," Dev was saying. "He loves her, so of course he's going to take her side."

Eliza shook her head at him. "I also heard him say he was telling the truth. I don't see any reason to doubt that. You didn't even deny what he said."

"Because...because...ah fuck it." He flung his arms in the air. "If you want to live in Lost Harbor, Alaska, I won't fight you, Megan."

"Really?"

"Yeah. Ruby does seem to love it. I don't have the heart to take it away from her. But I will be closely monitoring her education."

Oh, so now he didn't have the heart? After putting her through this? She opened her mouth to blast him, but felt Lucas' warning glance. Leave it be. She'd won. "Fine. Then I guess we have an agreement."

"So it seems." Dev shoved his papers into his briefcase and rose to his feet. While not exactly gracious, at least he wasn't sneering at her. "I'll say this, Megan. I never thought you'd last up there. I thought you'd be begging to come back to Palo Alto and let me take care of things."

"Well, I guess I'm stronger than you think." Even she hadn't believed in her own strength. But Lucas had, from the very first moment they met.

*Lucas.*

He too was rising to his feet to shake Eliza's hand in goodbye. *Wait a minute.* He was just going to walk out of here as if nothing had happened? As if he hadn't said that he loved her—under oath?

Yes. He was. Before she could collect herself, he'd left the office and headed for the elevator.

She scrambled to her feet and gathered up her bag and the papers she'd pulled from it at the start of the meeting. Without even bothering to put them back in their folder, she bolted for the door. "Bye Eliza, bye Dev, hold that elevator!" she shouted all in a burst.

She barely made it inside before the doors closed behind her. In fact, one of her papers fluttered away and got sandwiched between the closing elevator doors. She hoped it wasn't anything important, like her sale agreement for the *Forget Me Not,* but didn't take the time to check.

Panting, she stood in the middle of the elevator and looked at

Lucas. Cool and composed, he leaned against the back wall of the elevator, hands in his pockets.

"Can we please rewind to what you said back there? Was that some kind of...tactic?"

"Tactic? What sort of tactic?"

"I don't know! You're...you...you really love me?"

He was watching her so closely, almost warily. She noticed a muscle ticking in his jaw and realized—he wasn't as calm as he looked. Dev had put him on the spot and now he was all alone out there on the "I love you" ledge.

The elevator doors opened again. Her paperwork fluttered to the floor. She snatched it up just as two office workers stepped in. Great, now they had no privacy. She edged around the two women so she could stand next to Lucas at the back of the elevator. She curled her fingers into his and felt the reassurance of his return pressure.

She searched for the right thing to say in the awkward strangers-crowded-together atmosphere of the elevator. All of this was too important to share with random office workers. "If what you said is true—"

"It is. I wouldn't have said it if it wasn't true."

"Then why didn't you say anything earlier? I thought we were just—" She glanced at the two office workers. The door opened on the next floor and more passengers got in. It must be lunchtime. "You know," she ended.

"I thought so too, but I guess things change."

"And that's why you came down here?"

"Yup, I came down here to barge into a meeting and get grilled under oath by your ex." His dry words caught the attention of the others in the elevator. "It was well worth the trip."

"I'm sorry about that. Not that it's my fault, because I had no idea because you never gave any *hint*." More glances from the other passengers made her realize she'd raised her voice.

"I didn't say it was your fault."

"Oh my God, are we *arguing*?"

"Yes, with innocent bystanders nearby. Lord help them." He gestured toward the now-crowded elevator. At least half of the passengers were openly watching them.

She raised her voice. "Sorry, everyone. No need for concern. Arguing is just a thing we do. It's like verbal foreplay for us."

At her side, Lucas choked slightly.

She kept going. "We compete with each other a lot, and neither of us likes to lose, and right now Lucas is one-up on me because he had to tell a stranger how he felt about me. I can't let that stand."

Turning to Lucas, she saw his eyebrows lift and that devilish smile flirt with the corner of his mouth.

"Therefore, in front of even more strangers, let me share the fact that I," her teasing tone shifted to one of hushed vulnerability, "love you too."

For a long moment he didn't react other than to study her face. But when his hand closed around hers with a tight grip, she knew he was deeply affected.

He lowered his voice, and she noticed out of the corner of her eye that people were leaning in to listen. "When you told me you were going to stay here, I decided not to tell you how I felt."

Her stomach dropped—or maybe that was the elevator zooming toward the ground floor with a full load. "But then you had to because you were under oath?"

"That, and I couldn't keep it in anymore. I love you, Megan. My sweet badass bird nerd. I love you and I want to have a life with you."

A sigh drifted from one of the other elevator passengers.

She snuggled closer to Lucas' solid warmth and rested her head against his chest as his arm came around her. A life with

Lucas...was such bliss really possible? "Okay. Yes. But we're going back to Lost Harbor, right?"

"Yeah we are. If I have my way, we're not going to spend another hour in this godforsaken state."

"Hey," said one of the office workers. "Was that really necessary?"

Megan laughed. "See? You're in enemy territory here, Lucas. No California bashing."

"I take it all back. From now on, California is the state where you told me you love me. Nothing but love for this place."

A scattering of applause from the other passengers as the elevator touched down on the ground floor. The doors whisked open and the others filtered out until only Lucas and Megan remained.

"Thanks for the entertainment," an office workers told them on her way out. "But you might want to think about a hotel room after this."

Good point, but Megan didn't want to move yet. She didn't want to separate from Lucas long enough to step out of the elevator.

"Is this real?" she whispered. "Did all this really happen? Ruby and I are going back to Lost Harbor, you love me, I love you...is it really possible?"

"I told you before. Strange things happen around Lost Souls." He took her chin in his hand and tilted her face for his kiss. A brush of his lips against hers and she knew that every bit of it was real. Just because it was magical didn't mean it wasn't real.

"We're not anywhere near Lost Souls," she pointed out in a murmur against his lips.

"Seriously? Right now, you want to argue?"

"Foreplay, baby. Foreplay."

# CHAPTER THIRTY-EIGHT

Even though things were perfect now that they'd publicly—very publicly—declared their feelings for each other, Lucas knew something was still bothering Megan. Even during their visit with Ruby at her summer program, he sensed she was holding something back.

"So we're really going to live in Lost Harbor? For good?" Ruby tugged her arm away from Megan, who was tut-tutting over the formulas she'd scribbled on her skin.

"Yes. That's what you want, right? If you don't, say something now, honeybunch."

"Of course I do. Can we finally get a dog?"

Megan exchanged a long look with Lucas. They'd discussed logistics on the drive to the campus. "Well, the thing is that we're going to live with Fidget."

"Live with Fidget? In his dog house?"

"No no. With Fidget and Lucas. We're going to look for a new house where we can all live."

Ruby's puzzled gaze swung over to Lucas. He winked at her and she finally put it together. "You're getting married?"

"Not yet. This is a big change for us so we're going to ease into it. We don't have to get married right away."

"But we are engaged to be married." Lucas felt he had to clarify that.

Megan squinted up at him. "I'd see it more as we've agreed to approach the idea of marriage when everyone's ready. Including Ruby."

If she wanted an argument, she wasn't going to get it from him. He was just happy they'd gotten this far. "How do you feel about expanding your family a little bit, Ruby?" he asked her.

"That's not a little bit." She flashed the fingers on her right hand. "Adding a man and a dog, that means our family will be twice as big."

"And the math whiz speaks," he teased. "What do you think about me and Fidget hopping onboard the Megan and Ruby train?"

"Well, I like Fidget." He felt his eyebrows lift. Didn't he and Ruby have a good relationship? Was there something he'd missed?

Then Ruby broke into a mischievous grin. "I like you too. But you have to stop killing so many fish."

"Done."

The promptness of his response brought both Megan and Ruby's heads swinging around. "Excuse me?" said Megan. "Are you going to start throwing them back?"

"No, I'm done with Jack Hammer Charters. It was never what I wanted anyway. I'm putting the *Jack Hammer* on the market and I'm moving on. I'm closing my office in Colorado and making it official. The Holt empire will be headquartered in Lost Harbor from now on."

"You have an empire?" Ruby asked in awe.

"It's a figure of speech," he told her. "With a touch of sarcasm."

"Is that why you're selling the *Jack Hammer*? So you can focus on your business?"

"I'll mostly be focusing on my campaign."

They both stared at him. "Are you running for president?" Ruby's eyes widened.

He laughed. "Close. I'm running for head of the Harbor Commission. And I'm hoping I can count on the support of the *Forget Me Not* crew."

And just like that, he stumbled across the one thing still bothering Megan.

"There is no *Forget Me Not* crew anymore. There's probably no *Forget Me Not* anymore either. I just hope it's part of a great movie, but we probably won't get that lucky." He started to answer, but she cut him off. "But you have our support no matter what. Although I was playing with the idea of running myself."

Ha! So Maya Badger had guessed right. No wonder she was such a good detective.

"Bring it on." Lucas grinned and spread his arms wide. "I welcome the competition. May the best candidate win."

"I admit, it's tempting. I'd love to see you up on a debate stage. At least then I'd get a chance to bring up my issues."

"If you want to run, seriously, I'll step aside. Competing was fun, but now I think I'd like to try being on the same side."

She snuggled her face against his arm. "Me too. We can save the competing for—" She broke off, turning a little pink as she remembered they were with Ruby.

"Anyway, don't you want to hear my platform?"

"I'm not sure, do I? Repairing oil tankers, getting rid of the waste bins, am I close?"

"I'll be running on a comprehensive plan to make the harbor carbon neutral by the next decade, with a focus on sustainable fishing practices and protecting our local wildlife. Happy now?"

She stared at him with wonder in her blue-gray eyes. "Are you just teasing me now?"

"Nope. You won me over."

"I *won*?"

"I'd say we both won." He tugged her close and dropped a kiss on the side of her forehead. "Right now, I definitely feel like I won."

"Okay, but I won a little bit more," she murmured even as she melted against him.

"Mom, look!" A grasshopper had landed on Ruby's thumb. Entranced, she stared at its fragile wings. "I have a new friend!" She climbed off her chair and wandered to the nearest tree. The grasshopper clung to her hand as she walked.

"Welp, we lost Ruby," said Megan. "She'll be chatting up that grasshopper for the next hour or so."

"She does have a way with wild things."

"But on the bright side, we have a chance to do this." With a light touch, Megan pulled his head down so his mouth hovered over hers. She pressed her lips against his, sending a rush of hot joy through him. This kiss felt different—honest, complete. As if there were no shadows between them anymore. Nothing but full hearts and sparkling horizons.

Over Megan's shoulder, he caught sight of Ruby. The sunlight glowed around her dark head as she murmured to the tiny creature on her hand.

And he knew that Megan was wrong. He'd won the most. He'd won the two of them, and nothing could beat that.

# CHAPTER THIRTY-NINE

"Surprise." Lucas took his hands away from Megan's eyes. She blinked at the familiar bright blue trim of the *Forget Me Not*. Her boat. In one piece.

"It didn't get blown up yet. What happened?"

"It's not ever going to get blown up. Unless you want to blow it up yourself because it keeps springing leaks."

She spun around and noted his smug expression, as if he knew a secret she didn't. "Why didn't it get blown up? Did you stop the sale for some reason? I need that money! Wait, I have that money already. They paid me so they could blow up the *Forget Me Not*...did you pay them more so they *wouldn't* blow up my boat?"

He tilted his head back in laughter. The movement of his Adam's apple under his tanned skin of his neck made her mouth water. "Close. I bought the boat from the studio about an hour after you sold it to them. I found them a better boat to blow up. I'd show it to you but it's...well, you'll have to watch the movie."

She drew in an awed breath. "You saved the *Forget Me Not*? Why? You always looked down on my old tub."

"It has historical value." He winked at her to take the sting from his words. "I know how much you love your boat. The *Forget Me Not* belongs here, just like you. Besides, we're going to need a boat once I sell the *Jack Hammer*. Can't go birding without one."

"So—" She still couldn't believe it was true. Her beloved boat still floated peacefully in its usual slip in Lost Harbor. It was like a miracle. "That must have cost you a lot of money."

"It did. Luckily, the *Jack Hammer*'s worth about twice as much so I'm not worried about it."

She turned to gaze upon the miraculous sight again. Tears sprang to her eyes as she realized how wonderful it was to see her boat again. She'd steeled herself to the sad fact of its demolition, but that didn't mean it wouldn't have hurt. "You did this for me."

"Yes. And for Ruby. And for all you nature-lovers." His voice took on that teasing tone that she loved. "Without your bird boat, how else would the rest of us make fun of you?"

"You don't fool me with your fake mockery, Mr. Future Harbor Commissioner and Caspian Tern Photographer."

"I guess you're onto me."

She wanted to be on top of him. Or him on top of her. Or any way it worked out, as long as they were alone together. But that would have to wait since a small crowd of harbor rats was hurrying down the ramp toward them.

"Megan!" Zoe arrived first, flinging her arms open. "You're back! We were hoping you'd see the light."

"I *showed* her the light," Lucas said. "Don't I get a little credit here?"

"Sure, sure." She waved him off. "Whatever it took. It's great to have you back, Megan."

"I'm really happy to be back. And my boat didn't get blown up."

"Of course it didn't. Do you think anyone here would blow

up your boat?" Zoe directed a glare at the others. Boris, Yanni, Hunter and his mother, Trixie from the ice cream shop. "I'm sorry, but when it comes to harbor feuds we should draw the line at explosives."

"No no, it was a movie studio, they wanted to buy..." Megan trailed off when she noticed that Zoe's attention had swung away from her. Her friend was staring at a small boat gliding into the harbor. A tidy white cruiser with a staysail at the stern. A tall man stood at the helm, handling it with piratical ease. He wore a navy wool watch cap and work pants, much like other fishermen—but this particular man wore them especially well.

"What the..." Zoe whispered.

"Who is that?"

Zoe didn't seem to hear. She pulled away and stood at the edge of the float, shading her eyes against the sun.

Lucas put his arm around Megan's shoulder and drew her close to his side. "We should probably go now."

"What do you mean? Why?"

Lucas called to the rest of the crowd. "Let's give Zoe a little space here, yeah?" He shepherded them down the float. "Happy hour at Captain Crabbie's, let's go folks."

As everyone trooped away, Megan took one more look back at Zoe. The breeze made her flour-sack apron cling to her curves and blew her black curls around her head. She made a romantic picture, alone there on the dock.

"What's going on?" She turned on Lucas as soon as they were safely out of earshot. "Is Zoe okay?"

"I don't know. She hasn't really been the same since he left. And now he's back. So I don't know how she is right now."

"Who is that man?"

"I guess you'd say he's the one who got away. That's Padric Jeffers."

It took her a moment for the name to sink in. "Padric Jeffers the singer?"

"He sells out stadiums in about two minutes, but sure. Padric Jeffers the singer."

She'd been only dimly aware of the music scene over the past eight years since Ruby was born. But she had heard of him, so he must be extra famous.

"If he's such a huge mega-star, what's he doing here?"

"Fun fact. He was born here. Grew up here until he was fifteen or so. He and Zoe were best friends. Childhood sweethearts, I guess you'd say."

"She's never even mentioned his name in the entire time I've known her."

"Nope. Sore topic. Recommend you avoid it."

"The hell with that. I want to know everything. I've never seen Zoe act like this."

He tugged her against him. She'd never get enough of the way his strong body felt against hers. "How about we go pick up Ruby and Fidget and take them to the beach? Old Fidget put on about five pounds while I was gone."

"Will you tell me the whole story on the way?"

"The whole story? It would take a while, and it's not mine to tell."

She shifted restlessly against his side, her curiosity still going wild.

"But there's another story I can tell. It starts at a Harbor Commission meeting. A very boring meeting, except there's a woman in the audience. A beautiful, idealistic woman who accosts me after the meeting's over."

"How rude of her."

"Oh no. Best thing that ever happened to me. Something changed when she looked at me with those indignant blue eyes of hers. I was never the same after that. Should have thrown in the towel right then and there."

They reached the top of the ramp and looked out over the harbor. Low clouds swollen with rain tumbled over each other as if racing to see who would arrive first.

"Storm coming," he said softly. "Guess we'll have to skip the beach walk."

"Maybe we can do it tomorrow. Or the day after that. Or the one after that, because oh my God, I live here—with you!" Sometimes she still had trouble believing that anything could be so perfect.

"It'll sink in one of these days," he teased her. "Marrying your nemesis, who would believe it?" He interlaced his fingers with hers and swung their clasped hands between them.

"Well, you know what they say. Strange things happen near Lost Souls."

He lifted her hand to his mouth and kissed it. "Strange...and wonderful."

For once, she had to agree with him.


*THANK you so much for reading! YOURS SINCE YESTERDAY, the next Lost Harbor, Alaska novel, will be coming November 2019. Want to be the first to hear about new books, sales, and exclusive giveaways? Join Jennifer's mailing list and receive a free story as a welcome gift.*

# ABOUT THE AUTHOR

**Jennifer Bernard** is a *USA Today* bestselling author of contemporary romance. Her books have been called "an irresistible reading experience" full of "quick wit and sizzling love scenes." A graduate of Harvard and former news promo producer, she left big city life in Los Angeles for true love in Alaska, where she now lives with her husband and stepdaughters. She still hasn't adjusted to the cold, so most often she can be found cuddling with her laptop and a cup of tea. No stranger to book success, she also writes erotic novellas under a naughty secret name that she's happy to share with the curious. You can learn more about Jennifer and her books at JenniferBernard.net. Make sure to sign up for her newsletter for new releases, fresh exclusive content, sales alerts and giveaways.

*Connect with Jennifer online:*
JenniferBernard.net
Jen@JenniferBernard.net

# ALSO BY JENNIFER BERNARD

**Lost Harbor, Alaska**

Yours Since Yesterday ∼ Book 2

**The Rockwell Legacy**

The Rebel ∼ Book 1

The Rogue ∼ Book 2

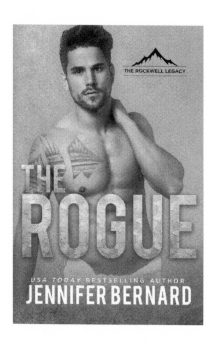

The Renegade ~ Book 3

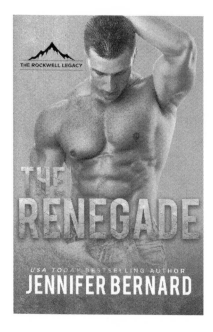

The Runaway ~ Book 4

The Rock ~ Book 5

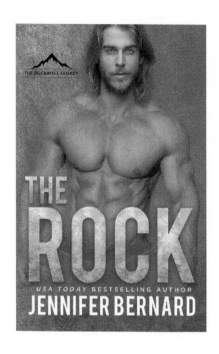

## Jupiter Point ~ The Hotshots

Set the Night on Fire ~ Book 1

Burn So Bright ~ Book 2

Into the Flames ~ Book 3

Setting Off Sparks ~ Book 4

## Jupiter Point ~ The Knight Brothers

Hot Pursuit ~ Book 5

Coming In Hot ~ Book 6

Hot and Bothered ~ Book 7

Too Hot to Handle ~ Book 8

One Hot Night ~ Book 9

Seeing Stars ~ Series Prequel

**The Bachelor Firemen of San Gabriel Series**

**Love Between the Bases Series**

Made in the USA
Monee, IL
31 December 2019